Trailblazer with a Tin Star

The day after tomorrow he'd take custody of six dangerous killers. It was nearly 250 miles to Fort Smith, and not a single yard of it would be easy.

The marshal smiled, rain beating on his lean, leathery face. As a youngster he'd pushed cattle along the Chisholm and Western trails, routes first forged by others. But now he was about to pioneer his own trail—northeast across plains, mountains, and rivers, a dust-and-cuss journey across an unforgiving land that offered nothing except a hundred different ways to kill a man. With an empty wagon, plenty of supplies, and good weather, the trip south from Fort Smith had been relatively uneventful. But heading back would be different now that fall was starting to crack down hard. Buff Stringfellow and his boys were no bargains either. Six desperate men who would do anything to escape the noose would be a handful.

"I'm blazing the Convict Trail," Kane said to himself.

Ralph Compton

The Convict Trail

A Ralph Compton Novel
by Joseph A. West

A SIGNET BOOK

SIGNET
Published by New American Library, a division of
Penguin Group (USA) Inc., 375 Hudson Street,
New York, New York 10014, USA
Penguin Group (Canada), 90 Eglinton Avenue East, Suite 700, Toronto,
Ontario M4P 2Y3, Canada (a division of Pearson Penguin Canada Inc.)
Penguin Books Ltd., 80 Strand, London WC2R 0RL, England
Penguin Ireland, 25 St. Stephen's Green, Dublin 2,
Ireland (a division of Penguin Books Ltd.)
Penguin Group (Australia), 250 Camberwell Road, Camberwell, Victoria 3124,
Australia (a division of Pearson Australia Group Pty. Ltd.)
Penguin Books India Pvt. Ltd., 11 Community Centre, Panchsheel Park,
New Delhi - 110 017, India
Penguin Group (NZ), 67 Apollo Drive, Rosedale, North Shore 0632,
New Zealand (a division of Pearson New Zealand Ltd.)
Penguin Books (South Africa) (Pty.) Ltd., 24 Sturdee Avenue,
Rosebank, Johannesburg 2196, South Africa

Penguin Books Ltd., Registered Offices:
80 Strand, London WC2R 0RL, England

First published by Signet, an imprint of New American Library,
a division of Penguin Group (USA) Inc.

First Printing, December 2008
10 9 8 7 6 5 4 3 2 1

THE IMMORTAL COWBOY

This is respectfully dedicated to the "American Cowboy." His was the saga sparked by the turmoil that followed the Civil War, and the passing of more than a century has by no means diminished the flame.

True, the old days and the old ways are but treasured memories, and the old trails have grown dim with the ravages of time, but the spirit of the cowboy lives on.

In my travels—to Texas, Oklahoma, Kansas, Nebraska, Colorado, Wyoming, New Mexico, and Arizona—I always find something that reminds me of the Old West. While I am walking these plains and mountains for the first time, there is this feeling that a part of me is eternal, that I have known these old trails before. I believe it is the undying spirit of the frontier calling, allowing me, through the mind's eye, to step back into time. What is the appeal of the Old West of the American frontier?

It has been epitomized by some as the dark and bloody period in American history. Its heroes—Crockett, Bowie, Hickok, Earp—have been reviled and criticized. Yet the Old West lives on, larger than life.

It has become a symbol of freedom, when there was always another mountain to climb and another river to cross; when a dispute between two men was settled not with expensive lawyers, but with fists, knives, or guns. Barbaric? Maybe. But some things never change. When the cowboy rode into the pages of American history, he left behind a legacy that lives within the hearts of us all.

—*Ralph Compton*

Chapter 1

Deputy Marshal Logan Kane was irritated. A man who had long since lost the habit of smiling easily, the face he turned to his elderly companion was masked by a ferocious scowl.

"I should have gunned him, Sam. I should have drawed my Colt an' put a bullet in his fat belly."

Up on the box of the prison wagon Sam Shaver leaned to his right, spat a stream of tobacco juice over the side, narrowly missing Kane's horse, and asked, "What fer?"

The fact that Sam chose to ignore the obvious irritated Kane further. "Highway robbery, damn it. That's what fer."

Sam was not by nature a questioning man, and now he held his tongue. For a few moments the only sound was the thud of mule hooves and the steady banging of the wooden water bucket that hung from a hook at the rear of the wagon.

Kane spoke into the silence, his voice cracking with

anger. "A dollar-ninety-seven to cross the Red. A dollar-fifty for the wagon an' mules, thirty-seven cents for me and my horse and"—his simmering outrage reached the boiling point and his voice rose to a shout—"he had the gall to charge ten cents for you. Said oncet you clumb down from the wagon you was considered a pedestrian."

Sam's eyes were on the forested landscape ahead. "In all my born days I never did meet an honest ferryman." He was quiet for a spell, then seemed to make up his mind about something. Finally he said, "You're right, Logan. You should've gunned him."

Somewhat mollified that Shaver had agreed with him, the marshal said, "Maybe on the way back. I'll put a bullet in his greedy hide and then we'll be on our way."

"Crackerjack plan, Logan. I'll swear on a stack of Bibles that he drawed down on you, to make it look good for Judge Parker, like." The old man smiled. "I never did cotton to a ferryman with a bald head an' red beard anyhow. Serve him right fer lookin' like that, I say."

To further justify his homicidal intent, Kane said, "When we go back the way we come, I know he'll charge us sixty cents for the convicts. He'll say them boys are pedestrians."

"Then you should gun him fer sure, Logan."

Kane was silent for a few moments, then said, "Of course, I could refuse to pay. Tell him, 'Send your bill to the judge and be damned to ye.' "

"You could do that very thing, Logan. Save a bullet thataway."

"I reckon it's something a man should study on for a spell, Sam. I mean, which way to go for the better."

"I reckon it is. But remember, it's no big thing to gun a robbin' ferryman."

"Well, I never shot one o' them afore," Kane said, turning the thought over in his mind.

"There's always a first time for everything, Logan. But if it does come to a killin', just don't let it upset you none."

Kane glanced at the sky, an upturned ceramic bowl of pale blue ribboned with streamers of scarlet and jade. The moon was already rising, transparent, hovering above the surrounding treetops like a white moth. "Coming up on dark, Sam," he said. "Best we find a place to camp."

"I been smelling water for the last two miles," the old man said. "We must be coming up on a creek."

The trail was a winding wagon and cattle path, cut through thick forests of pine and hardwood, mostly crowded stands of elm, oak, dogwood and ash. Among the tree trunks grew cacti, ferns and wild orchids that nodded their bonneted heads in a gusting wind. The untouched timber around him had a serenity and permanence that reminded Kane of the columns of an old Spanish cathedral he'd once seen down in the Mexican Durango country. That he'd splattered the church's ancient oak doors with the blood and brains of the bank robber Pancho Ramos had done nothing to spoil his appreciation of the holy place, then or since.

Now, among the trees, he experienced the same relaxed inner peace he'd felt in the ancient cathedral, only tonight the stars would substitute for candles, and the smell of orchids for the blue drift of incense. He had postponed his decision on the crooked ferryman until later, and he wouldn't have to deal with the six dangerous convicts he had to escort back to Fort Smith until tomorrow.

For the present, he was looking forward to coffee, crisp fried salt pork, skillet bread and his blankets.

As good as he felt, he dared to hope that just maybe the dream would not come tonight. His mouth tightened under his mustache. Maybe tonight it would leave him alone . . . they would leave him alone.

"Wash up ahead, Marshal," Sam said. He was leaning forward in his seat, his eyes searching into the shadowed distance. "Maybe you should ride on ahead an' take a look-see."

Kane kneed his sorrel into a trot and rode up on the wash. Both banks were broken down by the passage of wagons and cattle, and only a trickle of water ran over the sandy bottom. He swung to his right and followed the stream into the trees. After a few yards the banks narrowed to less than two feet, but here the water ran clear and several inches deep. The stream gradually arced to the north, through a clearing about half an acre in extent, roofed by a leafy overhang of elm and post oak. There was grass enough for the pair of mules and his horse, dry firewood aplenty and space to park the big prison wagon. It would do.

Kane rode back to the road, waved Sam forward, then returned to the clearing and swung out of the saddle. He was a tall, lanky man who moved with an easy, loose-limbed grace. A blue Colt hung on Kane's right hip and his marshal's star was pinned to his cartridge belt, left of the buckle and covered by his black leather vest. None of Judge Parker's deputies wore their stars in plain sight. In the Indian Territory a man with a badge was a prime target for bushwhackers, and there was no point in hunting for trouble.

As Kane stretched a kink out of his back, Sam Shaver drove into the clearing and looked around. "Good a place as any to make camp, Logan."

"It'll do," Kane said. "Unhitch the mule team and I'll rustle up a fire."

It was fully dark by the time the coffee bubbled and salt pork sizzled in the skillet. The crescent moon had risen higher in the sky, horning aside the first stars, and the coyotes were talking.

"How's the coffee, Sam?" Kane asked.

The old man lifted the lid off the pot, peered inside, then said, "Let 'er bile fer a spell longer."

Kane rolled himself a cigarette, lit it with a brand from the fire, then stretched out, leaning on one elbow. Shifting scarlet light played over the hard, lean planes of his face, and his eyes were lost in the shadow of his hat brim. "Back bothering you any?"

Sam shrugged. "It comes an' goes. All depends on where that dang Comanche arrowhead decides to shift. If she digs into my backbone, she do punish me some until she moves again."

"Well, if it gets bad, you ride and I'll drive the wagon."

The old man shook his head. "I don't trust that big American stud o' yours. If I get th'owed, I could be in a heap o' trouble. Besides, you're the deputy an' I'm the mule skinner. That's how the old judge set it up."

Kane managed a rare smile. "And I'm glad to have you along, Sam."

The compliment was sincerely given. Sam Shaver had been an army scout, buffalo hunter, saloon owner and sometime mule skinner. He was in his early seventies but was still a man to be reckoned with. A year before, back in the Nations, he'd outdrawn and killed the Texas gunman Elijah Hawks, a man nobody considered a bargain.

When he wanted a man to work for him, Judge Parker had few qualms about overlooking the odd killing. He had been impressed enough with Sam's toughness to sign him up as a wagon driver and camp cook at the same salary as a deputy, six cents a mile to the place of arrest and ten cents a mile for the return trip. The old man had since transported prisoners for famous marshals like Bass Reeves, Frank Canton, Zeke Proctor and Heck Thomas. Kane didn't know if Sam included him in that elite bunch and he'd never asked.

As tall as Kane, and just as lanky, Sam checked the coffeepot. "She's biled, Logan." He poured a cup for each of them, then removed the salt pork from the fire, forking the meat onto a plate. He mixed flour, sourdough starter and salt into the pork fat, then added water. When the bread mix was ready, he laid it near the fire to bake.

"Grub will be up soon," Sam said.

Kane was building another smoke. "I can sure use it," he said. His eyes angled to Sam's bearded face; he was hesitant to ask the question on his mind lest it imply fear, or at least apprehension. Finally he asked it anyway. "Sam, you're around the other marshals a lot. What do they tell you about Buff Stringfellow?"

The old man looked surprised. "You don't know about him your ownself?"

"Only what the judge said, and he's not an explainin' man. He said Stringfellow and five others were arrested for murder, rape and robbery, and sentenced to twenty-five years hard labor at the Little Rock penitentiary in Arkansas. Along the way Stringfellow led an escape in which two guards were killed. Then he and the others lit out for Texas, riding double for a spell until they murdered a rancher and stole horses." Kane licked his cigarette closed. "Five days ago rangers captured the fugitives without a fight at a brothel in the Boggy Bayou red-light district in Dallas."

Sam turned the skillet so the bread would bake evenly. "Rangers don't give up prisoners easy, but they reckon there's a chance Stringfellow an' the others might escape the rope in Texas. But they know fer sure them hard cases will hang in Fort Smith. Judge Parker is not a forgiving man when it comes to the killin' of his deputies."

"How come they didn't swing the first time around?"

Sam shook his head. "Don't know. But the judge can be notional by times. Maybe he figgered that twenty-five years in that Little Rock hellhole was worse than hanging. Men are sent there to be forgotten by other folks and smell the stink of their own rot." He watched Kane's eyes. "You ever been in prison, Logan?"

The marshal smiled. "No, I can't say as I have."

"A penitentiary is a wheel within a wheel, a prison within a prison. Them wheels turn real slow and they steal a man's youth, and then his soul."

"How come you know so much about it, Sam?"

"I did three years in Detroit when hard old Zebulon Brockway was prison governor."

"What fer?"

"A shootin' scrape an' a killin'."

"Was it fair?"

"Was what fair? The three years or the killin'?"

"The killin'."

"A man was coming at me with a Greener scattergun in his hands an' death in his eye."

"I'd say it was a fair fight."

"So would I, but the jury didn't see it that way. Happened that I'd gunned the town's only blacksmith, an' that cut them boys up considerable."

"Three years is a long time. But I don't see no scars on you, Sam."

"Maybe so, but I got them just the same, deep inside where they don't show. Maybe Stringfellow knew about Little Rock and decided the rope was better. *Quién sabe?*"

A restless wind rustled among the trees and set the fire's flames to dancing. The coyotes were yipping closer, drawn by the smell of cooked meat, and far out in the moon-slanted darkness an owl asked his question of the night.

"As to Buff hisself, he's not a man—he's a dangerous animal," Sam said. "And them with him are just as bad. I guess that's why we're taking them back in an iron cage. Them boys can't be around civilized folks. Over to the Ruby Mill Canyon country ol' Buff shot a Cherokee farmer. Then he and the others raped his wife and daughter. The girl was only fourteen and she didn't live through it. They murdered her mother afterward. Last I heard, Buff had killed eighteen men, including them two deputies, and I believe it. He's one bad hombre an' a dangerous combination—a born killer who's slick with the Colt."

Kane dropped the butt of his cigarette into the fire. "If he makes any fancy moves on the trail to Fort Smith, I'll gun him fer sure."

"Trouble is, Marshal, if'n he makes a fancy move, you could be the last to know. Buff is fast, mighty fast, an' sneaky as a hound in a smokehouse." Sam thumped the bread with his knuckles. "She's ready," he said. "Let's eat."

Logan Kane lay back on his blankets and said from under the hat tipped over his face, "A fine meal, Sam'l. Now I think I'll turn in."

The old man was scouring the skillet with sand. He stopped and glanced at the sky, where dark clouds chased across the face of the moon. "I'm smelling rain, Logan. Maybe you should spread your blankets under the wagon."

Kane raised his hat and looked at the sky. "Clouding up, right enough. An' I thought I heard thunder a minute ago, but it was a fur piece away." He wriggled his shoulders into a more comfortable position. "I reckon I'll stay right where I'm at, at least for the time being."

"Suit yourself," Sam said. "I'm all through telling marshals they should at least show enough sense to come in out of the rain. Why, I mind the time when I was drivin' fer big ol' Heck Thomas an'—"

"Hello the camp!"

The voice sang out of the darkness—a woman's voice . . . and she sounded troubled.

Chapter 2

Kane rose to his feet, and not being a trusting man, he kept his right hand close to his holstered Colt. "Come on ahead!" he yelled. "Slow an' easy, like you was visiting kinfolk."

The gloom parted and a woman stepped into the clearing, holding a blanket-wrapped bundle in her arms. Behind her Kane heard the creak of a wagon and the fall of hooves.

"I need help," the woman said. Her voice was frightened, cracking around the edges like thin ice. "My daughter is sick, Mister. She's awful sick."

Gun trouble Kane could handle, but a child with a misery was a thing beyond his experience. He stood speechless for a moment, but Sam Shaver filled the void.

"Bring her over to the fire, ma'am. What ails her?"

"She has a fever," the woman said. "Mister, she's burning up."

Kane found his voice. "It ain't the plague, is it?"

Sam answered for the woman. "No, Marshal, it ain't the plague. There's a wagon out there in the dark an' I'm guessin' she an' whoever is with her are travelin' folks. Bad food and bad water probably done it, but it's not the plague."

The old man laid his palm on the girl's head. "She's hot as a burning stump, all right." His eyes lifted to her mother's face. "How long has she been like this?"

"I don't rightly know. I figured she was asleep in the back of the wagon. I found her like this an hour ago, maybe longer than that."

"Come a fur piece?" Sam asked.

"From down Fort Worth way." The woman hesitated a heartbeat. "My husband had . . . business there."

The skin of Sam's face stretched thin over his cheekbones. "Ma'am, if'n we don't get this fever broke, your young 'un will die." He shook his head. "I don't mean to be rough of speech, ma'am, but what I just spoke was a natural fact."

"Help her, Mister," the woman whispered. She looked like she'd been slapped. "Save my child. She's all I've got."

Kane had kept his eyes from the fire, fearing temporary blindness if he had to shoot into the dark. Now he stepped closer to the edge of the clearing. His hand was still close to his gun. "You in the wagon," he yelled. "Drive on in at a walk."

"Scared, huh?" came a man's voice, as high, harsh and cutting as the cry of a screech owl.

Kane talked into the wall of blackness between the trees. "You don't want to get me scared, Mister. When I get scared, I get violent an' bad things happen."

A few moments passed. Then a pair of huge gray Percherons emerged from the dark hauling a box wagon, the rear half of the bed sheltered by a hooped canvas cover.

"I reckon now I don't scare you so bad after all, huh?" the driver said. He was a small man, thin, and his wasted legs seemed too short and spindly for his body.

Kane ignored the remark. He said, "Your daughter is mighty sick, so sick she could die. We have to see to her."

The small man shrugged. "She ain't my blood. I don't care one way or t'other." He grinned. "Name's Barnabas Hook, by the way. I'm headed for the Territory."

The coldness of Hook's reply hit Kane like a bucket of ice water. The marshal liked to say that by nature he was not a particularly caring man. But those who knew him soon realized that this claim was undercut by a fondness for children and a sincere, if bungling, respect for women.

Kane's voice held level, the Westerner's obligation to hospitality overcoming his revulsion. "I'm Deputy Marshal Logan Kane and the mean old coot by the fire is Sam Shaver. Light an' set. Thar's coffee on the bile."

"Lorraine! Chair!" Hook's demand slashed across

the fire-stippled darkness like the crack of a bull-whip.

The woman's eyes lifted to Hook, a tangle of emotion on her face, a quiet desperation uppermost. "Barnabas, Nellie is sick."

"Chair!"

Lorraine shoved her daughter into Sam's arms and hurried to the back of the wagon. In the fleeting glimpse he caught of the woman, Kane saw fear, and something more . . . hatred maybe.

Husband and wife this pair might be, but happiness was obviously not a part of their marriage agreement.

"Marshal, will you step over here?" Sam asked.

Kane stepped beside the old man and looked down at the girl. Nellie was older than he'd thought, a small, pretty child with lustrous dark hair, and long lashes lying on her cheekbones like Spanish fans. She was unconscious, her face flushed as the fever ravaged her, and her breathing was fast and shallow.

Kane took a knee and laid the back of his hand on the girl's cheek. His glance met Sam's and he saw his own concern mirrored in the man's eyes. "She's hot," he said. "Her skin's burning."

"If we don't get the fever down, she'll die, Logan. That is, if she ain't dying already."

"You seen this afore?"

"Oncet. When I was scoutin' for the Army I seen it in a Comanche village north of the Mogollon Rim after the cholera hit."

"Well, what happened?"

"For a lot of them, nothin' happened. They just

died. The youngest of them was buried in Arbuckle coffee boxes."

"Hell, did any of them live?"

"A few."

Kane's exasperation showed. "I swear, Sam'l, sometimes talkin' to you is like talkin' to a shadow. How come some of them survived?"

"Well, it had been snowin' up there. So along comes this young army doctor an' he packs the young 'uns that are still alive in snow until their fevers break. Some of them lived after that."

The marshal's face fell. "We don't have no snow."

"I reckon. But we have the creek an' the water's cold."

"Then let's get it done," Kane said.

He looked around for the woman. To his surprise, Lorraine was pushing a wicker wheelchair toward the front of the wagon. She stopped and waited until Hook edged over on the seat. Then she reached up and lifted him in her arms. She laid him gently into the wheelchair, placed his feet in supports and covered his wasted legs with a blanket.

"Shotgun. Then push me to the fire," Hook said.

Lorraine reached into the wagon and dragged out a shotgun from under the seat. Hook laid the gun across the arms of his chair as his wife pushed him close to the fire. He turned his head to her and said, "Coffee."

A small rage flaring in him, Kane rose to his feet. "The coffee can wait. There are other, more important things to be done here."

Hook ignored him. "Lorraine, coffee. Now!"

The woman saw Kane's rising anger and she shot him a beseeching look, her eyes pleading with him not to judge her husband harshly. The marshal recognized the look for what it was, took note of its intensity and said only, "I'll bring you a couple of cups from our wagon."

Kane returned with the cups and handed them to Lorraine, who immediately poured coffee for Hook. She handed the cup to the man, then rushed to Sam Shaver's side.

"How old is the young 'un, ma'am?" he asked.

"Twelve years," the woman answered. Then by way of explanation she added, "She's small for her age."

"Twelve, good. Then she ain't quite reached the age o' modesty yet. Get her clothes off, ma'am. We're going to lay her in the creek an' see if we can get the fever broke." Sam lifted cold eyes to Hook, who was sipping his coffee, staring into the fire. "Seems to me we've wasted enough damned time already."

Lorraine didn't question the old man. She quickly removed Nellie's clothes, then stood, the naked child in her arms. Hook did not even glance in their direction.

"Let's get goin'," Sam said. He looked at Kane. "You comin', Marshal? If you are, better grab our slickers. It's goin' to be a wet one."

Kane nodded, still on a slow burn. He very much disliked Barnabas Hook and with Logan Kane, that much dislike often led to a killing. But the man would leave a widow and an orphan behind. That very thing had happened so often in Kane's past that he could not bring himself to consider it now. Still, as he retrieved his and Sam's slickers from the prison wagon and followed the old man and the woman to the creek, his ill feeling for Hook rankled, and set his jaw at a jut.

The little girl moaned softly as Sam placed her naked body in the stream. The grassy banks were a couple feet apart and the cold water ran fast and shallow over a bed of sand and small pebbles.

"Water's got to be deeper," Sam said. He was using his cupped hand to pour water over the child's chest and stomach. His eyes lifted to Kane. "Logan, see if you can dam her up downstream a little ways."

Kane looked at Lorraine, who was holding her daughter's small hand in hers. "Woman, how you doin'?" he asked.

"I'm breaking all to pieces, Marshal. I never knew fear like this. I swear, if Nellie dies, I'll lie right down beside her and die myself."

"She won't die," Sam snapped. The old man was feeling the strain and his voice was sharp. "Leastways, if a certain feller ever gets the creek dammed up."

Kane touched his hat to Lorraine and stepped downstream a few feet. He walked through bladed moonlight, looking around to see what he could find. He wanted rocks or large pieces of fallen tree branch.

The night was cool, a stiff breeze riding point for a thunderstorm rumbling to the north over the craggy peaks of the Ouachita Mountains. Already probing fingers of black cloud were reaching into the violet sky, slowly blotting out stars, and the moon was threatening to take a header into darkness.

Kane smelled the coming rain and the ozone tang of lightning that flickered in the distance. The night seemed fragile as crystal, as if a single blast of thunder would shatter it into a million shards that would catch the blue fire of the lightning and fall to earth like diamonds.

He intensified his search and soon had an armful of small rocks that he dropped into the creek, then tried to arrange into a dam. The water bubbled over his hands and the rocks, heedless of his attempt to halt its flow. He rose and found more rocks and some thick branches. This time his rickety dam held better and suddenly the water began to pool behind it. But after a few minutes the force of the pent-up stream swept the wood away and the creek chattered over the pebbles as before.

Kane rose, defeat slumping his shoulders, and looked at Sam. "I can't dam it. The wood won't hold."

The old man was still pouring water over the girl with his hand. His head lifted. "Wash out the coffeepot. I'll use that." As Kane turned to leave, he said, "Logan, we don't have much time. Best we ain't a-squatting out here in a lightning storm."

As thunder growled to the north, Kane realized the urgency. He stepped to the fire and grabbed the pot.

"Hey, don't take the coffee away," Hook said.

Kane ignored the man. But a moment later he paid

heed to the twin shotgun barrels pointed right at his belly. "I said, don't take the coffee away." Hook's eyes gleamed in the firelight like hot coals and there was death in his voice.

But Logan Kane was not in an accommodating mood. Without a second of hesitation he threw the boiling-hot contents of the pot into Hook's face, then reached down and wrenched the scattergun from the man's grasp.

Hook screamed and his hands flew to his already-blistering face.

"Mister, if you wasn't a family man an' crippled an' all, I'd a drawed down on you and put a bullet in your belly," Kane said, his hard blue eyes lending truth to the statement.

Hook took his hands from his fiery, blistered face and looked at them intently, as if he expected to see blood. His eyes lifted to the marshal. "Damn you to hell, Kane. Someday I'll kill you for this."

The marshal smiled. He broke open the shotgun and removed the two red shells, then dropped the weapon at Hook's feet. "I'd like to cuss an' discuss that with you, Hook, but I got to be going," he said.

Hook's swollen, blistered lips looked like stained pillows. "Heed me well, Kane," he yelled at the marshal's retreating back. "One day soon I'll kill you."

After washing out the coffeepot in the creek, Kane handed it to Sam. "What happened to Hook?" the old man asked. "We couldn't see from here."

"Nothing," the marshal said, his face bland. "He just wanted more coffee."

Sam filled the pot in the water and poured it over Nellie. The girl's eyes fluttered open and she looked into her mother's face. "Ma, what—what are these men doing to me?"

"Making you better, child. You have a fever an' we must chase it away."

"Ma . . . Ma . . . I don't want . . ."

Nellie's eyes closed and Sam said to her mother, "I'm worried, ma'am. She's still way too hot, burnin' up something fierce."

"Pour the cold water over her," Lorraine said. "We must keep trying."

Thunder banged, closer now, and skeletal fingers of lightning scrawled across the dark sky. Sam looked up for a brief moment but said nothing. His face was like stone.

Lorraine took her eyes off her child for a moment. "Marshal," she said, "I heard what my husband said to you—about killing you, I mean. Be on your guard."

Kane smiled. "Lady, I've heard that a passel of times."

The woman shook her head. "Don't take Barnabas lightly. He's killed men before; more men than you could ever imagine."

Lightning flared on the woman's face and Kane saw that her eyes were wide—and very frightened.

Chapter 3

The storm struck with tremendous power, earsplitting thunder, sheeting rain and venomous lightning. Suddenly it seemed to Kane that the whole world was on fire, that when the new day came aborning, it would see only a wilderness of smoke and ashes.

He kneeled opposite Sam and the woman, rain running in torrents off his hat brim and the shoulders of his slicker. Nellie looked pale blue in the flame-streaked darkness, her head supported in Sam's right hand. The girl's hair was plastered across her face and every now and then she moaned softly.

Sam splashed a pot of water across the child's chest, then another. "If the fever don't break soon—" The rest of what he said was drowned in a clap of thunder, but his meaning was clear.

Over by the dead fire, Barnabas Hook was screaming for his wife, mouthing curses and threats. Searing white lightning flashes shimmered around him and the racketing rain pounded him mercilessly.

Sam laid his hairy cheek against Nellie's forehead and held it there. Finally he lifted his eyes to Kane, then to the woman. "She's gettin' cooler. I think maybe she is."

Hope flared in Lorraine's eyes. "The fever is breaking!"

"Wait!" the old man yelled over the thunder. "I said maybe she is. I don't know fer sure."

The strain of being outdoors in the middle of a dangerous storm and the sight of the child's pale-lipped face was getting to Kane. "Then don't speak again, old man, until you know fer damned sure!"

"Doin' my best, Marshal Kane," Sam said. It was a small rebuke, but it stung.

Kane swallowed his irritation. "I know you are, Sam. It's just that . . . well . . . I know you are."

"I reckon maybe it's the cold rain that's a-coolin' her," Sam said. "Comin' down hard enough, a reg'lar duck drencher, you might say."

Kane put the back of his hand in the middle of Nellie's chest. "I think you're right, Sam. She don't feel as hot." He looked at Lorraine. "What do you think, missus?"

Lightning raked the sky with skeletal fingers of silver flame, and thunder bellowed as the woman cupped her daughter's forehead in her hand. After a few moments she said, "Yes, she's cooling down." Then, with a note of desperation she added, "I jes' know she is."

Only then did Kane notice that the woman's dress was soaked. He unbuttoned his slicker and spread it over her shoulders. "It won't make you dry, ma'am, but it will he'p you from getting any wetter." He smiled. "About now you look wet enough to bog a snipe."

Lorraine threw Kane a grateful smile, then glanced toward her wagon where Hook was screaming her name into the night, cursing her for leaving him to die in the storm.

"Logan, we can attend to the young 'un," Sam said. "Maybe you should see to that bellyachin' man. I already got half a mind to walk over thataway an' gun him."

"Hell, let him fry." The words came unbidden out of Kane's mouth and he instantly regretted them. Lorraine looked at him, but said nothing. He sighed and shook his head. "Hell, I'll get him into the back of the wagon."

The marshal walked across the clearing under a sky that roared as it was being torn apart, and rain drove hard into his face. Barnabas Hook meant nothing to him, but in some strange way he felt he had a duty to help his woman and her daughter. As a man, Hook was nothing much, but the fact remained that he was Lorraine's husband and the little girl's pa, and nothing could change that.

Hook saw Kane coming and spoke first. "Tell my wife to fog it the hell over here."

Kane ignored that and said, "Sam thinks Nellie's fever is breaking. He's seen it afore."

"I already told you the kid means nothing to me. She's some other man's get, not mine." The eyes

Hook lifted to Kane, a hard-faced man standing tall and grim in the rain, were filled with hatred. "Send Lorraine over here."

"She's busy trying to save her child's life," Kane said. He didn't wait for Hook to make a comment. "I'll roll you to the back of the wagon and it's up to you from thar."

"Think you're tough, Kane, don't you? Mighty tough."

"I'm as tough as I need to be."

"Maybe so, but one day I'll cut you down to size."

Kane smiled, anger hacking at his insides like a knife. "That's big talk, Hook, coming from a man in a wheelchair."

Lightning shimmered on Hook's face, deepening the shadowed hollows in his eyes and cheeks. When he grinned, showing bared teeth, he looked like a dead man, and he spoke with the voice of a dead man. "Kane . . . I'm hell on wheels."

Walking through a wall of thunder, the marshal pushed Hook to the rear of the wagon, feeling an emotion he'd never experienced before.

Was it fear? Kane dismissed the notion. If his years as a puncher and then a lawman had taught him anything, it was that he was a hard man to scare.

Dread? A good word and maybe that was it. It was as if death had just spoken to him and had written his name in the book. For a moment, in the harsh glare of lightning, Barnabas Hook had looked less than human, a thing of rancid evil.

As he watched the man struggle out of the wheelchair, Kane shivered and his fingertips touched the cold blue steel of his Colt. That, at least, was reassuring. He had killed eight men with the revolver and it represented security. With a gun in his hand Kane believed he could handle anything the world threw at him, and that included Hook.

"Are you just going to stand there watching me, or are you going to help?" Hook was trying to lift himself into the back of the wagon and under the canvas cover, noisy with the drumroll of the rain.

"You're doin' all right," Kane said. "I got to be heading back to he'p Sam."

His useless legs dangling, Hook managed to lift himself onto the wagon gate. Behind the man, Kane saw a couple of blanket-covered pallets and an oil lamp. Only a small part of the wagon was covered, but it looked dry and snug enough.

"Thanks for the help, Kane," Hook said, his tone spiteful.

The marshal grinned under his dripping mustache and waved a careless hand. "Anytime." He pointed to Hook's scowling face. "The sovereign remedy fer them burn blisters is fresh butter. If you got none o' that, then axle grease will do in a pinch."

He'd tried to sound relaxed, but as he walked away from the wagon, the skin on his back felt like it was crawling with ants.

"We're winning, Logan." Sam Shaver grinned when Kane took a knee beside him. "The young 'un's fever is down fer sure."

Kane felt the girl's forehead. "Uh-huh, it certainly is," he said. He looked at Lorraine and smiled. "I'd say Nellie is going to be all right."

"Thanks to you two," the woman said. "I'll be beholden to you forever."

The child's eyes were open and now she was aware of where she was. She looked up at her mother. "Ma, I don't like it here in the water. I'm cold."

"She'll do." Sam grinned. He said to Lorraine, "If'n I recollect rightly, that cavalry doctor said it was dangerous to warm up the Comanche young 'uns too fast after their fevers broke. He wrapped them loose in a blanket and let them set thataway fer an hour or more." His eyes shifted to Kane. "Logan, we have dry blankets in the wagon."

"I'll get one," Kane said, wondering at how easily he had adapted to the change from gun-handy lawman to sick child's nurse. There was, he decided, no end to life's strangeness.

The thunderstorm was moving, flashing and grumbling to the south, but the rain was still falling, heavy and relentless. Kane was soaked to the skin and he shivered in the cool wind. Suddenly he found himself yearning for the comfort of his own blankets, wet or no.

Tired as he was, he had a feeling the dream would not disturb his sleep tonight. He hoped not. He wished for it to stay far away from him and eventually lose itself in memories.

The prison wagon was a converted Mitchell and Lewis Company farm wagon that had been fitted with a wrought-iron cage and hinged door made by a Fort Smith blacksmith. The man had been paid sixty dollars for the work, the money coming out of Judge Parker's own pocket. The comfort of prisoners was not a consideration and the wagon box was only ten feet long and forty inches wide. Like old Charlie Goodnight's famous chuck wagons, it had a box for supplies and a boot to the rear featuring a number of shelves and drawers to hold what Sam Shaver would need to feed the prisoners. A water barrel big enough to hold a two-day supply was roped to the side of the wagon along with a shovel, pick and the precious American Enterprise coffee grinder.

Since wood was often hard to find on the trail, Sam had slung a canvas under the wagon hammock-style where he could throw any fuel he collected during each day's drive. There was also a wagon box where he and Kane kept their bedrolls, spare blankets and shackles. No bedding was provided for prisoners.

The wagon was sturdily built and was fitted with steel axles that could last up to five months on the trail, as marshals and drivers often stayed out that long. Judge Parker had written a letter to the Mitchell and Lewis Company declaring that their wagon was "a marvel of modern engineering, first-rate in every way." What his prisoners thought of the prison wagon has not been recorded.

Kane took a folded blanket from the wagon box and bent over, holding it against his chest to protect it from the hammering rain.

He handed the blanket to Lorraine. "It's dry, mostly." The woman lifted her daughter from the creek and wrapped her in the blanket.

"Remember, don't get her too warm, ma'am," Sam said.

Kane helped the woman to her feet. "I'll walk you back to your wagon."

The marshal held Lorraine's elbow as they made their way to the wagon, stepping through darkness and rain. Lightning shimmered to the south, but the voice of the thunder was stilled.

"Brung you back your woman, Hook," Kane said when he reached the tailgate. "Make room there."

Grudgingly the man made a space. He glanced at Nellie. "She all right?"

"Her fever is down," Lorraine answered, attempting a smile that quickly died on her lips.

"Woman, you ever disobey me again, I'll throw you and the brat out, no matter where we are, desert, mountain, swamp, wherever," Hook said. "Without me you'd both starve to death in weeks."

Lorraine's face didn't change, but her eyes were wounded, lifeless. She handed Kane his slicker, then took her place on the pallet beside her husband and bent her head to the child, whispering soothing words.

"Lorraine," Hook snapped, "did you hear me?"

"I heard you, Barnabas," the woman said quietly.

The man grabbed a handful of his wife's hair and forced her to look at him. His red, blistered face was twisted in fury. "Then heed me well. You were a two-dollar whore before I took you in and I can send you back to being a whore tomorrow."

"I'm sorry, Barnabas," Lorraine said meekly. "I promise, I'll heed you from now on."

Kane had seen enough. It was not his place to intervene between husband and wife. He stepped away from the wagon and walked into the night, the rain hissing around him like an angry dragon.

Why had Lorraine married such a man? Was it an act of desperation by a woman who reckoned her child needed a father?

Kane had no answers and he tried to dismiss the woman from his mind. She was none of his business and he had problems enough facing him. The day after tomorrow he'd take custody of six dangerous killers. It was nearly 250 miles to Fort Smith, and not a single yard of it would be easy. Now was not the time to think about a woman, and a married one at that.

The marshal smiled, rain beating on his lean, leathery face. As a youngster he'd pushed cattle along the Chisholm and Western trails, routes first forged by others. But now he was about to pioneer his own trail—northeast across plains, mountains and rivers, a dust-and-cuss journey across an unforgiving land that offered nothing except a hundred different ways to kill a man. With an empty wagon, plenty of supplies and good weather, the trip south from Fort

Smith had been relatively uneventful. But heading back would be different now that fall was starting to crack down hard. Buff Stringfellow and his boys were no bargains either. Six desperate men who would do anything to escape the noose would be a handful.

"I'm blazing the Convict Trail," Kane said to himself.

Despite its dire implications, he liked the sound of that.

Chapter 4

Kane and Sam bedded down in the wagon, their slickers spread on top of the cage to keep out the worst of the rain that continued to fall ceaselessly. They spent an uncomfortable night and slumbered little, but the dream had stayed away and for that Kane was grateful.

The dawn shaded gray from night and when the marshal woke from a shallow sleep, Sam was already up and had coffee on the fire.

"They're pullin' out, Logan," the old man said as Kane joined him, stretching knots out of his back.

"So I see," the marshal said. He glanced at the Hook wagon and then the ashen sky. "At least the rain has quit."

"For a spell at least," Sam said. His eyes lifted slyly to Kane. "Sleep all right, Marshal?"

"Did I call out?"

"Nah. Not a sound. First time in a while, mind you."

"Then I slept all right."

Kane squatted and built his first cigarette of the day. The trees around him were ticking water and the creek had spilled over its banks, swollen by the storm. The air was cool and smelled of dampness and decaying vegetation.

Lorraine had hitched the Percherons, and Hook was up on the box, the reins in his hands. The man had some kind of grease on his face, and the eyes he turned to Kane were cold and hostile.

Sam saw it and said, "Step careful around that man, Logan."

"He don't worry me none."

"He should. He's a back-shooter, an' you can take that to the bank."

Kane thumbed a match into flame and lit his smoke. Lorraine, smiling, was walking toward him.

"Nellie is resting," she said. "I want to thank both of you for saving her life." The woman kissed Sam on the cheek, then got up on her toes and did the same to Kane. "I'll never forget you, Marshal," she said.

Kane shook his head, his eyes questioning. "Lorraine, why that man?"

The woman took the question in stride, showing no surprise. "Barnabas told the truth. I was working the line in Abilene when he found me. He married me and gave my daughter his name."

"Nellie Hook," Kane said. "Was it worth it?"

Lorraine took a quick glance over her shoulder, then turned back to the tall lawman. "Logan, look at me. I'm a homely woman, no great catch. When Barnabas asked me to be his wife I jumped at the chance. I was already getting too old to work the line, so what was ahead of me? A hog ranch at best, dead from disease or some drunken cowboy at worst. What would happen to my child then?"

Lorraine unbuttoned the top of the shirt she was wearing and pushed it off her shoulder. Her skin was laced all over with the pale scars of bite marks. "Is living with Barnabas really any worse than this?"

Kane was shocked into silence, the tracery of arced scars more eloquent than any of the woman's words. Finally he managed, "Lorraine, I'm sorry. I'm not by inclination a questioning man."

The woman buttoned her shirt. "You got nothing to be sorry for, Marshal. You didn't put the scars there. Men who visit girls on the line act like animals." She shrugged. "And animals bite. I reckon it's just a fact of nature."

Sam had been listening and watching, and now he said, "Coffee's biled, ma'am, if you'd care fer a cup."

Lorraine shook her head. "No thank you, Sam. I have to get back. Barnabas is eager to leave."

"Where you headed?" Kane asked.

"The Territory."

"Them's badlands up there, ma'am," Kane said. "It just ain't safe for a lone man to be travelin' with a woman and child. What's your husband's line o' work anyhow?"

The woman's quick eyes revealed her unease. "Marshal, maybe you should ask him your ownself."

"Logan, if'n you won't, I will," Sam said. "Why would a crippled man take a white woman and her young daughter into the Indian Territory? It don't make a lick o' sense."

"No, it don't," Kane agreed. "Maybe I can talk to him."

A painful look crossed Lorraine's face and she laid her fingertips on Kane's arm. "Be careful. Barnabas loaded his shotgun again."

The marshal smiled and touched his hat. "It always pays to be careful, ma'am."

Hook's welcome was less than cordial. "What the hell do you want, Kane?"

"Your woman says you're taking her and Nellie into the Territory. Is that wise?"

"What business is it of your'n?"

Kane pulled back his vest, uncovering the star pinned to his gun belt. "This makes it my business."

For a few moments Hook was silent, making up his mind about something. His scattergun was beside him, propped against the seat. Finally he said, "All right, then I'll let you meddle in my affairs for the last time." He motioned with a hand to the wagon bed. "The wooden box back there behind the seat— open it up, see what you see and be damned to ye fer a bad egg."

Ken stepped behind Hook and found a box of rough-planed mahogany. He lifted the lid on the box and looked inside. A dozen hemp ropes were neatly coiled, already noosed with the hangman's knot and next to them, made from rough cotton, was a pile of black hoods. A worn Bible lay on top of lengths of rope long enough to bind a man's hands and feet, and under those lay a .38 caliber Smith & Wesson revolver.

Kane stepped to the driver's seat again, puzzled. "What the hell are you?"

"Ain't it obvious?"

"No, tell me."

"I'm what you might call a traveling hangman. That's why I'm bound for the Indian Territory."

"Judge Parker administers the Territory and he has his own hangman."

"I'm aware of that. But you'd be surprised how many settlements need a helping hand. In every town there's always somebody nobody likes or a troublemaker who keeps getting into scrapes or a nuisance that's tetched in the head. It makes folks feel real good about themselves to hire me and know they're hanging a man legal-like."

Kane's eyes hardened. "You don't have a legal right to hang a man in the Territory."

"Damned if I don't. I got me a letter signed by a federal judge in Texas giving me the legal right to hang a man in any state, territory or protectorate where our flag flies."

"Hook, that letter isn't worth the paper it's written on. You know that."

"The hell it isn't."

"You paid some drunken old judge to write it."

"That's neither here nor there. It's a legal document an' nobody has ever questioned it before, 'cept you."

"How many men have you murdered with a rope, Hook?"

The man looked sly, warning Kane what to expect. "Legally executed, you mean. At last count, twenty-seven men and one woman. Each and every one of them a thief, murderer or no-account."

"How can a cripple in a wheelchair hang grown men?"

Hook smiled. "The locals haul me up the gallows steps and then I make the condemned kneel for the noose. Once they're cut down to size, I can get to their necks just fine."

"Why, Hook?"

"For money, of course. And the satisfaction of ridding the earth of undesirables."

"You're a paid killer, Hook, and a poor excuse for a man. If I hear of you hanging a man in the Territory, I'll come after you, arrest you and take you back to Fort Smith. The Honorable Judge Isaac Parker will deal with you at his convenience."

Anger flared in Hook's eyes. "Kane, you won't be around to arrest anybody, for I intend to kill you." His fingers drifted to his blistered face. "For this."

"Hook, if you're pondering the scattergun, I wouldn't. I can draw and shoot the iron on my hip faster'n you can blink."

"My time will come, Kane. Revenge is a dish best served cold. I'll wait."

Hook's stare moved beyond Kane. "Lorraine," he said, "get up here. We're pulling out now."

The woman stepped beside Kane. "Once again, Marshal, thank you for everything," she said.

"My pleasure, ma'am," Kane said. He took Lorraine's elbow. "Let me assist you into the wagon."

"She doesn't need assistance," Hook said.

Kane ignored the man and walked Lorraine around the stamping Percherons to the seat. He helped the woman climb up beside her husband, then said, "You're wrong about being homely, ma'am. You got pretty brown eyes and your hair catches the morning light an' turns it into spun gold." Suddenly embarrassed, he said, "Well, I jes' thought you'd like to know that."

Lorraine smiled at him but said nothing. Kane stepped back as Hook slapped the horses into motion and watched until the wagon left the clearing and turned onto the trail.

Suddenly Sam was at his elbow. "Marshal," he said, "one day soon you're going to have to gun that man."

Kane stared at him. "Shoot a cripple?"

"He's poison," Sam said. "Don't ever take him lightly."

"I feel as mean as a mule with a toothache this morning," Kane said. "I ain't in the mood to take anything lightly."

"You're feeling mean on account of how you haven't had your coffee yet. Come an' get it afore it biles away."

Kane glanced at the sky. "Fixin' to rain again, I reckon."

"Rain, shine, it don't matter, Logan. We got prisoners to collect."

Kane was silent for a moment, then stared at Sam. "How come I don't feel good about that no more? Since I woke this morning, it's like I've been expecting something real bad to happen. Maybe a thing I can't handle."

"Marshal, you're an ol' curly wolf from way back, an' you can handle anything throw'd at you. You jes' need your coffee is all."

Sam was smiling, but his eyes were troubled.

Chapter 5

The Texas Rangers had arranged to meet Judge Parker's deputies a few miles north of the boomtown of Clarksville. The location was an abandoned railroad station that had been built in anticipation of a Texas and Pacific Railway branch line. The rails had never arrived, and the station and the tent-and-tarpaper settlement that sprang up around it had been quickly abandoned.

Logan Kane and the wagon came down through trees along one side of a pasture that showed signs of having once been earmarked for cattle pens. Five horses and four mules grazed on the thin grass and a convict wagon without a cage stood to one side, its tongue raised. The station itself was an ornate, gingerbread structure that had been painted red at one time. Now its timber had reverted to a silvery gray and the peaked roof sagged, most of its wood shingles long since taken away by winds. Two windows stared blankly out into the pasture, all of their glass panes gone but one. Some ranny had taken a potshot at the surviving pane, but had succeeded only in putting a hole in it. The fractured glass around the bullet hole spread out like a spiderweb.

Beyond the station, all that was left of the town were a few grassy mounds and broken pieces of lumber. A waterwheel had rusted into immobility and at its base a rotting, fly-specked coyote lay tangled in death.

Up on the wagon box, Sam looked around him but said nothing. He reined the mules to a halt as Kane rode closer to the station.

A short, bearded man wearing a grubby collarless shirt and a suit coat three sizes too big for him stepped onto the platform. A .44-40 Yellow Boy hung from the crook of his left arm. Unlike its owner, the rifle was well cared for and its barrel gleamed with an oily sheen.

Kane drew rein as the small man studied him with hard blue eyes, then said, "State your business."

"I'm Deputy Marshal Logan Kane, acting on behalf of Judge Isaac Parker's court. I'm here to take delivery of six prisoners."

The small man looked surprised. "You and who else?"

"Me an' my teamster, feller by the name of Sam Shaver."

"Mister, there's nigh on three hunnerd miles of rough country between here an' Fort Smith."

"I know the trail. It's the way I came south."

"They sent only you?"

"And my teamster."

"Then God help you, Marshal. That's all I can say. You're either a damned fool or brave too much. Me, another four men an' a driver escorted the prisoners up from Tyler, an' I reckoned five rangers wasn't near enough. In the event, we was lucky, that's all."

The short man hesitated, looking at Kane. He said, "I'm Corporal Dan Hayes, D Company, Texas Rangers. Climb down, then come inside and inspect your prisoners. I expect a receipt, testifying that they were transferred to you in good condition."

Kane swung out of the saddle and followed Hayes into the station. The interior walls were gone or had never been built and there was only one cavernous room with a warped, green timber floor. The place was dusty and smelled of decaying wood, and an untidy packrat's nest lay in one corner.

Six men sat on the floor, their backs against a wall. All were dressed in nondescript range clothes and battered, shapeless hats, except for one who seemed to be the oldest. That man wore striped pants tucked into high boots, and a fancy embroidered shirt that once had been white but was now stained and dirty. He wore a brown derby hat with an eagle feather stuck in the band, and a large silver ring graced the little finger of his left hand.

The convicts looked what they were, cold-eyed killers who had long since forgotten if they ever had a conscience and slept without dreams. They closely studied Kane as he walked into the room, measuring him from hat to heels, six dangerous, predatory animals hunting for any sign of weakness.

Hayes introduced Kane to the four other rangers, hard-bitten, unfriendly men with worn Colts on their hips, their lips thin and tight under sweeping dragoon mustaches. The tough eyes of the lawmen were an even match for the tough eyes of the prisoners and just as measuring. Kane, a cold-eyed man himself, looked right at each one, lawman and outlaw, and did not take a step back from any of them. Over the years, along a hundred dangerous trails, he had written the book on toughness. And he knew it showed on him.

"Come, meet your charges," Hayes said, a bemused smile on his face, as though he knew Kane had just fought a successful skirmish in the battle to be acknowledged bull of the woods. He reached into the inside pocket of his coat and produced a folded sheet of paper.

Hayes cleared his throat, then said, "From the left: Buff Stringfellow—convicted of murder, rape and robbery."

Stringfellow hawked and spat, narrowly missing Kane's boots.

"Kills with a Colt but will use any weapon to hand," Hayes said.

"Bennett Starr—murder, rape and robbery. Kills with the Colt.

"Hick Dietz, murder, rape and robbery. Used a rifle in most of his killings.

"Amos Albright—murder, rape and robbery." Hayes' eyes angled to Kane. "All of his seven victims have been whores. Uses his hands as weapons.

"Reuben Largo—murder, rape and robbery. Calls himself a preacher and kills with a bowie knife.

"Joe Foster—murder, rape and robbery." Again Hayes turned to Kane. "Don't let his baby face fool you. He's worse than any of them. Fancies himself a fast man with the Colt and has killed at least six men trying to prove it."

"How old are you, boy?" Kane asked Foster.

"What's it to you?"

"Well, for one thing, if I end up killing you, Judge Parker will expect me to put your age on my report."

"I'm eighteen, and I've killed seven men. I like to shoot big men like you. They make a louder noise when they fall. Sometimes, if I'm in a grouchy mood, I plug them in the belly so I can hear them scream."

The other convicts laughed, and Stringfellow yelled, "That's tellin' him, kid!"

Hayes ignored the men, as though he'd heard it all before. "Marshal, would you like to address the prisoners?" he asked.

Kane nodded. "My speech will be short and sweet an' this is it: Any man who tries to escape between here and Fort Smith, I'll shoot off his right thumb. Any man who gives me back talk or sass, I'll shoot off his right thumb. Any man who kicks out at, or in any way abuses or impedes my teamster as he applies or removes shackles, I'll shoot off his right thumb. Any man who interferes with or in any way harms the civilian population we might encounter on the trail, I'll shoot off his right thumb. That is all I got to say."

Hick Dietz, a tall, heavy-shouldered man with blazing black eyes, jumped to his feet. "Damn you, I'm all through with chains. Your man ain't putting the shackles on me, an' if he tries I'll kick his face in."

A second ticked past, then another. Kane looked confused, as though he was thinking of something to say. Already a smirk had appeared on Stringfellow's face.

Then Kane summed it up. He drew and fired, and Dietz's right thumb disappeared in a sudden fan of blood and splintered bone. Kane spoke into the stunned silence that followed the roar of his gun and the shriek of the wounded man.

"I don't usually repeat myself, but I'll say it one more time: Any man who kicks out at, or in any way abuses or impedes my teamster as he applies shackles, I'll shoot off his right thumb. I have just made good on that rule. Don't let it happen again."

Dietz was sobbing. He looked down at Stringfellow and wailed, "Buff, he shot my thumb clean off. He took it away, Buff."

Stringfellow lifted his eyes to the man. "I know, Hick, I know. Just keep in mind that it's a long way to Fort Smith." Stringfellow's eyes angled to Kane. He said nothing, but his burning stare spoke of hatred and death.

Kane turned and stepped to the door. He called out, "Sam, you've got doctoring to do."

Sam was standing beside the mules. "Figgered that when I heard the shot. You plug somebody?"

"Uh-huh. He done broke the rules."

Hayes stepped beside the marshal. "Mighty sudden with the iron, ain't you, Mister?"

"Dietz was notified."

"I'll need that receipt. I'll need it signed, saying that the prisoners were in good shape afore you started shootin'."

"You'll get it."

A big ranger in a black shirt and hat slapped Kane on the shoulder. "Hell, Marshal, you did good in there."

Kane nodded. "Dietz knew how I felt about things, and if he didn't, he should have."

He glanced at the gray sky. In the distance birds were singing and insects were making their small sounds in the grass. And it had started to rain again.

Chapter 6

Sam Shaver bound up Hick Dietz's thumb, then applied leg irons to the prisoners. Kane tore a page from the tally book he always carried, laid it on his knee and wrote:

I rode a sorrel hoss down to Texas and I taken charge of six convicts har at the old trane station. They was as fit as a fiddle and had no gripes comin.

He signed the receipt and handed it to Hayes. The ranger looked the note over, folded it twice and shoved it into the pocket of his coat.

His eyes were level, looking at Kane as a hard rain ticked on the station roof.

"Marshal, I got to be pulling out. But here's some advice: You and Shaver sleep in shifts an' sleep light. When it comes feeding time, don't take your eyes off them boys for one second. They'll be looking for an edge and they'll kill you if they can."

"I'll surely give that some considerin'," Kane said, though the ranger was telling him a thing he already knew.

Drips from the roof plopped on Hayes' hat. He ignored them as he studied the marshal's face as though looking for the answer to a question he hadn't asked yet. Now he asked it. "You heard tell of an hombre *malo* who goes by the name o' Jack Henry? By nature, he's a quarrelsome man, especially in drink."

Kane nodded. "Heard tell of a hired gun out of El Paso by that name. Last I heard he was ridin' with the James boys an' that tough bunch."

"Henry split from Jesse an' them a year or two back. Now he's in business for his ownself. Two months ago, sixty-one miles west of St. Louis, him and three others, identities unknown, robbed the Katy Flier, dynamited the safe an' killed a Pinkerton guard. Ol' Jack put a bullet into a passenger who sassed him, but I read in the newspaper that the man was expected to live. But, like I said, that was two months ago, so who knows if he did or not? I don't."

The ranger was a talking man and Kane was irritated. "Hayes, when you're done pumpin', let go of the handle. Get to the point."

"Hold your horses, I'm getting there. Henry an' Stringfellow are close kin, weaned on the teats of the same wet nurse you might say. Now, they belong to a mighty close-knit clan and word gets around. It could be that Henry already knows you're taking his cousin on the trail to Fort Smith and he just might come a-gunning for you. I don't know that for a fact either."

Kane was not alarmed, but he was concerned enough to ask, "This Jack Henry feller, is he as good with the iron as they say?"

"Well, again that's a thing I don't know, but given the line of work he's in, I'd reckon he's as good as he needs to be."

"Well, thanks for the warning," Kane said.

"It's something to keep in mind," Hayes replied.

"Yup, sure is," Kane said.

"We're pulling out now, Marshal," Hayes said. "I regard riding in the rain with considerable displeasure, but we're due back in Tyler in a couple of days and I don't have much option." He stuck out his hand. "Well, good luck an' a safe trip."

Kane took the little ranger's hand and nodded his thanks. "Maybe one day our trails will cross again."

"Could be. Lawmen are a close-knit clan as well."

Sam Shaver was guarding the prisoners as Kane watched the rangers leave, an odd sense of loss in him. Now he and Sam were on their own and they had it to do.

He stepped into the station and said, "Let's load 'em up, Sam. We've a fur piece to go and we might as well get started."

Sam nodded and made a motion with his rifle. "You heard the marshal. On your feet."

"Hell, it's raining," Stringfellow said. "You can't drag a man out in that."

"Don't give me sass, Stringfellow," Kane said, drawing his Colt. "You won't melt. You ain't that sweet."

The six men shuffled out of the door, their iron chains chiming. Bent over, Hick Dietz held his wounded hand close to his belly and looked at Kane. "A helluva thing to do to a man, shoot off his thumb."

"Think yourself lucky," Kane said. "I could've just as easily shot off something else."

The mule team stood heads down in the lashing rain as Sam stepped out quickly and opened the cage door. He beckoned the prisoners forward.

Stringfellow, awkward in his shackles, scrambled into the wagon first, followed by the others. Sam clanked the door shut and turned the key in the lock. The convicts had no protection from the downpour and they were quickly soaked. They sat in the bed of the wagon, hunched and miserable, though Stringfellow's cold, calculating eyes never left Kane.

The marshal shrugged into his slicker and Sam did the same. Kane swung into the saddle, waited until Sam climbed up on the box, then waved him forward.

"Only a couple of hundred miles to go, Sam." He grinned.

"Logan, that's all I been thinking about fer days, an' now I've come to it, having them boys back there is making me real nervous."

"Me too, Sam. Me too."

The afternoon was raked with rain, gloomy and

dark, as though the night was impatient for the day to end. Kane rode point for the wagon, dropping back now and then to check on the prisoners. The going was easy, across flat, grassy country broken up by swampy playa lakes and stands of timber where shadows gathered. Heavy clouds had dropped so low, they settled on the high plains like an iron gray mist and the land seemed empty, shrouded in silence.

After Kane estimated they'd covered six miles, he cantered ahead to hunt up a place to stop for the night. The flat country offered little and he briefly considered returning to the spot where he and Sam had made camp the night before. But there had been no shelter from the rain in the clearing and his searching eyes reached into the darkening distance, hoping for something better, out of the rain.

Kane swung his sorrel into the pines and rode parallel to the trail, the big horse picking its way through the trees. He found what he was looking for a few minutes later and stared at it in disbelief, surprised as the widow woman who prayed for a man, then discovered one sitting at the foot of her bed come morning.

It was a roofless sod cabin but, incredibly, the door was intact, banging open and shut on its rawhide hinges at the whim of the wind. Around the cabin the tops of the pines were strung with mist, and rain filtered through their branches, falling to the ground with the sound of a ticking clock. Kane rode closer, then swung out of the saddle.

The cabin had never been roofed, he could see that.

He scouted around and saw no source of water. Kane decided that someone had started to build the cabin and had then abandoned it, perhaps intimidated by the need to dig a deep well.

But Kane did a rethink when he found a rusted, strap-iron arrowhead embedded in the door. He also saw that the rough timbers were perforated by a dozen bullet holes. A settler had made a last stand here, most likely against marauding Apaches or Kiowas riding north from Texas.

A few minutes later, he found the settler's body, or what was left of it, lying at the bottom of a shallow depression at the rear of the cabin. Some of the yellowed bones had been scattered by animals, but the skull, rib cage and arms still remained. There was enough to tell the man's story. He had been dragged out of the cabin, spread-eagled on the ground and then tortured to death. The ivory jaws of his skull were wide-open and the memory of his last, agonized shriek remained, echoing in dreadful silence among the pines.

The settler, whoever he was, had died a death Kane would wish on no man, and he felt sadly depressed as he rode out of the trees and waited for Sam on the trail.

Kane stretched his slicker over a corner of the cabin and held it down with small rocks he found lying around. "See if you can build a fire under that, Sam," he said. "The wood I picked up is damp, but it will burn. Eventually."

"Smoke some too, Logan." The old man stood inside the cabin doorway and nodded to the prison wagon. "You bringing them in?"

"Long enough to feed them. Then they go back."

"Mighty wet."

"That's their problem. It's going to be wet in here."

"We cross the Red tomorrow. Going to feel good to get out of Texas, seem like we're finally headed somewhere."

"Seem like."

"Will we make it, Marshal?"

"We'll make it. Maybe we'll arrive with no prisoners because I've had to gun them all, but we'll ride into Fort Smith with our hides intact, nineteen, twenty days from now."

"The judge doesn't want them rannies dead. He wants them to hang."

"He doesn't always get what he wants, Sam."

"Hope our grub holds out."

"It'll hold out. If it don't, I'll kill some meat along the trail."

The old man shook his head. "Ain't like me to hear footsteps in the fog, but Fort Smith . . . well, it's a long ways from har to there."

Kane smiled. "It's a long ways from har to anywhere."

"I'll get the fire started. Coffee, salt pork an' pan bread for supper, same for breakfast, until the flour an' coffee run out."

Kane's smile stretched into a rare grin. "Sam, what would I do without you?"

"Starve to death, most likely."

The marshal left the cabin and walked to the wagon. The rain was still heavy and lightning shimmered in the dark clouds without sound.

Kicking aside a tangle of legs and feet, Stringfellow moved closer to the side of the cage. "How long you gonna keep us out here?" he demanded.

"Not too long, Stringfellow. Once Mr. Shaver has the grub ready, I'll take you into the cabin and feed you."

"The old coot is mister, an' I'm Stringfellow."

"Uh-huh, that's about the size of it."

"The cabin don't have a roof, damn you. We'll be as wet in there as we are out here."

"Stringfellow," Kane said, "I'm not concerned with your comfort. I was ordered to escort you to Fort Smith. How you get there was left up to me."

"Hey, Kane!" Joe Foster yelled from the rear of the wagon, his young face made old by hate and anger. "If I ever get an even break with you, I'll—"

"You wouldn't even come close," Kane interrupted, smiling. "All over the West, Boot Hills are full of tinhorns like you."

Foster opened his mouth to speak again, but Stringfellow cursed him into silence. "Your time will come, Joe," he said finally. "Maybe not tonight, maybe not tomorrow, but it will come. Now shut your trap."

Amos Albright looked at Kane, then ran a slimy tongue over his top lip. "Hey, Marshal, you gonna find us a woman soon, maybe a little Indian gal, huh? All you got to do is th'ow her into the back o' the wagon an' let's have at her."

Albright had the face of a cadaver, a tallow skin that never took the sun and red-rimmed yellow eyes. His wet, loose-lipped mouth always hung slack, as though his jaw were broken.

Kane said, "You enjoy abusing women, don't you, Albright? You ever bite them on the shoulders?"

"Sure I do, an' I bite hard. Hot little gal expects that from a man. What do you do, Marshal, huh? What do you do to a woman?"

Albright started to cough, gagging on his own lust. Kane ignored him and stepped into the cabin. "I seen your smoke—smelled it too," he said to Sam.

"She's smokin', all right, but there'll be enough fire to bile the coffee an' cook the grub." The old man handed Kane the coffeepot. "Fill that from the water barrel, Logan. I'd do it my ownself, but this danged rain is a misery. My old knees is stiff as a frozen rope with the rheumatisms."

Kane took the pot and said, "You set close to the fire an' warm up them bones, Sam."

"Know what I really need, Logan? Brown paper, vinegar and an Irish potato. You soak the paper in vinegar and then make a poultice of shredded potato. Spread the poultice on the knees and cover with vinegar paper. It's a sovereign remedy for the rheumatisms."

"We don't have any o' that, Sam."

"I know we don't, so getting me the coffee water will have to do." His eyes lifted to Kane's face. "You be careful out there, Marshal. I heard them boys talk-in' to you an' none of them has a good story to tell."

Kane walked to the wagon, lifted the tin lid of the water barrel and filled the pot. The convicts sat soaked and miserable in the wagon, saying nothing, but all eyes were hard on the marshal, their hostility hanging like black bile in the air, crowding Kane so close he could almost smell its vile stink.

He made to step back to the cabin but stopped in his tracks when he heard the soft fall of hooves on the wet ground behind him. Kane carefully laid the coffeepot at his feet and turned, his hand close to his holstered gun.

"Trusting man, ain't you?" a voice said from the darkness.

Kane spoke in that direction. "You ought to know better than ride into a man's camp without announc-ing yourself."

"Never occurred to me."

Leather creaked and hooves thudded as the man rode closer. But now, as the darkness opened up, Kane saw three riders, not one as he'd first supposed.

"Stop right where you're at," he said. "I can drill ya clean through from here."

The rain hissed around him as the riders drew rein. He made a quick study of the three men. They were wearing yellow oilskin slickers and looked alike as peas in a pod. All wore black plug hats, broadcloth pants tucked into English riding boots, and in the V formed by the lapels of their slickers, Kane saw rounded, celluloid collars and tightly knotted ties.

All sported sweeping mustaches and thick burnsides, but they didn't seem to be Western men, although the Winchesters across their saddle horns looked frontier enough. They sat their saddles, patient men, watching Kane with shadowed eyes, as if the steel-bladed rain that hammered on their hats and shoulders did not exist.

"Behind you, Marshal. On your left."

Sam's voice carried across the distance. Kane did not turn, knowing the old man would be standing outside the cabin with his rifle.

"What can I do for you fellers?" the marshal asked. "I can offer you coffee, not much else."

"We're traveling," the only rider who had spoken so far said. "We'll pass on the coffee."

His accent was hard to place and Kane wrestled with it.

The man tilted his head, his chin jutting in the direction of the wagon. "Who are they?"

"Convicts." Kane pulled back his sopping vest and showed the star. "I'm Deputy Marshal Logan Kane. These men are on their way to a hanging at Fort Smith."

"The American people hate to see that," the rider said. "White men caged like animals."

"They'd hate it a sight worse if them white men ever got loose."

Stringfellow and the others were crowded close to the wagon's iron bars, intent on the three riders as though they thought their saviors had arrived.

Never a man to stand in one place for too long,

especially in a downpour, Kane was all through with it. "Mister, state your business or ride on."

"State my business?"

"Did I just hear an echo?"

The rider eased himself in the saddle. His gaze slid off Kane, moved to Sam and lingered for a moment. Then he sighed and said, "My name is Carmine Provanzano. These are my brothers, Vito and Teodoro. We're from New Orleans."

"Fur piece off your home range, ain't you?" Kane said.

"Like I told you, we're traveling."

"Well, it's been right nice talking with you," Kane said. "But I've got prisoners to feed."

He moved to lift the coffeepot, but Provanzano's voice stopped him. "Marshal, my brothers and I are part of a large and successful business family. Mostly our commercial interests are centered on the New Orleans docks, but in recent years we've branched into the banking and hospitality industries, among others."

Kane badly wanted his coffee and the scant warmth of Sam's smoky fire, and now he was irritated. "Mister, what's all that to me, huh?"

One of the other men spoke. "We're hunting a man. We think you might have seen him."

Despite himself, Kane was interested. "What man might that be?"

Carmine waved a dismissive hand at his brother. "Later, Vito. I'll tell him when the moment arrives. First a little background on our . . . ah . . . problem,

Marshal. After hearing me out, you may be more inclined to help." He leaned forward in the saddle. "Have you ever heard the word 'Omerta'?"

"Can't say as I have."

"It's the code my family lives by. It is a strict rule of honor that is never taken lightly. But one of our family recently broke that code."

"And now you're lookin' to get even, huh?"

"No, that man is dead, but not at our hands."

Carmine's horse tossed its head, the bit chiming. The mounts of the other brothers moved restlessly, perhaps scenting coyote or bear in the wind. Lightning shimmered, illuminating the planes of Carmine's face, making the shadows pooled in his cheeks and eye sockets darker.

For an instant, Kane thought he was looking at a skull. "If the ranny who broke your rule is dead, why are you huntin' another man?"

"The man who shamed us was married to our sister. He used this relationship to steal a considerable amount of money from the family, thirty thousand dollars to be exact. He left our sister and fled New Orleans, then headed for Texas, thinking he could lose himself in that vast land. But he was wrong. A man like him, dressed as a gentleman and spending money freely, is always noticed and commented upon. Before long, word got out, all the way to New Orleans, and when he was told of this, the man panicked and made his way to a dung heap called Fort Worth."

Kane picked up the coffeepot, a signal that he was no longer interested. Carmine saw this and spoke with more urgency. "In Fort Worth, the man was befriended by a cripple named Barnabas Hook, an executioner by trade."

Now Kane was listening intently, the coffeepot in his hand.

"Hook, if that was his real name, promised the man he would protect him, that he could travel with him to a place of safety in the Indian Territory. Later, the local constabulary found the man dead, cut in half by a shotgun. His money and all his possessions were gone and there was no sign of Hook. All this we were told in Fort Worth."

"So now you're hunting this man, Hook?"

"We want our money back. It belongs to the family."

The man called Vito said, "Did you meet Hook on the trail? He's already a dead man from the waist down and he travels with a woman and young girl."

Kane had made up his mind about two things: the three men facing him had a killing in mind, and he would say nothing to endanger Lorraine and Nellie.

"There are many trails in and out of the Territory," he said. "I never came across a man who fits your description."

A sudden flare of anger in his face, Vito opened his mouth to speak again, but Carmine cut him off. "Then we will take up no more of your time, Marshal. You have your duties and we have ours."

But the man didn't leave right away. He kicked his horse into motion and rode up to the cage. "Are any of you men *Siciliani*?" he asked.

The six convicts were silent, their faces puzzled. Kane guessed they were probably trying to figure out what "*Siciliani*" meant, as was he.

"No? Then that's too bad. There's nothing I can do for you."

Carmine swung his horse away from the wagon, touched his hat to Kane, then led his brothers into the black cavern of the night.

The marshal was uneasy. He had the feeling he'd meet the Provanzano brothers again, and their next meeting would not be so civil. He was certain they knew he'd lied to them about Hook and they were not men to forget such a slight.

Chapter 7

Kane fed the prisoners two at a time, herding them into the cabin under a sky splintered by lightning and heavy with rain. Later he spread Sam's slicker over the top of the wagon cage and added some fallen pine branches. It was a meager shelter, but it kept out the worst of the downpour.

Stringfellow and the others made no complaint, a fact that bothered Kane. He was more troubled still when the prisoners huddled together after they were returned to the wagon, Stringfellow's whisper thin as a razor in the darkness.

Standing as close as he dared to the wagon without seeming to listen, Kane could hear nothing. But then Stringfellow's voice rose a little and he heard the man say, "Joe, you're gold dust, true-blue." He looked around the circle of shadowed faces. "Ain't that so, boys?"

A murmur of agreement . . . then silence.

The rustling pines were alive with wind, and rain

hissed on the grass like a snake. Despite the constant shimmer of lightning that filled the clouds with golden fire, there was no thunder and the quiet night closed around Kane, mysterious and oppressive. The air was thick, hard to breathe and smelled of decay and the memory of ancient death.

The marshal walked back to the cabin through a wind-tossed darkness that slapped at him and gave him no peace.

Sam Shaver looked up when Kane stepped inside. "Get them boys bedded down for the night?"

Kane nodded. "They'll be snug enough, I reckon."

"Got your plate ready. Set and eat." The old man's eyes wandered over Kane's rangy body. "You're soaked to the skin, Logan. Get that vest an' shirt off'n you and I'll be dryin' them at the fire."

"I'll be all right."

"For oncet do as I say, Marshal. Last thing the old judge needs is a deputy with the rheumatisms."

Kane crowded beside Sam, under the token shelter of his spread-out slicker. He was suddenly tired and didn't feel like arguing with the old man tonight. He stripped off his vest and shirt, revealing the roped muscles of his wide shoulders and the flat planes of his chest. His upper body bore the white, puckered scars of three bullet wounds, and, unseen under his canvas pants, there were two more.

He took the coffee and plate of salt pork and bread Sam passed to him and set the cup on the floor between his legs. He had no appetite for food, but ate quickly, just to put it away and please Sam. After he'd eaten, Kane built a cigarette and lit it from the fire. He dragged deep, then laid the back of his head against the wall, tendrils of blue smoke curling slowly from his nostrils.

Sam had spread out Kane's steaming shirt near the fire, and now his eyes angled to the marshal. "Something bothering you, Logan?"

Kane did not make light of it. "Heard Stringfellow whispering to the others. He's up to something, and I think it involves Joe Foster."

"Two of a kind," Sam said. He held the shirt up to the feeble flames of the fire. Without lifting his eyes, he said, "We got our hands full, Logan, an' no mistake. Men like Buff Stringfellow and them others, they weren't born with a sense of what's right and what's wrong. They see themselves as the strong an' they figure they have a God-given right to prey on the weak, an' they exercise that right often. A man like ol' Buff, he'll kill a man, woman or child with nary a twinge of conscience. Destroyin' a human being means no more to him than gunnin' a jack-rabbit."

Sam's eyes sought Kane's in the shifting, scarlet gloom. "Men like them out there, they don't know the meaning of mercy. They don't give it an' they don't expect it for themselves. We can't try to understand them, because men like us can't begin to comprehend what they do and why they do it. Up in the Territory when they raped that Cherokee farmer's wife and daughter, they kept using the girl's body even after she was dead. Amos Albright an' Joe Foster did that. Reuben Largo, the one who calls hisself a preacher, used his knife on the mother and hung what he'd cut off'n her in a tree where she could see it while she lay bleeding to death."

Kane tossed the stub of his cigarette into the fire and immediately began to build another. "What do you do with men like that, Sam?"

"Just what we're doin'. You hang 'em if you can, an' if you can't do that, you put them away in jail until they rot." He smiled slightly. "Hell, I'm philosophizin' so much, I sound like the judge."

Often God's tender mercies seem so small, they go unnoticed. But when he woke, Kane whispered a prayer of thanks that the dream had again not haunted his sleep. Despite the rainy discomfort of the cabin, he felt rested and refreshed as he buttoned into his damp shirt and vest and stepped outside for the coffee water.

The prisoners were fed breakfast and loaded in the wagon without incident. Kane helped Sam hitch the mules and an hour later, under a gray sky, they reached the Red.

Kane was still smarting over the dollar-ninety-seven the ferryman had charged him and he planned to lower that price considerably on the return trip.

The ferryman's name was Bill Young, but his regular customers called him Fat Willie and he didn't seem to mind. He was a beached whale of a man with pouched slits for eyes and a shaved head that looked like a bullet.

"River's high," Sam said to him from his perch on the wagon. "Ain't that unusual for this time o' the year?"

Young, wearing only filthy red long johns tucked into a pair of untied work boots, scratched his belly and said, "Yeah, it's unusual, an' so is the rain we've been having. It's getting so a man can't even depend on the weather no more." He looked up at Sam. "You crossing?"

"Don't that seem obvious?" Kane growled, the very sight of the fat man irritating him beyond measure.

"I long since learned that nothing about folks is obvious," Young said. His eyes wandered over the prisoners in the back of the wagon, revealing speculation, greed maybe, but no surprise.

Kane decided that a man in Young's line of work must have seen everything, good and bad, of which the human race is capable. He leaned forward in the saddle. "I'll pay you a dollar-fifty to take us across."

The fat man laid one of his chins between his thumb and forefinger and frowned. "That don't cut it, Marshal. What we have here goes under the category of dangerous cargo, I mean them prisoners an' all. I charge a premium for that."

"How big a premium?" Kane felt his anger simmer somewhere under his hatband, but it was quickly coming to a boil.

"Well, I'm always one to help the law. Let's say two-dollars-fifty-cents, an' that's with the regular customer discount, since you crossed afore."

Kane tried to speak, but his tangled words sputtered to outraged silence on his lips and he fell silent. He swallowed hard, then tried again. "Mister, that's out-an'-out robbery."

Young shrugged. "Suit yerself." His smile was unpleasant. "Maybe that iron wagon will float accrost, but I doubt it."

Kane lurched back in the saddle, rage in his eyes. "Mister, get haulin' on the rope of that scow and take us across for one-fifty or get a bullet in the belly. The choice is your'n."

"Figured you might say something like that, Marshal, an' that's why my woman is over there at the cabin with a Sharps .50 aimed right at your brisket."

Kane turned his head and saw an Indian woman wearing Cheyenne braids at the door of Young's ramshackle cabin. He'd been telling the truth about the Sharps, and the woman was holding it to her shoulder as though she knew how to use it.

"We had you pegged as a troublemaker the first time you crossed," the fat man said, a smug walrus in long johns. "And I'm a cautious man. Live longer that way."

"Logan, maybe we should just pay him his blood money," Sam said. "Hell, you're bound to ride this way again. You can shoot him then."

"Yeah, Marshal," Stringfellow yelled. "Pay the man his money!"

The others laughed and Kane felt his face burn. He was well and truly buffaloed and he knew it.

"Mister, the next time I'm down har, I'll gun you

fer sure," Kane said, the taste of yet another defeat at the hands of the bandit ferryman like dry ashes in his mouth.

Young smiled. "Me an' my woman will be waiting." He slapped his hands together. "Now, are you ready to cross? Cash in advance, Marshal, if you please."

Kane's shoulders slumped. "Sam, get the wagon on board." He stood in the stirrups and reached into his pocket, his breath sighing through his lips like a mournful wind.

After he paid Young, Kane led his horse onto the ferry. He stood at the side of the wagon, watching Young with resentful eyes as the man took up the slack on the rope and prepared to haul. The hole the missing two dollars and fifty cents had left in his pocket made Kane's pants feel light and he nursed his anger to keep it warm.

The Cheyenne woman, not pretty but lithe and slender, had moved closer to the ferry. The Sharps was now slanted across her breasts, but her black eyes never left Kane's face. She was obviously ready for anything that might happen.

As the ferry pulled away from the gravel bank, Amos Albright pushed his face against the iron straps of the cage and yelled at the woman, "Come on over here, li'l squaw. See what I got fer you." The others laughed and hooted. Emboldened, a grinning Albright stuck his arm through the bars and wiggled his fingers in a suggestive manner. "Come here, honey. Just a li'l closer now."

Kane's gun cleared the leather fast and he brought the barrel down on Albright's wrist. The man yelped and pulled his arm back. "What the hell did you do that fer?" Albright demanded, his lips pursed as he clutched at his bruised wrist.

"I get seasick," Kane said. "Makes me a might testy."

The Cheyenne woman lowered her rifle and held it across the top of her thighs. Kane wasn't sure, but she didn't seem as ready anymore. There might even have been a hint of a smile on her lips.

The ferry ground to a halt on the opposite bank. Scattered pines and hickory almost reached the water's edge, covering a gradual slope that rose from the river. This early in the fall, pink and blue flowers still showed among the grass and a few wild orchids were in bloom. The wind gusted cool from the north and carried a fragrant reminder of the wetlands and cypress swamps that clung close to Oklahoma's eastern border with Arkansas. The sky had cleared and was now a hard blue, streaked with misty ribbons of white cloud.

Sam slapped the backs of the mules with the reins and they scrambled up the grade, the wagon bouncing behind them.

"Hey, you!" Stringfellow yelled, holding on to the cage with white knuckles as the others tumbled around him. "Slow down, damn you!"

Sam grinned and ignored the man. He hoorawed the team onto the flat, then drew rein, looking behind him for Kane.

The marshal swung into the saddle and put the sorrel to the slope. He'd reached the top when he heard Young call out after him, "Nice doin' business with you again, Marshal. Hurry back now, y'heah?"

Kane caught the note of mockery in the ferryman's voice and something snapped inside him, so loud he heard it twang in his head. He swung his horse around and saw the fat man standing at the bottom of the rise, the self-satisfied grin on his face wide enough to make his slitted eyes disappear entirely.

Kane kicked his mount into motion and hit the slope at a gallop, a wild, Southern yell ripping from his lips. Sudden panic gripped Young. The fat man's mouth made a startled O, and he turned and broke into a waddling run, his enormous buttocks giggling.

Young attempted to run to his right, along the bank, looking over his shoulder. But the sorrel was an excellent cutting horse, and Kane cut the fat man off and herded him back toward the river. For a moment Young stood at the water's edge, uncertain, but Kane was bearing down on him, and the man turned and floundered into the Red.

Kane went after him, his horse kicking up cascading plumes of foamy water. Terrified, Young waded deeper, then tripped and disappeared. He surfaced like a broaching sperm whale, spluttering, his face and bald head dripping slimy river mud.

The marshal drew rein, the sorrel standing in water up to its knees. Kane grinned. "It's about time you took a bath, Young. You stink like the business end of a polecat."

The man angrily slapped the water on each side of him. "Damn you, I won't fergit this. You're banned from my ferry for life. You hear that, lawdog? Banned for life!"

Kane's grin grew wider. Then he lifted his eyes from Young to the Indian woman on the opposite bank. She stood still, holding the Sharps over her right shoulder, her face impassive. The marshal waved, but the woman did not wave back.

Kane swung his horse around and cantered up the rise. Behind him Young started to wade out of the river, fell, then waded again. He stumbled onto the bank and fell on his belly, his chest heaving.

Sam looked at Kane, his eyes twinkling, and said, "Drownin' is a sure cure for bad habits."

"Ain't it, though," Kane said.

"Happy now?" Sam said.

"As a kid pullin' a pup's ears," Kane said.

"That's what I figgered," Sam said.

But Kane's attention was suddenly elsewhere. On the opposite bank a rider sat his horse, his face shadowed by a black, wide-brimmed hat. A far-seeing man, Kane took note of the holstered revolver on the man's hip and the booted rifle under his left knee. The guide rope of the stranger's pack mule was in his gun hand and he seemed relaxed and unthreatening.

But still, there was something about the rider that made Kane uneasy. It seemed Sam shared that feeling.

"He's a gun all right, Logan," he said, as though Kane had asked him a question. "Ain't nobody else but a named man sits that arrogant in the saddle, except maybe a Yankee cavalry colonel."

"Recognize him?"

Sam shook his head. "Nah, I can't peg him."

It was Buff Stringfellow who answered Kane's question. The man had bullied his way to the door of the cage and his mouth was pressed between the bars. "Jack!" he bellowed. "It's me, Buff!"

For a moment Kane thought the man hadn't heard, but then he slid his rifle from the scabbard and brandished it over his head.

"I'll be lookin' fer ya, Jack!" Stringfellow yelled.

Even from a distance, Kane saw the white grin on the face of the man called Jack.

Sam turned all the way around in his seat and called out to Stringfellow, "Hey, Buff, who's yer friend?"

"That's for me to know, old man."

"I know who he is," Kane said. "He's a drunken killer an' train robber who goes by the name o' Jack Henry." The marshal's eyes lifted to Sam. "It don't come as too much of a surprise that him and Stringfellow are pea patch kin."

"Correct on all counts, Marshal." Stringfellow grinned. "An' if you ain't boogered by now, you should be. Jack is a heller from way back. Why, I mind the time him an' ol' Jesse—"

"Shut your trap, Stringfellow," Kane said. "Another word o' sass an' you'll be building your smokes with your left hand."

"Suit yourself, Kane," the man said. He looked

around at his companions. "Won't be long now, boys." Every man's eyes turned to the marshal. All six of them were grinning, like cats who had just eaten the canary.

Sam climbed down from the wagon and stepped beside Kane, his hand on the bridle of the marshal's horse. "How you want to play this, Logan? You cain't get lard less'n you boil the hog. Want to wait on this side for ol' Jack, lay up for him an' shoot him right out of the saddle?"

Kane sat his saddle, his brow wrinkled. He said nothing.

"Marshal?"

"I'm studying on it, Sam. I'm studying on it."

Chapter 8

Kane watched the sloshing wet Bill Young clamber onto the ferry and take up the rope. On the opposite bank Jack Henry had dismounted and stood by his horse.

"Well, Logan, what do you think?" Sam prompted. "Do we stash the wagon someplace and bushwhack that feller?"

Kane had already made up his mind. "Move 'em out, Sam."

"But—"

"Henry won't cross on the ferry until we're gone, and a man in his line o' work ain't likely to ride into our rifles."

"Then how do we play it?"

"For now, we watch our drag, left flank, right flank an' point."

"That's it?"

"That's it."

"Atween us, we don't got that many eyes." Sam

shook his head. "I sure hope you know what you're doin', Marshal."

Kane's smile was tight. "So do I, old-timer. So . . . do . . . I."

After they left the Red, Kane dropped back, leaving Sam to follow any trail he could find. The marshal rose through rolling country, the ground thickly carpeted with buffalo and grama grass, and here and there patches of sand bluestem and prickly pear. Vast forests of pine, hickory and wild oak grew everywhere and sometimes glades of tumbled white boulders were visible through the trees. The sky was blue as carbon steel, the morning clouds burned away by the flaming sun. Kane saw where the tracks of Sam's wagon swung wide around peat bogs and stretches of wetlands where water lilies floated on shallow ponds like ancient galleons. The old man was a first-rate teamster and his experienced eyes constantly searched the terrain ahead, wary of places where the wagon could get stuck or shatter a wheel.

Three miles north of the river Kane rode up on the wagon. Sam had stopped at a slow-running creek bordered by cottonwood and elm. At first the marshal thought the old man was about to water the team, but the mules were standing head down in the traces and Sam was fifty yards downstream, looking around him.

Kane rode closer and then saw what the old man was seeing.

Sam looked up at him. "Small herd, no more'n

five hundred head, headin' north. Watered here, oh, maybe two, three hours ago."

At this point both sandy banks of the creek had been broken down by the passage of the herd. The smell of cow dung and dust still lingered in the air.

Kane offered no response, and Sam said, "Safe bet they're headed for the Territory. Army is always ready to buy beef to feed the Indians."

The old man stuck his hands in his pockets and kicked at the grass at his feet. He looked at Kane again and grinned. "You thinkin' what I'm thinkin'?"

"Sam, I never know what you're thinkin,' " Kane said. "But if you're thinkin' we should fall in with them drovers, then you're thinkin' what I'm thinkin'."

"That's what I'm thinkin'," Sam said. "Small herd like that should make ten miles a day easy. We could stay with them until we reach the mountains, unless they decide to go over instead of around."

Kane shifted in the saddle, then took the makings from his shirt pocket. There was safety in numbers, and Texas drovers were a tough bunch. The thought of Jack Henry on his back trail rankled him, to say nothing of the Provanzano brothers. He was sure they thought he was protecting Barnabas Hook, and in a way maybe he was. They might even figure Hook had given him the family money for safe-keeping.

Kane thumbed a match into flame and lit his cigarette. "Water the mules, Sam, and let's see if we can catch up to that bunch."

He finished his smoke, then swung out of the saddle and walked back to the wagon, where Sam was already unhitching the team.

"Hey, Kane," Stringfellow yelled, "we're burnin' up in here. Let us out so we can set in the shade fer a spell."

"You thirsty?" the marshal asked.

"Hell no. We're not thirsty—we're hot. Look at that sun, you damned idiot. It's scorching our hides."

Kane nodded. He got the water bucket from the back of the wagon and filled it at the creek. He walked back to the wagon, smiled at Stringfellow, then threw the contents of the bucket in his face. "That ought to cool you down some."

Stringfellow spluttered and shook his head, spraying water. "Damn you, Kane, you're as mean as a curly wolf."

"Good thing for you to remember, Buff." The marshal pulled his vest away from his gun belt. "When it comes to downright meanness an' cussedness, the only thing that separates me from you is this here badge."

The day had begun its shade into night when Kane and Sam caught up with the herd. The cattle, Herefords mostly with a few longhorns, were bedded down along a creek surrounded on three sides by a shallow arc of pine and hardwood forest. To the west, the setting sun was a scarlet pool making its way down a draw between swollen, purple rain clouds. The air smelled of trees and the dusty heat of the dying day.

The drovers had made camp about a hundred yards from the herd, on a bend of the creek where grew tall cottonwoods and a single willow that trailed its branches into the water. There was a small remuda and a chuck wagon, a canvas canopy rigged on one of its sides.

As Sam swung in that direction, with the casual interest of a former cattleman, Kane took time to check out the herd. The cows all looked to be in excellent shape, fat and glossy with some yearlings among them. But one thing struck a jarring note in the marshal—even in the waning light he counted six different brands, and there were probably more.

That meant nothing in itself. Small ranchers often banded their herds together to make a drive, though the railroads were rapidly making such arrangements a thing of the past. But the suspicion that this was a rustled herd was strong in Kane. He was going only on that sixth sense all experienced lawmen have, the little, nagging voice at the back of the head that warns them to be wary.

When he was twenty yards from the camp, Kane drew rein, but it was Sam who took it on himself to observe the proprieties. "Hello the camp!"

Four men, backlit by the flickering red glow of a fire, had watched them come. Now one of them called out, "Come on in, real easy an' slow like."

It was not a friendly greeting, Kane decided, but

it wasn't all that unfriendly either. Kind of some-where in between. He kicked his horse forward, then stopped when he was a few feet from the drovers. It was only then he saw that one of them was a woman. She was tall, angular, her hat hanging on the back of her shoulders from a string around her neck. She wore a split, canvas riding skirt, a white shirt and a black-and-white cowhide vest. It was the woman who spoke.

"Passing through?" Her voice was light, pleasant, almost musical.

Kane saw the woman's head move as her eyes angled to the convict wagon. She took note of it but said nothing more.

Kane ignored the woman's question. "Name's Logan Kane, Deputy Marshal for the Indian Territory, out of the Honorable Judge Isaac Parker's court."

"Did you say Logan Kane?" This came from a tall, rangy young man whose face was shaded by the wide brim of his hat. The man wore two Remingtons, butt forward in crossed belts. It was an unusual gun rig, the first Kane had ever seen. Whoever or what-ever he was, he didn't look like a thirty-a-month drover, that was for sure.

"You heard the name right," Kane said. For some reason a small anger was flaring in him. These were turning out to be right inhospitable folks.

"We don't much cotton to lawmen around here, Kane," the young man said, "especially killers who hide behind a badge. But you might have guessed that already."

"You're right. I done guessed that when I saw the brands on your herd," Kane said.

The man took a step forward and now Kane could see his face. He was flushed with real or pretended rage, his mouth a tight, hard gash under his mustache. "What the hell is that supposed to mean?"

Kane smiled. "You know what it means." The smile quickly faded and the marshal's eyes iced. "A word of warning, boy, don't sass me. You're gettin' mighty close."

"Hyde, let it go," the woman snapped. "See to the herd."

The man called Hyde stared at Kane, a challenge in his eyes. But finally his gaze slid from the marshal's face and he turned on his heel. "Ed," he said to a short, stocky puncher as he walked away, "mount up. We'll check on the herd like the lady says." Then, to another man, older, with a mournful face split by a ragged mustache, he said, "Buck, start rustling up the grub."

The woman waited until the men had left, then said to Kane, "Marshal, we seem to have gotten off on the wrong foot. Let's start over again, shall we?"

"Fine by me," Kane said. His eyes were still on Hyde, who was swinging into the saddle of a paint. The kid was either a named man or a wannabe. Either way, it was worth keeping an eye on him.

"My name is Mae St. John, a rancher from down around the Nacogdoches country, and I'm bringing beef to the Army," the woman said. "I was instructed by letter to meet a military representative at Fort Smith—a Colonel Brennan. Do you know him?"

Kane shook his head.

"Really? That's a surprise. Evidently he's quite a well-known Indian fighter."

Kane shrugged. "I wouldn't know. I've never fit Indians."

Mae St. John smiled. "Now, as to those mixed brands you alluded to—"

"I what to?" Kane asked.

"Mentioned, the brands you mentioned. As you know, Marshal, times are tough in Texas right now. With my last few dollars I bought those cattle cheap from ranchers who are already scraping the bottom of the last barrel. I intend to sell the herd at a good profit to Colonel Brennan."

Mae's smile grew even more dazzling. Kane thought she looked like a young girl who had just walked into the brightly lit hall at her first cotillion. "Now you understand why there are so many different brands."

"It's a long drive to Fort Smith," Kane said. "Why not ship your beef in the boxcars?"

The woman laughed, a good sound to Kane's ear. "Marshal, the railroad quoted me a price of forty dollars a day and couldn't guarantee the trip would take less than ten days. I don't have that kind of money. As it is, my drovers are working for a percentage of the profits, so I can just about cut it."

As though she'd suddenly remembered something, Mae said, "Please don't let Hyde Larson get to you,

Marshal. He's a top hand, but he can be a hothead by times."

Kane opened his mouth to speak, but the woman's apologetic laugh stopped him. "Goodness gracious, what am I thinking? Where is my Texas hospitality? Light and set, Marshal, and pull your wagon in beside ours. Please join us for supper. We don't have much, but what we have we're willing to share." Her eyes moved to the wagon again. "Are those men all prisoners?"

Kane had stepped out of the saddle and now he stood near the woman, the sorrel's reins in his hand. "Apart from Sam Shaver up on the box, they're condemned criminals, ma'am. I'm taking them to Fort Smith to be hung at Judge Parker's convenience."

May's hand flew to her mouth. "Oh, how perfectly horrible!"

Kane nodded. "A hangin' ain't purdy, ma'am, that's fer certain." He turned. "Sam, bring 'em in. Lay alongside the other wagon, but where I can see 'em, mind."

The old man slapped the reins and the mule team lurched into motion. When he got closer he stopped, measuring distances for a turn.

"Good to see you, Mae. It's been a long time."

Startled, Kane swiveled his head and glanced at the wagon. Stringfellow's face was pressed against the bars and he was grinning hugely.

It took the woman a moment; then her eyes widened in surprise. "Buff, is that you?"

"As ever was."

Mae stepped to the wagon and Kane said, "I wouldn't get too close, ma'am."

She ignored him and said, her eyes wandering over the cage and the ragged men inside, "I see you're prospering, Buff."

"They're planning to hang me, Mae."

"So I heard." The woman turned to Kane. "What are the charges, Marshal?"

"Murder, rape and robbery."

"Rape? Still can't keep your hands off women, Buff, huh?"

"Right now I wish my hands were on you."

"Damn you, Buff, get in line," Amos Albright said. His lips were wet and his eyes were hot on the woman.

Stringfellow's backhand was vicious. His hard, scarred knuckles smashed into Albright's nose and Kane heard bone break. The man let out a bubbling, piercing scream and fell to the bottom of the wagon, his mustache and beard red with blood.

Stringfellow looked down at Albright. "You keep your dirty mouth shut. This woman ain't anybody's whore."

Albright groaned but made no reply.

Sam leaned from his seat. "You all through, ma'am?" he asked.

Mae nodded and took a step back.

The wagon rolled past, Stringfellow never taking his eyes off the woman. For his part Kane was troubled. Stringfellow and Mae St. John had been friends once, probably a lot more than that. If she was a respectable rancher as she claimed, why would she be on first-name terms with an outlaw and vicious killer like Buff Stringfellow?

The implications were not pleasant to contemplate and Kane looked at the sky as though to find the answer to his question there. He saw only the hollow moon herding a gathering of dark storm clouds.

Chapter 9

"I cain't expect you to feed the prisoners, ma'am," Sam said to Mae. "There's a passel o' them."

The convicts were sitting, lined up, at the base of a cottonwood. "Only five of us, old man," Stringfellow said, grinning. "Amos seems to have lost his appetite."

Albright had his face in his hands, his shattered nose bubbling blood. Beside him, Hick Dietz nursed his ruined hand, looking at Kane, hate in his eyes.

"Sorry-looking bunch, ain't they, ma'am," the marshal said. "If I get them to the gallows in one piece, I reckon it will be a miracle."

Joe Foster lifted his head, his pale blue eyes blazing. "Kane, I'm asking. Give me an even break with you. Put a gun in my hand and see what happens."

"Some men make big reputations gunning drunks an' greenhorns, kid. I don't think Marshal Kane cares to risk his in a fair fight." Hyde Larson sat his horse at the rim of the firelight. He was smiling, but he was still and cold as ice.

Quickly, Sam tried to salvage it. "The only place other folks make a name for themselves is on a tombstone, young feller. Them's words of wisdom and maybe you should back off a ways an' study on them for a spell."

But Kane was not annoyed and his smile was genuine, if thin. "Larson, you're up on a hoss. If it comes down to it, how fast do you think can you skin them Remingtons from there?"

"Fast enough. For somebody like you, anyways."

"I'll give you some advice," Kane said evenly. "Backin' up hard words with gunplay is dangerous business, unless you're a top hand at it. Miz St. John says you're a top hand with cattle—she didn't say nothing about guns."

"Enough!" Mae said. She left Kane and Sam standing at the fire and stepped beside Larson. "Hyde, Buck says the grub is nearly ready. Come to the fire and eat." She laid the tips of her fingers on the young man's knee. "There will be no gunplay. I'm depending on you to get the herd to Fort Smith."

The woman could have read uncertainty in Larson's eyes, because her voice suddenly hardened. "Do as I say!"

Larson made no answer, but he touched his hat to Mae and rode into the blue darkness beyond the circle of firelight.

Mae stepped back to Kane and the old man. "I'll

feed your prisoners tonight, Sam," she said. "And you and the marshal. What have you been giving them? They look kind of sharp set."

"Salt pork, ma'am, an' pan bread. An' coffee of course, though I just bile up the grounds fer them."

Mae turned to the man called Buck who was standing over the fire, stirring a blackened pot. "What's for supper?"

"Bacon an' beans," answered Buck, a sour-looking man in his mid-forties. "Like always."

"I'd say it's a step up from salt pork," Mae said.

Kane thought she looked too eager to please, like a woman who was not by nature or inclination friendly but was going out of her way to be pleasant.

Sam missed that, or appeared to. "Haven't had bacon in a coon's age, ma'am." He grinned. "Thankee fer the invite."

Kane sat with his back against a tree where he could keep an eye on the prisoners. When Sam brought him a plate, he propped his rifle upright beside him.

"Fixin' to storm again, Logan," the old man said. "Looks like."

"An' it smells like. Sure as shootin' there's sulfur in the air."

But Kane was only half listening. His gaze was on Mae St. John. Sam had fed the prisoners, including Albright, who had apparently decided he could sit up and take nourishment, but the woman had insisted on fixing Stringfellow's plate.

"Only for old time's sake, you understand," she'd said.

Now the marshal watched Mae as she carried food to the outlaw. Stringfellow was at the end of the line and the woman sat beside him. She handed the man the plate and for a moment Kane saw their fingertips touch, like furtive lovers.

Stringfellow began to eat. Then he bent his head close to Mae and whispered something in her ear. The woman listened intently, but her expression did not change. She looked across at Kane and smiled.

Whatever she was, or had been, the marshal decided that Mae St. John was a woman who would play her cards close to her chest. What had Stringfellow just said to her? Kane had no way of knowing and the woman would not tell him.

The sky flashed with blue electricity and a wind was rising, setting the cottonwoods to whispering. Something big plopped in the creek, and out on the high plains the coyotes were talking back and forth.

Over by the fire, Hyde Larson was drinking whiskey steadily, a bad omen that set Kane on edge.

After scraping up the last of his beans the marshal set the plate aside and began to build a smoke. But he stopped when Mae left Stringfellow's side, walked past the fire and sat beside him. Up close she was a handsome woman. Her hazel eyes were large and lustrous and her auburn hair was thick, hanging over her shoulders in glossy curls. The woman's mouth was too wide for true beauty and little arcs formed at the corners of her lips when she smiled.

Mae looked askance at the untidy makings in Kane's fingers. "Here, let me do that," she said. "I've yet to meet the man who could roll a cigarette properly."

She finished building the smoke with deft, sure fingers, then sealed it shut with the tip of her tongue. Mae put the cigarette between Kane's lips. "There, see how easy it is?"

Kane thumbed a match into flame, lit his smoke and inhaled deeply. "I'm obliged to you," he said. He turned his head to the woman. "Tell me about it."

"About Buff, you mean?"

The marshal nodded.

"I first met him about three years ago. I'd just inherited the ranch after my pa died. The range was overgrazed and the herd was in poor shape, and I was having a hard time making ends meet. Then, one evening just before supper, Buff rode in."

Mae pulled up her legs and wrapped her arms around them. Her eyes were shining with memories.

"Oh, you should have seen him then, Marshal, mounted on a tall, black American stud, more silver on his saddle and gun belt than I'd ever seen in one place at one time. He wore a red shirt and black pants and had a big, white sombrero on his head with a silver band." Mae laughed. "My, but he was a grand sight to see."

Nothing about the woman's speech pleased Kane, but he let it go. "Did you know he was an outlaw?"

"No. But back then I wouldn't have cared. I asked

him to step down and he did. He lived for three months with me and helped me put the ranch in shape. Well, him and Buck that is. Buck was my only hand back then."

"And one day he just rode out."

"I woke one morning and Buff was gone. I never saw him again until today."

"So he never told you why."

Mae shrugged. "A man like Buff can't stay long in one place. It would be easier to try to fence the wind." Her gaze moved to Kane's eyes and held there. "Marshal, I don't believe what they say about Buff. A woman can't share her life and her bed with a man for months and not get to know him. He's capable of many things, but he would never harm a woman. That's—that's just too hard to believe."

"Hard to believe, all right," Kane commented, his face emotionless.

"Logan!"

Sam Shaver's voice, sharp with warning, cut through the night. He'd been picking up the prisoners' plates and now he was standing still, watching Larson, who was now on his feet, swaying slightly. His eyes were intent on Kane.

Sam took it on himself to provide commentary to go along with the young man's actions. "Kid's on the prod, Marshal."

Kane's awareness sharpened as it always did before a scrape. He was aware that the prisoners were leaning forward, their tense faces hungry. Stringfellow was grinning like a wolf. Beside him, Kane was aware of Mae's sharp intake of breath. She rose slowly to her feet, her eyes on Larson.

The marshal stayed where he was, prepared to play out whatever hand was dealt to him.

Larson adjusted his gun belts on his lean hips and stepped away from the firelight. He stopped when he was a few yards from Kane, but his eyes went to Mae. "I'm ordering that man out," he said, nodding to the marshal. "I don't want him around here no more."

"That's the ticket, kid," a prisoner laughed.

"Hey, Larson, what about us?" said Stringfellow.

"You can stay." The man's eyes dropped to Kane. "He goes."

The marshal smiled. "Don't like lawmen much, huh?"

"I hate the breed, especially you. I heard about you, about your big rep. Well, now I'm going to take it all away from you. Get to your feet."

His voice even, Kane said, "Kid, if I stand up, I'll kill you. Don't make me do that."

Mae St. John took a step toward Larson. "Hyde, you've been drinking. Go sleep it off. Now!"

"I'm not backing down, not this time, lady. Kane has a choice—drop his guns and ride out of here with his tail between his legs or die where he lays. The proposition ain't real complicated."

The marshal's gaze lifted to Larson's face. "You've spelled it out clear enough." Kane rose to his feet, death in his eyes. "All right, let's see what you got, boy."

Larson's hands dropped to his Remingtons. He never made it. A single shot, and his head exploded into a scarlet and white fan of blood, brain and bone. There was enough time remaining in the man's life for a single, terrified scream. Then he staggered a few steps and crashed onto his back.

"You killed him!" Mae shrieked.

Stunned for a moment, Kane glanced down at the unfired Colt in his hand. His eyes darted to Sam, but the old man's arms were dangling at his side and his face bore a shocked expression. Finally Sam recovered enough to point across the clearing where the rustling pines were lost in darkness. "It came from the trees, Logan. Rifle shot."

"Sam, put your scattergun on the prisoners!" Kane yelled. Without waiting for a reply, he sprinted across the clearing and pulled up when he reached the tree line.

His Colt ready, the marshal stepped warily. There was little underbrush to slow him and he walked on a carpet of pine needles. Ahead he saw an impenetrable wall of blackness. Only when the soundless lightning flared did the trees momentarily come to life, their trunks shimmering with a ghostly sapphire light.

Kane stopped, listening into the silence. His mouth was a thin, hard line and his ragged mustache drooped to cheeks that were drawn tight against the bone. He moved again, cursing under his breath when the crown of his hat scraped against a tree branch and was swept from his head. Kane took a knee and fumbled about in the darkness, found the hat and jammed it back on his head. He rose to his feet, then froze.

Someone or something was running fast toward him. Ahead of him Kane caught a blur of motion and his Colt came up fast. A few small branches cracked and then whatever it was almost landed right on top of him.

But the deer sensed danger and bounded to its right. The marshal had a fleeing impression of wide, frightened eyes and a flash of tan coat. Then the animal was past him, vanishing into the night.

His heart hammering in his chest, Kane stood for a moment to regain his composure, then walked on, feeling his way around the tree trunks. A moment later, not far ahead of him, he heard the pounding of retreating hooves; then the echoing silence crowded around him again.

Kane hurried his pace, helped by lightning that flashed more frequently now, shading the darkness among the pines from black to purple. Gradually the forest thinned and he looked out on the plain that mocked him with its emptiness.

On the way back to camp, Kane paced off the distance. He came up with eighty yards, maybe a little more. The bushwhacker, whoever he was, had made an excellent shot under difficult circumstances, hitting a small, moving target in poor light.

The marshal was impressed—and more than a little troubled.

But what if there was another possibility? Perhaps the marksman was not as good as Kane gave him credit for and the bullet had been aimed at him.

That thought was not calculated to help a man sleep well o' nights.

When Kane returned to the campfire, Mae St. John and her two remaining hands were standing over Larson's body. Sam was by the prisoners, his shotgun cradled in his arms.

A huge chunk of Larson's skull had been blown away and his open eyes still showed his fear and surprise at the time and manner of his dying.

Mae's eyes lifted to the tall marshal. "Did you see anything?"

"Heard a hoss."

The woman looked at the man called Ed. "Get out to the herd. We'll bury Hyde in the morning."

The man touched his hat. "Anything you say, ma'am." He hesitated a moment, then said, "Leaves us shorthanded though, don't it?"

"Maybe I can pick up a drover along the way."

"Ain't likely, ma'am," Ed said. "Not in these parts."

All at once the horror of Larson's death caught up with Mae, and her anger flashed. "Ed Brady, don't tell me what I can't do. For a change try telling me what I can do."

Chastened, the man touched his hat. "Yes, ma'am. I'll study on that very thing."

A few moments later Brady rode out to be with the herd and Sam stepped beside Kane. He looked at Larson's body and said, "That boy must've made a mighty powerful enemy."

Buck pointed at Kane. "Either that or he has a mighty powerful friend. I reckoned the kid was gonna gun him fer sure." His old, red-rimmed eyes swept the marshal's face. "Heaven's lookin' out fer you, boy." He paused. "Or hell."

"Sam, start loading the prisoners," Kane said wearily, a sudden tiredness in him. "Buck, let's me an' you move the kid's body away from camp."

"Coyotes around."

"They don't eat their own kind."

The drover shook his head. "Death on a drive has always boogered me. I never did know any good to come from it."

But the dying wasn't over.

Not that night.

Chapter 10

Sam Shaver had just ordered the prisoners to their feet when Bennett Starr made his break.

Starr had been quiet and uncomplaining since he'd left Texas, which caught Sam and Kane by surprise. He was a small, thin man with dark, brooding eyes, his nose and cheekbones cobwebbed by red, broken veins, and his teeth were few and black.

The man hobbled away from the cottonwoods, desperately seeking the cover of darkness. Like the others, his ankle chains were long enough to allow him a shuffling walk, but too short for running.

"Starr!" Sam yelled, and fired a shotgun blast over the prisoner's head.

The man kept on going, glancing fearfully over his shoulder as he took quick, choppy steps along the creek bank. Lightning splashed around him and now, for the first time that night, thunder rumbled. Ahead of Starr the looming darkness was a welcoming cloak ready to shelter him.

But he was destined never to reach it.

Kane ran after the man, then stopped and drew his gun. "Starr, halt right there!" he yelled. "Or I'll shoot!"

Starr ignored the warning, his ankle chains chinking as he staggered forward.

The marshal raised his Colt to eye level and fired.

For a moment Starr kept going. Then his legs buckled and he fell flat on his face and lay still. Kane walked to the man's side and rolled him over with the toe of his boot. Starr's eyes were open . . . but he was staring into nothingness.

The marshal grabbed the dead man by the back of his shirt and dragged him into camp. Kane's teeth were bared under his mustache, his eyes ablaze with a terrible anger. The prisoners were lined up at the rear of the wagon and he hauled Starr's body in front of them, then let the man's shoulders thud to the ground.

Straightening, he yelled, "This man tried to escape. Now he's dead. From this moment onward I'll kill any man who tries to make a break." He looked at the sullen, angry faces of the convicts. "Do you understand that?" There was no answer and Kane said, "Stringfellow, do you understand that?"

"You shot him in the back," the man growled.

"He gave me no choice. Now answer my question, damn you. Do you understand what I just told you, told all of you?"

Stringfellow looked along the line at the others.

Then he answered for all of them. "Yeah, Kane, we understand you only too well."

The marshal turned his head slightly, his glare still fixed on the prisoners. "Sam, load these men into the wagon. Get them out of my sight."

The red mist had cleared from Kane's eyes and his burning anger had cooled, leaving only a sickly, tangle of loss in his belly and the realization that his killing of Bennett Starr had not been a victory.

"He made his play and he lost." Kane said it to Mae, who was looking at him in horror. "If he'd reached the darkness he could've got down on his belly and crawled for miles. I would never have found him."

"No, Marshal, you know you didn't have to kill him. I saw what happened and it—it was cold-blooded murder."

Kane's voice was level, almost reasonable. "Ma'am, like the rest of them, Bennett Starr was a killer—a wild, dangerous animal. Ask Sam what he and Stringfellow and the others did to a Cherokee farmer's wife and daughter up in the Territory. You don't take a chance on men like these gettin' loose among decent folks. You go after them and if you have to, you kill them."

Kane saw shutters close in the woman's eyes. She turned on her heel and walked away toward the awning at the side of the chuck wagon.

He had the feeling that when it came to Buff Stringfellow and the rest of them, Mae would believe nothing he said.

Kane saw that Buck was looking at him, an expression on his face that could have been fear. The old puncher shook his head. "Hell has come to this place," he said.

The marshal smiled without humor. "Old-timer, I got the feeling hell was riding drag for this outfit long afore I ever got here. Now, help me put this body beside the other one."

"No, Marshal," Buck said. "Lay out your own dead."

Kane took the first watch and let Sam sleep. Mae St. John was wrapped in her blankets under the awning and Buck was stretched out near the chuck wagon. Ed Brady was still with the herd, but Mae was due to spell him in a couple of hours. Now that she was down to two hands, the woman seemed determined to pick up her share of the work. Kane had overheard her tell Buck that, against the accepted practice of a trail drive, tomorrow his wagon would take the point and she and Brady would ride flank, dropping back every now and then to cover the drag.

It was a far-from-perfect arrangement, but Kane was sure that if anyone could make it work, it was Mae St. John. She was a strong, capable woman with only one flaw to the marshal's thinking—a blind spot when it came to Buff Stringfellow. Where that might lead, Kane did not know, but it continued to worry him.

Kane sat with his back to a tree near the creek

where he had an unobstructed view of the camp, his rifle across his belly. The thunderstorm had passed quickly, with only a few drops of rain. The blushing moon was covered and uncovered by scudding clouds, driven by a belligerent wind, performing a shy dance of the seven veils for the heedless night.

Carefully keeping his eyes away from the fire, Kane built a smoke. The camp was quiet, the cries of hunting coyotes but distant yips in the stillness. The marshal inhaled deeply and listened into the darkness. Wood crackled in the fire, shifting now and then, sending up a shower of sparks that briefly winked red, then died.

The tall, rangy shape of Sam Shaver emerged from the darkness and walked around the circle of the firelight, moving stiffly. He carried his shotgun, a holstered Colt, on his hip. The old man stepped to Kane's left, not wishing to obstruct the marshal's view of the camp.

Kane's eyes lifted. "Can't sleep, huh?"

"No, I reckon not. There's something in the wind I don't like, Logan. It's telling me things I don't understand." He shook his head. "It's like there's a ghost at my elbow, whispering in my ear."

"Old-timer, we're all on edge tonight. Still fur to travel an' one of the prisoners dead already. It's a time for a man to trouble his mind thinkin' about haunts an' sich. Maybe so."

As Sam squatted on his heels, Kane asked the question uppermost on his mind. "Was I right to gun Bennett Starr?"

Sam made a show of thinking about an answer. He said, " 'In the performance of his duty, and only if the appropriate warnings to halt have been issued and ignored, a marshal has the right to bring down a fleeing fugitive by any and all means necessary.' Them's ol' Judge Parker's words. I heard him say that with my own ears."

"What do you think, Sam?"

"I just done tole you what I think."

"No, you told me what the judge thinks. What do you say?"

The old man reached out, took the cigarette from between Kane's lips and inhaled. He passed the smoke back to the marshal and said, "What I say don't matter."

"It matters to me."

The words he was about to say seemed painful to Sam Shaver. He grimaced as though they were stuck like rocks in his chest. "I don't think you needed to kill that man. Starr was hobbled with chains an' I reckon you could've gone after him afore he got too fur. Seems to me you could have buffaloed him, then drug him back to camp." The old man hesitated a heartbeat. "That's what I think, Logan. Fer what it's worth."

Beyond the campfire, the prison wagon creaked, then creaked again, louder this time. Kane looked in that direction. "What's going on over there?"

Sam shrugged. "Somebody stirring in his sleep, I reckon. Them boys won't give us any trouble while they're locked in the wagon. They know I could up my rifle an' clear that cage quicker'n scat."

Kane ground out his cigarette butt on the grass beside him, then immediately began to build another.

"You riled at me, Marshal?" Sam asked.

"No, Sam. I asked you to speak your mind an' you spoke it. But I'm studying on something. Stringfellow, Joe Foster an' them others, when you get right down to it, I'm no different from them, am I?"

The old man said nothing.

Kane thumbed a match into flame and lit his cigarette, his eyes distant. "Afore I signed on with Judge Parker, I killed men for money. The better the money, the more men I killed. I didn't give a damn about their wives or children or if they was in the right or in the wrong. I was hired for gun work an' I did it to the best of my ability.

"One time, down to Old Mexico, I gunned a man at the door to the mission where he was about to get hitched. His bride was a-standin' there, watching, wearing a veil an' a white dress. She looked at me like I was some kind of animal. To my dying day I'll never fergit her eyes, how they judged and condemned me."

"Logan, you don't—"

"Wait, Sam, let me finish." Kane spoke through a cloud of blue smoke. "Oncet, when I was ridin' the grub line for the first an' only time in my life, I held up a Bain and Company stage down on the Concho. This gambler feller objected to bein' robbed of his

money an' watch an' drew down on me." Kane
dragged on his cigarette. "I killed him too."

He turned his head to look at Sam. "I've been sitting here thinking that I'm no better and maybe a
sight worse than the men in the cage over there. A
tad luckier maybe, but no different." Now Kane's
gaze searched the old man's face. "Is that how it
be, Sam?"

He could see by the still pools of Sam's eyes that
he was not hunting in his mind for an answer. The
old man rose to his feet. "I only drive the wagon,
Marshal." He looked down at Kane for a moment.
"Stretch out, get some sleep. I'll keep watch for a
while."

"Sam, I reckon that's how it be."

"Get some sleep, Marshal."

The dream came to Logan Kane that night, while
Sam kept watch and the tossing trees were alive
with wind.

The four of them stood outside the old sod cabin
where he'd been born and raised: Ma in the patched
calico dress she always wore; Pa in his overalls, his
black beard fanning over his chest; his twin sisters,
the way he remembered them, two years younger
than he, Patience and Prudence, both pretty as
pictures.

But they were all dead these twenty years, taken
by the cholera.

They stood still, looking at Kane, eyes accusing in
faces as white as bleached bone.

As always it was Ma who spoke. "Logan, why did you leave us?" she asked. "Why did you just ride away?"

"I was scared, Ma, scared of the cholera." Kane tried to walk toward his mother and take her in his arms, but he couldn't move. A gray mist was gathering, coiling around him.

"We don't lie in the earth, Logan," Ma said. "It ain't right for Christian people not to lie in the earth."

"I'm sorry, Ma," Kane said. He felt like he was tightly bound with rope. "You were all dead, Ma. I didn't know what to do no more."

"Son, you should have buried us decent," Pa said. "Our bones lie on top of the ground, scattered by coyotes. We will be forever denied our eternal rest until we sleep in the good Texas earth."

The mist drifted over Pa, then all of them. From somewhere in the shifting grayness, Kane heard his mother's voice calling out to him. "Logan . . . don't leave us. . . . Don't leave. . . ."

"I'll be back, Ma!" Kane yelled. "I'll find you! I'll find you!" The echoes of his last shouted words still echoed around camp as Kane jerked upright, his heart hammering in his chest, sweat hot on his face.

He looked around him. Mae St. John had been saddling her horse and now she was looking at him, her eyes wide and startled. Over by the chuck wagon, Buck was propped on one elbow, staring across camp, a man just rudely wakened from slumber.

Kane saw Sam stride toward him, concern on his

face. "Marshal, you were callin' out in your sleep again like the gates of hell had just opened up fer you."

With trembling fingers, Kane reached into his shirt pocket for the makings. "I'm fine now, Sam. Thanks. Yeah, just fine." He'd tried to keep his voice steady, but he knew he'd failed.

The old man squatted and took paper and tobacco from the marshal's trembling hand and quickly built his cigarette. He handed the rolled paper to Kane and said, "All you got to do is lick it."

Kane did as he was told and Sam lit the smoke for him. "Sit quiet, Logan," he said. "You weren't asleep for no more'n an hour afore you started hollerin'."

Across camp, Buck had rolled in his blankets again, but Mae was still looking at Kane, the look on her face hard to read. Then she swung elegantly into the saddle and headed out for the herd at a canter. She had not said a word.

"You got demons haunting you, Logan," Sam said. "I'm only the driver, but this much I'll say to you: find your folks, anchor them deep in the earth an' you won't search for them in your sleep no more."

Kane nodded. "I will, Sam. One day soon I will."

Sam smiled. "I bet ol' Buck will be glad to hear that. He's a mite tetchy about his rest gettin' disturbed, an all."

Chapter 11

At first light Ed Brady rode in from the herd and he, Buck and Kane buried the dead. Mae St. John, as was her right and duty as trail boss, read the prayers from the Book. No one had anything to say, good or bad, about either man. Mae sang "How Firm a Foundation," the hymn sung at the funeral of General Robert E. Lee, then noted that both men were now with God. Then it was over.

After Sam fed the prisoners, Kane poured himself coffee and stepped over to Mae, who was standing near the chuck wagon talking to Buck.

He had thought about apologizing for crying out in his sleep, but had dismissed the idea. What was done was done, and in any case he didn't have the words to explain it.

The marshal touched his hat. "Mornin', ma'am."

Mae's eyes were cool, so distant they were unreachable. She said, "What can I do for you, Marshal?"

"Me an' Sam figgered we might throw in with you, at least until we reach the Ouachita peaks. I guess you're planning to head west an' drive the herd around them."

"No, I'm going over all the mountains in my path between here and Fort Smith, Marshal. As to throwing in with us, it's a free country and you can do as you please. But I'd rather you didn't. I can't afford to lose my remaining hands."

Kane let that slide. "Ma'am, you're headed for some rough country filled with road agents, rustlers and outlaws of every stripe. You might be grateful for an extry rifle by the time you reach Fort Smith."

"We can make it alone, I assure you, Marshal," the woman said. "Both Buck and Ed are accomplished marksmen, so I really don't think we have anything to fear from road agents and cattle rustlers."

Kane recognized defeat when he saw it and his talking was done. He touched his hat. "Well, good luck to you then, ma'am."

"Wait," Buck said, his old eyes shrewd. "You ever work cattle, huh?"

"Some. I went up the trail for the first time with Charlie Goodnight when I was fourteen and twicet after that with different outfits. One time ol' Charlie his ownself told me he reckoned me a fair hand."

Buck turned to Mae. "Boss, you an' Ed will have problems aplenty driving the herd. If this feller is even half the puncher he claims to be, we can sure use him." He looked at Kane. "You willin' to ride drag?"

Punching cows was not quite what Kane had in mind when he offered to ride with the herd, but with the Provanzano brothers and Jack Henry somewhere along his back trail, there was a measure of safety in numbers, few though they were. "Me an' Sam was going to do that anyway, drop back and keep our eyes on what's behind us, like."

Mae bit her lip and thought that through. Kane believed she was a practical woman who was already well aware of the problems facing her. She was headed into the high plains, and beyond soared the rugged barrier of the Ouachita Mountains. She must know that, shorthanded as she was, the herd could get strung out for miles crossing high rim country and in the end she might lose most of them.

The woman lifted her eyes to Kane. Even at this early hour of the morning she was enough to take a man's breath away. Her full breasts pressed against the thin stuff of her shirt and morning sun was tangled in her hair.

"What about your"—Kane saw her momentary reluctance to use the word, but then she said it— "prisoners?"

"Sam Shaver keeps a Greener scattergun up on the box. He ain't likely to be troubled."

Mae made up her mind. "A dollar a day, Marshal. To be paid in full when we reach Fort Smith. Take the drag and keep the herd closed up. If a cow gives birth, shoot the calf and drive the cow back to the herd. Any questions?"

"No, ma'am. I've rode drag afore."

"Good. You can ride Hyde Larson's string."

The woman dismissed Kane with her eyes. "Buck, Ed, let's move 'em out. Buck, keep the remuda on point with you. From time to time I'll check in to see how you're doing."

Sam had been standing by the wagon and Kane told him of his arrangement with Mae St. John. The old man's only comment was to look glum.

"Out with it, Sam, what's eatin' you?" the marshal said.

The old man cocked his head like a bird. "You really want to know?"

"That's why I'm askin'."

"First thing, riding drag ain't no job fer a white man, and it sure ain't fer one of Judge Parker's deputy marshals an' his teamster."

"It's necessary, Sam. A necessity under the circumstances, you might say."

"An' second thing," Sam said, as though he hadn't heard, "this is a bad-luck outfit. I'm tellin' ye, Logan, there something in the air, something wicked that's new aborning, an' it's comin' up on us fast." The old man pointed to the south. "It's headed from there and it's on its way."

Sam Shaver was a hard man to scare, but the dread in his eyes infected Kane like a disease and the marshal shivered. "Jack Henry?"

The old man shook his head. "Not him, and not them furrin'-lookin' New Orleans fellers either. This is worse, Logan, much worse. What's a-headed our way is hell on horseback."

"Sam, let it go," Kane said irritably. "Your crazy talk is startin' to clabber my blood."

"It ain't crazy talk, Marshal. An' if you're scared, well, you got every right to be."

Mae St. John planned to make twelve miles the first day.

The cattle crossed rolling plains that were constantly in motion, like waves on a sea. Shadows cast by passing clouds chased one another over the restless grama grass and for most of the long afternoon the sun hung like a molten ball, burning the color out of the sky.

Recent rains had settled the worst of the dust and Kane rode the drag without choking or spitting black grit or getting an inch of the stuff between his clothes and skin. Mae St. John was paying him a dollar a day to outthink a cow, and he earned his wages, keeping the herd bunched and tight. The Herefords were fat and lazy, already trail broke, and they moved along placidly enough. But the longhorns were ornery and wild as deer. Kane cussed them loudly and with gusto each time he had to bust one out of the brush between the nearby pines or drop back to round up a straggler.

Three times that morning, when he'd passed Mae on his way to the point to throw his saddle on a fresh pony, the woman had studiously ignored him, looking straight ahead, her face like stone under the brim of her hat. Kane had tried waving, but not once had she waved back.

The sun had reached its highest point in the sky when Kane returned to check on a Hereford that had been in the process of giving birth to a calf. Sam was a mile behind the herd and he jerked a thumb over his shoulder as the marshal drew rein beside the wagon.

"If you're lookin' fer a Hereford, she's back there, Logan. Got a bull calf on the ground."

Kane nodded. His eyes moved to the cage, where the prisoners were sitting with their knees drawn up, looking miserable. "Behavin' themselves?" he asked.

"When they ain't talkin' about what they're gonna do to you when they get free, they're complainin'. Another few miles, an' I'll water them."

"Keep the scattergun close," Kane said.

"Always do, Marshal."

Kane kicked his horse into motion, but Sam's voice stopped him. "Passed some Apaches back there a ways, Mescaleros by the look of them. Old man, three young women an' a couple o' boys. They don't look like much. Hungry-lookin' bunch though." Sam smiled. "I'd get that fat Hereford movin', Logan."

The Apaches were trudging north alongside the tracks of the herd. The young women were bent over, carrying heavy loads of firewood on their backs. The old man and the two boys were wearing the blue headband of the Mescaleros.

Their clothing had long since disintegrated into rags and all were gaunt with hunger. By then the Apaches were a defeated people, and even old Geronimo, the last and the most stubborn of them, was gone, locked up in the middle of a Florida swamp.

As Kane rode past, the women and boys ignored him, but the old man stopped and laid a blue-veined hand on his skinny chest. "God bless," he said, his voice thin and dry with age. "I love Jesus. Jesus wants me for a sunbeam."

In the presence of a white man, the old Apache was paying lip service to the religion that had failed to prevent his destruction.

The marshal smiled and nodded and rode on. The Apache called out after him, "I love Jesus." They were probably about the only words of English he knew, but he had been taught them well.

One of the more disagreeable tasks drag riders faced on a long drive was to shoot calves dropped by pregnant cows. No outfit, large or small, had the time or inclination to take care of an animal that couldn't keep up with the rest of the herd.

Kane found the Hereford with her bull calf nursing at her side. He started to push them north, the calf running to keep up. When the Apaches came in sight, he dabbed a loop on the calf and handed the end of the rope to the old man.

The Apache's face lit up. "God bless," he yelled. Even the women and the sullen boys were smiling.

Kane nodded and pushed the Hereford forward. The cow was bawling for her calf and continually tried to cut back, but the sorrel anticipated her every step and kept her moving.

The marshal had few principles, but those he had were uncomplicated and direct: do not abuse a woman or child, feed the hungry and never ignore the pleas of a man with the tobacco craving and no makings. They were the simple principles of a plain man, but in as much as he could, he had tried to live by them.

As he reached the drag, he smiled to himself. It had been tough on the mama cow, but the Apaches would sleep with full bellies that night.

At dusk they made camp in the open on a patch of good grass cut across by a wide, muddy stream. Despite being heavy with silt, the water was sweet and good to drink. A single oak, its ancient, gnarled roots sunk deep, stood close to the stream bank and night birds were already rustling in its branches. As he unsaddled the paint he'd been riding, Kane figured the creek had its origins to the east, running off the Little River, in turn a tributary of the Red.

They would have to cross the Little late on the next day or the day after that. Sometimes the river showed white water, other times not. He fervently hoped it would be one of the other times. If it wasn't, the Little could play hob with a herd.

The cattle were downstream, about two hundred yards beyond the camp. They milled around the water for a while, then settled down to graze. Most of the herd had bedded down by the time the moon came up, but throughout the night they would rise restlessly to their feet and graze some more.

Kane sat at the fire and accepted the coffee Sam poured for him. Opposite, Buck had beans simmering and was frying bacon. Mae sat under her awning, a book in her hand. Ed Brady was already with the herd and in the distance Kane could hear him crooning "Bold Sam Bass." The marshal was not much of a one for singing, but he liked to listen when it was done well, and Brady was a hand at it.

The sky was clear, dusted with stars, its breadth vast. A rising wind stirred the long grass and set the flames of the fire to dancing. The coyotes were talking, but far off in the darkness.

Kane's eyes lifted to Sam, who stood with the coffeepot in his hand, listening into the night. "Still boogered, old-timer, huh?" He had made light of the question, but a part of him dreaded the answer.

Sam said nothing. Then he said, "I'll have me some coffee an' then feed the prisoners." The old man's eyes moved to Mae St. John. "That's a right handsome woman over there."

Kane nodded, a half smile on his lips. "That she be. She's made it plain enough that she doesn't want anything to do with me though."

"Oh but she will. Soon, Logan, soon. See, a man can set an' calculate what's ahead o' him on the trail. But one thing he can't do is calculate on them who will cross his path an' make their troubles his, especially purty females with a hex on them."

Kane's grin was genuinely amused. "Sam, you fixin' to start in on some more o' that talk about haunts?"

"Logan, I'm no longer a young man an' I know you reckon it's a mite late for me to be boogered by fancies," Sam said. He squatted beside Kane and lowered his voice so Buck, who always seemed engrossed in his cooking chores anyway, could not hear.

"My ma, an' her ma afore her, were mountain folk, them black-eyed witchy women who can look into the fire an' see pictures of the future as clear as though they was printed in a book. It's a gift, Logan, or a curse, dependin' on how you care to look at it."

"An' you have the gift, Sam? Do you see pictures in the fire?"

The old man shook his head. "Just sometimes, but mostly I see them in my mind." He rose to his feet, his knees cracking. "See the woman over there?"

Kane nodded and Sam said, his voice hollow, "She'll be dead before we reach the Little River. And others with her."

The prisoners ate in silence, now and then lifting their heads to glance at the starlit sky as though its blazing, crystal beauty had the power to touch even their calloused souls.

Mae took her plate and sat next to Buff Stringfellow. Sam was standing close by with his shotgun, and the woman's move made his long body tense. The old man's eyes fixed on the outlaw and did not shift from him. Alone in the darkness, Brady was softly singing the plaintive "She's More to Be Pitied

Than Censured," a song Kane thought appropriate for the occasion.

The woman and Stringfellow had their heads close, whispering quietly to each other, and once she kissed him lightly on the lips, a transgression that brought a warning growl from Sam.

Kane finished his food and rose to his feet, picking up the rifle that lay beside him. He strolled across camp to Sam and said, "It's time to lock 'em up."

"Hey, we've haven't finished eating yet, Marshal," Stringfellow said. Beside him Mae smiled and said, "Just a few more minutes."

"Finish the grub or I'll throw it out," Kane said. His eyes shifted to the woman. "Ma'am, I'd appreciate it if you'd get back to your wagon."

Joe Foster chewed on a mouthful of beans, then spit them over the scuffed toes of the marshal's boots. "This pig swill ain't fit for a man to eat anyhow." The gunman's insolent grin held a challenge. Stringfellow and the others sat in tense, amused anticipation, anxious to see what would happen next.

It was not long in coming.

Briefly, Kane glanced at the mess on his boots, then at Foster. His kick, driven by all the raw power of his lean, muscular body, slammed into Foster's face, just below the man's left cheekbone. The sound of boot meeting flesh was like a gunshot; Foster's grin vanished as his head snapped back and he smashed onto the grass behind him. For a moment the man lay stunned, his bruised face already swelling. Then he rolled on his side, drew up his knees and began to whimper softly.

Kane didn't spare a glance for the moaning Foster. His eyes quiet but hard as blue steel, he said, "I won't take sass, back talk or impertinence. This man should have remembered that, or if he did, he chose to ignore it." He turned to Sam. "Put the prisoners back in the wagon."

Mae threw her plate aside and sprang to her feet, her eyes blazing. "It's you who should be locked in a cage, Kane! You're a whole sight worse than the men you're planning to hang." The woman opened her mouth to say more, but the words choked in her throat and she dissolved into tears. She brushed past Kane, ran to the awning and threw herself on her blankets.

Her sobs were loud in the quiet.

"Pick that up and carry it inside," the marshal said to Stringfellow, nodding at Foster. "He racked a round into his Winchester. "An' I'll kill any man who makes a move I don't like."

Stringfellow put his arm around the waist of the whimpering Foster and helped him stagger to the back of the wagon. He turned his head. "Mae is right, Kane. You're no better than me, damn you, no better than any of us here."

"Tell that to the Cherokee farmer whose wife and daughter you raped and murdered, Stringfellow," Kane said. "I wonder what he would say."

Chapter 12

Logan Kane spread his blankets away from the circle of the firelight. He dozed, fearful of a deep sleep that would bring the return of the dream and the demands of the dead.

He woke to full darkness. The fire was guttering, burning the last of the wood, and a brooding silence hung over the camp. Somewhere a horse stamped and blew through its nose. The wind had dropped and the moon sailed high in the sky, ringed by a halo that looked like blue mist.

Kane put on his hat, then tugged on his boots. He picked up his rifle and stepped to the fire where he threw on a few more pine branches. The flames immediately licked around the wood and a thin column of smoke rose into the air, straight as a string. He hefted the coffeepot, then tested its temperature with the flat of his hand. It was still warm. The marshal poured himself a cup and stood, a nagging restlessness riding him as he sipped the coffee.

Right then, unshaven and grim-faced, Kane looked what he was, a rough-hewn, hard-grained man who had led a life where nothing had come easy and lessons had not been cheap. Behind him lay only violence and blood and little tenderness. No one had ever been glad at his arriving or sad at his leaving. Ahead, looking into the scowling night, he saw nothing. He was a man who owned a horse, a rifle, a revolving Colt and nothing else. It was not much of a foundation on which anyone could build dreams of the future.

Across the fire from Kane, Ed Brady lay in his blankets, snoring softly, his hat over his face. Mae was asleep under the awning, so Buck must be on night herd.

Kane tossed away the dregs of his coffee, his mind made up. He was on edge, and his instinct told him the cause of his unease was behind him, somewhere on his back trail.

As he walked to the remuda, irritated, he wondered about that. Was it really instinct, or had Sam's talk of haunts and folks dying got to him and scared him worse than he cared to admit? The old man had said death was coming from the south, and that's where Kane was headed.

As he threw his saddle on the sorrel, the marshal shook his head. He would scout to the south because he was wary of enemies on his back trail, Jack Henry and the Provanzano brothers. There was no other reason.

*   *   *

Kane covered nearly four miles in the first hour, keeping to the trail that was a wide scar across the virgin landscape, clearly visible in the moon-splashed darkness. To the east lay the unbroken forests of pine and hardwoods, and once he heard the howls of a hunting wolf pack as they moved like ghosts through the trees.

Another hour passed, and Kane began to think he was on a fool's errand. Around him there was endless, empty prairie, the only sound the rustle of the wind bending the grass. The moon was sinking in the sky and long shadows were darkening the land.

He drew the sorrel to a halt and stood in the stirrups, listening into the night. Nothing. It was time to go back and tell Sam his phantoms were all in his head.

Kane swung his horse around, but drew rein immediately. He lifted his nose to the wind that was blowing warm from the south. There! He smelled it again, the fleeting tang of wood smoke.

Were the Apaches he'd seen earlier that day camping nearby? He immediately dismissed that idea. You seldom caught scent of an Indian fire, and besides, they would have covered more ground by this time.

Then where was the smoke coming from?

Kane rode south again at a walk. After ten minutes the sorrel swung up its head and its ears pricked forward, aware of something ahead. Wary now, the marshal slid his Winchester from the boot and propped the brass butt plate on his thigh. The horse nickered softly and the marshal stroked its neck. "Easy boy," he whispered. "Easy now . . ."

The smell of smoke grew stronger and Kane's eyes tried to penetrate the darkness ahead of him. He was a far-seeing man, but the moon was hidden behind a cloud and he was riding into the black wall of the night.

Following the musky odor of the smoke, Kane left the trail but found his way blocked by pines. He swung west, following the tree line. The moon reappeared and a faint, opalescent light spread across the plain and touched the pine branches and long grass. The wind was rising, talking, and the long grass murmured back. High above Kane the star-filled sky looked like splintered ice, impossibly cold and remote, giving him no counsel.

A haunted sense of unease tugged at him, as though the eyes of the night were watching his every move. His restless fingers opened and closed on the Winchester as the tree line thinned, then petered, giving way to empty prairie. The marshal swung south again. The sorrel was nervous, its ears twitching, the bit chiming as it tossed its head.

Then Kane heard what had been alarming the horse.

The rough voices of men carried in the wind, rising often into laughter, and a growing sense of danger warned Kane to ride no farther. He turned the sorrel, backtracked the way he had come for a hundred yards, then stepped out of the saddle. He looped the reins around a pine trunk and walked south again, his rifle slanted across his chest.

He kept close to the trees that now stretched ahead of him, stepping carefully. Here many of the pines and hardwoods were scorched, evidence of some recent prairie fire, and a few had fallen, sprawled on the ground like stricken giants. The voices were louder now, and close enough that Kane heard the clank of bottles.

Whoever those boys were, they were celebrating late—or working themselves up for something.

The timber line began a gradual curve to the east and the marshal followed it. His mouth was dry as chalk and the pounding of his heart was loud in his ears. Gradually the curve grew sharper. Kane stopped and looked behind him but saw only darkness. He walked on, then halted again. The trees continued to curve, describing an arc around a clearing. Three large campfires flared a few yards out from the very middle of the bend. Kane dropped to one knee, watching.

Flickering silhouettes of men, many men, passed back and forth in front of the flames. Their voices and laughter, rough from alcohol, were raucous. A bottle arced from near one of the fires, sailed into the woods and shattered against a tree, followed by a roar of merriment.

The marshal's eyes moved beyond the circles of firelight to where horses were picketed. In the dim light he could not see them well, but there seemed to be as many as there were in Mae St. John's remuda back with the herd.

Kane's eyes strained to see into the darkness. Were they horse soldiers? This was an undisciplined bunch, so cavalry was highly unlikely. A posse maybe? It was possible, but unlikely. Those boys by the fires were drovers and a fair piece off their home range. The family men who formed the bulk of posses never cared to wander far from their wives and kids.

Then who the hell were they?

A tall man walked away from the fires a few yards toward Kane, fumbled with his pants, then arched his back and relieved himself. As far as the marshal could make out, the man wore the typical waddie's rough range clothes, but his wide-brimmed, white sombrero and batwing chaps spoke loudly of Texas.

Was it possible these men were returning to the home ranch after delivering a herd and were now letting off steam? The plains were vast, and the punchers could have passed Kane and the others on the trail without being seen. Or were they headed north?

As the man he'd been watching buttoned up and stepped back to the fires, Kane told himself there was one way to find out—he could go ask.

But something held him back, a sense of wrongness about the men, as though their loud talk and laughter were not expressions of joy, but of threat. Kane had the feeling they were liquoring themselves up for a task they would not normally care to carry out sober. Over by the fires, men were dancing, holding bottles. To roars of approval, a few started shooting into the air.

Kane swallowed hard. This was not a group of high-spirited punchers; it was a drunken mob. And in his experience that always meant only one thing—hemp ropes, shooting and killing.

But who could they be chasing in this wilderness?

Unbidden, a thought crept into Kane's mind.

How had Mae St. John really gathered her herd?

Chapter 13

Logan Kane retrieved his horse and rode north under a brightening sky. The night was shading into dawn as he rode into camp and put up his horse.

Buck was already awake and had the coffee on and a mess of sourdough biscuits baking on the fire in a Dutch oven.

Kane looked around him. The lean-to was empty but there was no sign of Mae. She and Ed Brady were probably out with the herd. Sam was packing his blanket roll into the wagon and for some reason Stringfellow was cursing softly.

Kane strolled to the fire. The eggshell blue sky was streaked with ribbons of scarlet and a single sentinel star was still awake to the north.

"Coffee ready?" Kane asked Buck.

The old puncher nodded. "It's biled." His eyes lifted to the marshal. "You been riding out." It was a statement, not a question.

Kane lied easily. "Thought I'd check the trail a few miles up ahead."

Buck absorbed that, blinking, then said, "Wind's from the south." He watched Kane nod, then said, "I'd say it's an ill wind."

Startled, the marshal stared at Buck, a reaction the man noted. "I got a feeling." He pointed to the star. "See that? It will come up a-lookin' fer me tonight, but it won't see me on account of I won't be here."

Kane managed a small smile. "Why, where you goin', Buck?"

The man dropped to a knee, lifted the lid on the oven and peered inside. "I don't know the answer to that question an' I never have," he said.

It seemed Buck was all through talking. Kane poured himself coffee. "Miss Mae around?" he asked. "Or is she with the herd?"

"She's close," Buck said, never a talking man in the morning.

Kane wanted to gauge the woman's reaction when he told her about the men he'd seen. He circled the camp and saw no sign of her. But then the sound of a woman's singing drifted from the pines and the marshal walked in that direction.

Shadows still lingered among the trees and only now were birds stirring in the branches. The stream meandered to Kane's left and he followed it, the sound of Mae's song reaching his ears from just ahead of him. She was singing "Aura Lee" in a high, sweet voice and for a moment Kane, who knew and liked the song, stopped, listening. Then he coughed loudly and moved closer.

Mae sat beside the stream, her naked back to him, running a wet washcloth over her breasts and shoulders. "Ma'am," Kane said. The woman did not turn her head, nor did she try to cover herself. "What is it?" she said.

"I surely admired your singing, ma'am."

"Thank you."

The marshal hesitated a moment, his eyes on Mae's smooth, ivory skin and the beautiful curve of her back as it narrowed to her waist. Her auburn hair cascaded over her shoulders, the ends damp and curling. He swallowed hard, then said, "We got riders on our back trail, ma'am. A passel of them an' real close."

Mae's hand stilled, but she betrayed no other emotion. "What manner of men?"

"If I had to guess, I'd say Texas punchers. All of them drunk."

"How many?"

"A bunch. Maybe eighteen or twenty."

"Rustlers?"

For some reason that thought had not occurred to Kane. His lawman's instinct had told him the men were not two-bit outlaws planning to lift a herd. They were something else . . . something more sinister and infinitely more dangerous.

"No, not rustlers. At least, I don't think so," he said. His eyes bored into the back of the woman's head. "Ma'am, how did you gather your herd?"

Mae still did not turn, but her back stiffened. "I

already told you, Marshal. Most of those cattle belong to my friends and neighbors from ranches surrounding my own."

"Ma'am, I got the feelin' your friends and neighbors are right behind us, an' that's a hangin' bunch if ever I seen one."

If Kane was hoping for a reaction, he wasn't disappointed. Mae reached for her shirt and buttoned into it. Then she turned and faced the marshal. "We're moving out, right now."

Right then, Mae St. John was more beautiful than Kane had ever seen her. Her damp shirt clung close to her firm breasts and the morning light slanting through the trees highlighted her hair with streaks of burnished gold. Her eyes shone with a light that was all their own, bright, luminous and achingly lovely.

"Ma'am, if that's a rustled herd and them boys want it back real bad, as I suspicion they do, you won't get far. They could be here in an hour, maybe less."

Mae's eyes hardened, in part anger, part determination. "The herd is all I have. It's all that stands between me and poverty, and I'm not giving it up to anybody." She took a step closer. "Marshal, let Buff and the others out of the cage. They're all top gun hands and we'll need their skill."

Kane shook his head. "I can't do that, ma'am. When those Texans get here, we'll give back the herd and hope that I can show my badge an' talk them out of a hangin'."

"They won't hang a woman."

"No, I guess maybe they won't. But they'll sure string up Buck and Ed Brady, depend on it."

"Let Buff and the others out of the cage, Kane, I'm begging you." Mae moved close and laid the tips of her fingers on the marshal's chest. She tilted back her head, met his eyes and smiled. "I saw how you looked at me back there at the stream. I can read it in a man's eyes when he wants what he sees. Believe me, Marshal, I can be grateful. I can show more ways to be grateful than you ever imagined."

"Mae," Kane said, using the woman's name for the first time since he'd met her, "you're giving back the herd you stole and we'll hope to God that's enough."

"Go to hell, Kane," the woman snapped. She brushed past him and then he heard her yell to Buck to break camp.

But Mae St. John was too late . . . too late for her and too late for Ed Brady and Buck.

The riders swept into camp from all directions, Brady with them, dragged behind a horse. As Kane stepped out of the trees he saw Sam was surrounded and had already unbuckled his gun belt. Mae stood beside Buck, her eyes scared, her lips white.

"Good to see you again, Mae." This from a big man riding a raw-boned black. "You sure played hob."

"Good to see you too, Clay," the woman said. She

was obviously scared but was trying desperately to brazen it out. "What brings you here?"

The man called Clay smiled. He was big in the chest and shoulders, dressed in expensive gray broadcloth. His face was ruggedly handsome, the lips under his blond mustache full and sensuous, with a hint of cruelty. He looked what he was, an arrogant, wealthy man who walked a wide path and was used to getting his own way.

"What brings us here?" the man called Clay said. "Why, Mae, I thought you knew. We came to take back the cattle you stole from us."

Kane walked to the edge of camp. The quick eyes of a small, thin man sitting his horse beside Clay flicked to the marshal, then lingered.

There were twenty riders in the bunch, a few swaying in their saddles, their faces ragged from whiskey and a lack of sleep. Perhaps, more than any of the others, old Buck saw where this was headed. "It's all a misunderstanding, Mr. Cullen," he said. "A mistake, you understand."

"You shut your trap," Clay Cullen snapped. "I'm talking to the lady."

"Talk to me," Kane said. He stepped closer to Cullen. The gaze of the small man followed him.

Cullen's head moved slowly in the marshal's direction, as though he was in no hurry to see who had just spoken. But when he did look, his eyes dropped to the gun on Kane's hip. "Who the hell are you?"

"Name's Logan Kane. I'm a deputy marshal for

Judge Parker's court." He eased back his vest, revealing his star. "I'm taking escaped prisoners to Fort Smith to be hanged at the judge's convenience."

"You throw in with this nest o' thieves?" Cullen asked.

"We're headed in the same direction."

The small man sat straighter in the saddle, suddenly interested. "You the Logan Kane that killed Jake Grant over to El Paso way?" he asked. He had an odd way of talking, a low, snake-hiss between his teeth.

"That was me."

"Ol' Jake was fast on the draw."

"Maybe so, but a man with a six-gun shouldn't go up against a man holdin' a Greener scattergun loaded with double-ought buck. I guess ol' Jake wasn't exactly sure about that rule."

Cullen turned his head to the small man. "Can you take him, Lewt?"

Without a moment of hesitation he answered, "Sure."

Cullen nodded, satisfied.

"Take back your cattle and then ride out," Kane said. "There's no need for violence here."

He knew the chances were slim that Clay Cullen would pay heed to him, but then Mae spoke and gave herself no chance at all.

"You're taking back nothing," she said, a flat statement that belied the temper hot in her face. "Clay Cullen, for years you and the rest of them with you here fenced off my best pastures, cut my water and slapped your own brands on my yearlings. You drove off my hands and rustled my cattle and finally pushed my back to the wall. Well, I've now taken what's rightfully mine."

In the abrupt silence that followed, Kane looked around the circle of riders. They were tough, sun-scarred men raised hard to survive in a land that offered nothing for the taking and where compromise of any kind didn't enter into their way of thinking. In their faces he saw much of the solemnity of judgment but little of understanding and mercy.

Cullen was smiling. "A pretty speech, Mae, and maybe there's a grain of truth in what you say." The smile slipped and the man's face turned to stone. "You're a rustler and horse thief, and I'm going to hang you, Mae. You and the two with you." He didn't look at Kane. "As to the lawman, I'll study on that for a spell."

Ed Brady, his face swollen from the beating he'd taken, spoke for the first time. "Cullen," he yelled angrily, "let me get closer to you so I can spit in your eye."

A kick in the head from the nearest rider sent Brady sprawling to the ground.

Time was running out on him fast and Kane had to make a play. Knowing it was hopeless even as he did it, his hand flashed to his Colt, catching the gunman called Lewt and the others flat-footed. "Cullen," he said, "rein in your hounds or I'll shoot you right off that hoss!"

A moment later something heavy and hard crashed into the back of Kane's head . . . and the ground opened up and swallowed him whole.

Chapter 14

The marshal woke to pain.

His head felt like an anvil being pounded by a hammer, and green and yellow nausea curled in his belly. His eyes fluttered open. A pale blue sky arched above him, smeared by wispy white clouds, and the sun rode high, gleaming like a white-hot double eagle . . . not that Kane had seen one of those in a long while. The judge paid in silver, and little enough of that. Why was he so penny-pinching all the time? Well, it must be said in his favor that the court depended on the federal government for funding that was seldom paid and . . . the judge liked his sherry wine. How much did sherry wine cost? Kane admitted that he didn't know, but he would have to find out soon. . . .

The marshal groaned as he stopped his mind wandering any deeper into the realm of the bizarre. He forced himself to return to sanity, to the thudding agony of his head and a memory that was broken all to pieces. Slowly, he began to fit the fragments together, like a child he'd once seen in Fort Smith do with one of Mr. Milton Bradley's newfangled jig-saw puzzles.

As the pictures moved together Kane began to remember, and the memory pained him worse than the trip-hammer clangor in his head. Clay Cullen and his riders . . . the man's threat to hang Mae St. John . . . his drawing down on him . . . and then the world going dark.

Alarm spiked at Kane. Where was Mae?

He rose to one elbow and the landscape around him immediately cartwheeled crazily, the labored cut of his ragged breath loud in his ears. The spinning slowed and stopped, and the camp shimmered into focus.

He was lying near the fire, on his back, his saddle under his head. He raised his hand to touch the place where he'd been hit and dislodged a wet towel that had been placed on his brow. Kane's fingers moved to the back of his head and felt crusted blood on his hair. The wound was raw and sore to the touch, but it had barely broken the skin.

Not a bullet then. A rifle butt probably, or a tree limb. Like a bumpkin selling pumpkins, he'd allowed someone to sneak up behind him and buffalo him good.

The marshal pushed himself off the grass, and when the earth settled again he saw vultures circle the sky, birds of ill omen that glided patiently under a black star.

His eyes moved around camp, past the prison wagon where men cowered, to the oak tree by the stream and the terrible fruit it bore. Three bodies dangled from ropes, swaying gently in the wind. Mae St. John's hair drifted over her contorted face, as though the breeze was aware of her ugliness in death and sought to shield her from prying eyes.

Sam Shaver stood with his back to Kane, the scattergun in his hands. A man sat at his feet, his back hunched, his head lifted to Mae's body. With a small twinge of anger, the marshal recognized him as Buff Stringfellow. He shouldn't be there. He should be in his cage.

Someone had shoved Kane's gun back in the holster. He settled the belt lower on his hips and walked unsteadily to the oak. Sam saw him, raised an eyebrow, but said nothing.

"Cullen?" Kane said.

"Who else?" Sam said. "Him an' some o' the others. Buck surprised them, put up a fight. The old man had sand."

Kane looked. One of Buck's eyes was swollen shut and blood from his smashed mouth stained his ragged mustache.

"When?"

Sam looked at Kane as though he thought the question strange. "Two hours back, maybe a tad longer."

"I been out fer two hours?"

"Out. At one time I thought you was dying, but then I remembered you've got a thick skull."

Kane had to direct his impotent anger somewhere. He pointed to Stringfellow. "What the hell is he doing here?"

"He asked. Once upon a time, him an' Mae were close."

"Get him back to the cage."

Now Stringfellow turned his head. "Damn you, Kane, she was my woman. Let me grieve."

"I ain't in the grieving business," Kane said. "On your feet an' get back into the cage where you belong. Stay down there a minute longer an' I'll shoot a thumb off you."

The outlaw struggled upright. When he looked at the marshal, his black eyes were glittering with hate, but he said nothing.

"Do your duty, Sam," Kane said.

"Yes indeed, Marshal Kane," Sam said. His cheeks were stained with red, like a man who had just been slapped. He motioned with the Greener. "Let's go, Buff. You can't do any good here."

Kane's gaze followed Sam as he locked Stringfellow in the cage, then returned to the oak. "You're a hard man, Logan," he said. "There's just no give in you, is there?"

"Stringfellow is still alive, ain't he? That's give enough."

Sam watched the circling vultures for a few moments. Then he said, "Your sorrel's gone. Cullen took it with the remuda. He left the wagon mare." The old man's eyes tightened on Kane's face. "We goin' on?"

"Only after I get my hoss back."

"That's not it. You want to kill Clay Cullen. He's nothin' to you."

"He done ill by me. I can't let that go. The man can boast he put the crawl on Logan Kane. People hear that an' think all kinds of strange things."

"No, Marshal, that's still not it, leastways not entirely. Mostly it's on account of how Cullen hung Mae St. John. What was she to you, except Buff Stringfellow's woman?" Sam stared at Kane. "I smell iron in the wind, an' that means winter's crackin' down on us and we still have mountains an' rivers to cross. We got to move on, Logan."

"I'll take the mare," Kane said. "Be back in a couple of days."

"There's twenty of them, only one o' you."

The marshal smiled. "That's Cullen's problem." He glanced at Mae's body, then back to Sam. "She does mean something to me. She was real purty an' she sang real sweet. She didn't deserve to die like this." His eyes lifted to the oak again. "We'll cut them down an' bury them decent. Then I'm riding out."

"And who's goin' to bury you decent, Logan?" Sam said.

They buried Mae, Buck and Ed Brady near the oak, but far enough away to avoid the tree's roots. As a reluctant concession to Sam, Kane allowed Stringfellow to stand at the graveside.

When the praying was done, the outlaw said, "She was a good woman, a decent woman, but they pushed her to the wall, all them rich ranchers who

wanted her miserable few acres." He looked at Kane.
"You going after Cullen?"

"He's got my hoss."

"Take me with you, Marshal. Give me a gun an'
let me put a bullet in him."

Kane smiled. "Stringfellow, I wouldn't trust you at
my back with a gun in your hand."

"Damn you, I never back-shot a man in my life."

"There's a first time for everything." Kane looked
at Sam. "Take him to the cage."

Stringfellow's eyes swung to the old man, desperately seeking an ally. "Tell him, Sam. Tell him it's
my place."

Sam shook his head. "Buff, you ain't got a hoss."

"Then I'll walk. I'll run."

"You'll walk to the cage," Kane said. "Then your
walkin' is done."

"Kane, when it's over an' Cullen is dead, you can
chain me up again, on my word of honor. Hear me,
Kane. I'm breaking apart here."

The marshal spat onto the ground at Stringfellow's
feet. "Your word of honor ain't worth that. Now, let
the dead lie quiet an' get back to the wagon."

A ragged, bearded man with sun-scorched skin
and hollow eyes, and stinking of his own rank sweat,
Stringfellow somehow managed to draw his dignity
around him like a tattered cloak. "Kane, the man
who rides next to Cullen is Lewt Mantles. There's
nobody better with a gun than him. You ain't comin'
back here."

Kane seemed to think that over. Finally he turned

to Sam. "If I don't come back, shoot Stringfellow. After that the others will follow you willingly enough."

"Marshal, if'n you want him dead that bad, why don't you shoot him your ownself afore you leave?" Sam asked. He looked irritated.

"Because I plan on comin' back. An' besides, the judge would take it hard if it turned out I killed a prisoner I didn't need to." Kane's eyes moved to Stringfellow. "Right you, back in the cage."

"Kane, I hope you burn in hell," the outlaw said. His raw hatred was a living entity, pushing against the marshal.

Kane smiled. "Then you better save a place for me, hadn't you?"

Kane tightened the cinch on the wagon dray, an ugly little mustang with a hammerhead and a mean eye. "Sam, I won't waste any time getting back. Don't take any chances with the prisoners. Feed them in the cage if you have to, and keep your eyes skinned for Jack Henry. Maybe he studied on how things were shaping up around here an' moved on, but maybe he didn't."

"He didn't move on, Logan. He's close. I can sense him."

"Then watch for him. I took Henry fer a bushwhacker an' a sure-thing killer." He looked at Sam. "What you seein' in the fire?"

"I ain't seein' nothing, an' that's what troubles me."

Kane swung into the saddle. The yellow mustang

halfheartedly bucked a few times to keep him honest, then settled down. It was an old horse and not much given to energetic displays.

The marshal looked down at the old man. "I'll be back soon, Sam. I meant what I said about Stringfellow. Don't take any lip, an' if it comes down to it an' you have to lead the prisoners north, shoot him first."

"I ain't like you, Logan," Sam said. "I'm not that hard."

Kane shook his head. "You may have to be."

Sam was quiet for a moment, his eyes measuring the younger man. Then he said, "Know what sits on that hoss? Pride. An' fer what? Because you let a man best you, an' now you can't let that go. It's false pride, Marshal. Ride out now and all you are is a droop-tailed rooster crowing on a dung heap."

"Then them people who was hung don't matter, huh?"

"They rustled cattle an' took their chances. Logan, you don't owe them a damned thing." Sam's talking was done. He reached down, slid his Colt from the leather and held it up to Kane. "Take this. If you get into close work, you may need it."

Kane nodded and shoved the gun into his waistband. "Be seein' you, old-timer."

Sam didn't say anything. But when the marshal swung his horse away, he whispered, *"Vaya con Dios*, Logan."

His eyes were very old—and very tired.

Chapter 15

Clay Cullen and his men were not difficult to track. He was driving the cattle along the same trail that had brought them north. He'd taken along the chuck wagon and it followed in the same ruts.

Kane rode under a pale blue sky. The sun was dropping lower and shadows were angling among the trees. The day was still hot and only a soft wind stirred the prairie grass. For the past hour the mustang had stepped out willingly enough, but it had a short-coupled, choppy gait and was uncomfortable to ride.

The marshal took off his hat and wiped his sweating forehead with the back of his hand. The air was astonishingly clear and he could see for miles across the high plains. Only in the far distance, where heat waves danced, could his gaze penetrate no farther. Once he saw a herd of antelope emerge from the haze; distorted by the shimmer, their legs stretched impossibly long and slender. As they came closer, they slowly returned to their normal shape and headed north, toward water.

Kane began to smell dust as the day shaded into evening. He swung out of the saddle and studied the cattle dung. It was moist and fresh, dropped no more than a couple of hours before.

He rode on as the night birds pecked at the first stars of night and an owl in the trees demanded over and over again to know his identity. With the coming of the dark, the wind rose, tossing the long grass, and the coyotes had begun to call back and forth.

An hour later, in full darkness, Kane saw the fires.

He rode closer, trusting to the gloom, and scouted the camp. This close, he heard the quiet talk of men. There was none of the drinking and carousing he'd heard the night before. Maybe the deaths of Mae St. John and the others were weighing on them. But more likely this was a crowd with a hangover, tuckered out by the rigors of a cattle drive.

The remuda was near to the tree line, the herd grazing close to him, upwind from the camp. In the darkness Kane detected no sign of water, but there must be a source somewhere since this part of the Oklahoma Territory was cut through by many streams that were fed by the Little and the fall rains.

Kane swung the mustang to the east, riding close to the trees. Nothing on his clothes or saddle reflected light, and the moon was hiding behind cloud. Over at the camp, men had already sought their blankets and the only movement was when somebody rose and reached for the coffeepot.

Used to men on horseback, the remuda did not stir as Kane got closer. A few raised their heads and looked at him, their ears pricked, but they soon ignored him and went back to grazing. A problem for Kane was that the horses slowly moved away from him as he rode among them, their footfalls stirring up the night.

But even in the darkness, a red horse is not hard to find. He shook out a loop, then dabbed it over his horse's head. The big sorrel balked, pulling back on the rope, and for a moment Kane's heart stopped in his chest; he feared the big stud would cut and bolt. He spoke softly to the animal and it calmed at the sound of his voice. He led the sorrel out of the remuda and back to the black wall of the trees.

When the cattle herd was between him and camp, Kane switched his saddle to the sorrel and looped a rope around the mustang's neck. He tied the little horse to a tree, then swung onto the sorrel's back. Then he stood and considered his options.

Logan Kane was not by nature a deep-thinking man. When presented with a situation he reacted to it instantly, heedlessly, without considering the consequences of his actions. It was this that had helped him establish a reputation as a named gunfighter who was mighty sudden on the draw and shoot. But it had impaired his relationships with the few women with whom he'd allowed himself to get close and had all but assured him of a life without wife or child. Kane knew this and, aware of the limitations his character imposed upon him, accepted it.

Now he sat his horse, alone in the sheeted darkness, tangling with his alternatives. He had his horse and Sam was alone with the prisoners. He should go back, not needlessly risk his life. Yet he couldn't get Cullen out of his mind. He owed the man, not only for a bump on the head, but for what he'd done to Mae St. John.

And the old man had been right. There was pride. It was the gunfighter's stiff-necked pride, the most important part of the code he lived by, and it was honored by the best of them—Hardin, Hickok, Thompson, Longley and the rest. He could not let Cullen go unpunished, not if he ever again wanted to hold up his head in the company of belted men.

It had to be done. Clay Cullen had chosen the dance and now he must pay the fiddler.

His mind made up, Kane's eyes reached through the darkness to the herd. He had to get them running, but there must be a night herder and maybe two or three. He kneed his horse closer to the cattle.

Unlike longhorns, Herefords were a docile breed not much inclined to be skittish, and it was possible only one man was out with the herd and he'd be as hungover as the rest. The night was on Kane's side. The dark sky quivered white with lightning and the rising wind was talking loud. The few longhorns in the herd might be feeling uneasy, and if they cut and ran, the Herefords would follow.

He walked his horse to the edge of the herd and drew rein, his gaze scanning the darkness. He waited, so much on edge he felt like his belly was being pulled out. He could get them running, he figured, but if the night herder was somewhere close in the darkness, he could be rifle-shot right out of the saddle. After a couple of minutes his patience was rewarded. A man rode toward him, slumped, his chin on his chest, his face hidden behind his hat.

"Howdy," Kane said. He rode close to the man.

The rider's head snapped up. "You sent to relieve me?" He was groggy from sleep, but suddenly his eyes widened. "Hey, who the hell are—"

Kane drew and shot into the middle of the man's chest. The herder immediately threw up his arms and fell backward off the saddle. "That was for Mae," he said.

Kane shoved his Colt into the air and fired, then fired again. Led by the longhorns, the herd started to run. To Kane's joy they were headed right for the camp where up until his first shot every man had been rolled in his blankets.

The cattle were running hard and Kane followed them at a gallop. Men scattered as the cattle charged among them, and the marshal saw one puncher go down, screaming as he was trampled under pounding hooves.

The night became a shambles of charging cattle, roaring guns, angry shouts and the flickering forms of running men backed by the firelight. Fractured images hurtled toward Kane at breakneck speed: open mouths that bellowed curses, orange muzzle flashes blasting near him, the backs of running men.

Then Clay Cullen's face, twisted in rage, swung

into Kane's line of vision. The rancher was bringing up a rifle. Kane's horse reared as he cut loose with both Colts. Hit hard, with scarlet blood suddenly thick in his mouth, Cullen called out, then went down. A shot split the air next to Kane's head, then another. Lewt Mantles was standing with his legs spread, calmly working his guns, his eyes red in the firelight, intent on Kane. The marshal fired at the man but missed. Heedless of the men around him, he rode right at Mantles, the gun in his right hand flaring. Hit, Mantles took a step back.

Kane's gun was empty. His reins trailing, he did a perfect border shift and Sam's Colt thudded into his hand. Kane was right on top of Mantles now. The gunman fired and Kane felt a sledgehammer blow to his right thigh. He leaned out of the saddle, shoved his gun into Mantles' face and pulled the trigger. Instantly the man's face turned into a crimson mask of blood and bone. Mantles staggered to his right, still trying to bring up his guns, but couldn't find the strength. He toppled into the fire, an upset coffeepot hissing over the coals around him.

Then Kane was through them, riding hell-for-leather into the gloom. Bullets zinged around him and one burned across the thick meat of his shoulder. The rest went wild. All at once he was swallowed by darkness, and the shooting staggered to a ragged halt.

His leg on fire, Kane rode into the plain, then looped wide around the camp and swung north. Behind him, borne on the wind, he heard men yelling.

Distance and darkness shredded the sound, and soon there were only the whisper of the prairie and the drumbeat hammer of his heart.

The violence Kane had wrought had been brief, shocking and sudden. It had been brought about by a man trained in arms, using the latest black-powder weapons of the time, designed to fire big, low-velocity lead bullets that inflicted terrible wounds. For a few brief, terrifying seconds he'd been a ravening wolf among sheep and his attack had been devastating.

He stared into the night ahead of him, but saw only the eyes of Lewt Mantles as the gunfighter died in the flame-streaked night. The man had not died clean and had breathed his last, facedown in fire. Somewhere, along the back trail of his years, Mantles had taken the gunfighter's path and had known and accepted the risks. But no man should meet an end like his.

Kane gritted his teeth against the pain in his thigh as he untied the mustang and led the little horse behind the sorrel. He turned his head, listening. He heard no sound of a chase, and he thanked God for it. There had already been enough killing.

Bitterly, Kane realized he could see no end to it. The vicious, mindless violence, the belted men dying hard and defiant, would go on and on . . . until the day he lay with his own face in the flames, his open eyes already staring into hell.

The prairie wind tugged at him, teasing, and the sky was black, without stars. A fine rain pattered against him and ticked through the trees, and he shrugged into his slicker.

It had to end, he knew that now. Kane had killed three men that night and their deaths weighed more heavily on him than any others. And he thought he knew the reason. He had acted out of pride, not a sense of justice. He'd used the deaths of Mae St. John and her riders only as an excuse to gun Clay Cullen. His fingers strayed to the star pinned to his gun belt. He could have arrested Cullen, taken him to Fort Smith and let Judge Parker deal with him. The chances were he would have died in the attempt, but the judge had already lost threescore deputy marshals in the line of duty and maybe that's what was expected of him. Maybe that was what the law expected of him.

The marshal was a troubled man as he rode through the rainy canopy of the night, because all at once he knew exactly who and what he was, and that knowledge cut deep, like a knife.

He was Logan Kane, the violent gunman, an outlaw with a badge.

Chapter 16

The night had turned cold and there was sleet in the rain as Logan Kane rode into camp. The fire was out and there was no sign of Sam Shaver.

He swung out of the saddle and let the mustang's lead rope drop. Then his eyes sought to penetrate the darkness, looking for movement in the shadows. Nothing stirred, the only sound the rustle of the oak and the distant cry of coyotes.

He drew his gun and limped toward the wagon, the pain in his leg beating at him. The cage loomed ahead of him, an obscene thing of wood and iron. It was empty, the open door creaking in the wind.

"Logan, is that you?"

Sam's voice, thin and strained.

"Behind the wagon, Logan."

The old man was lying on his back, his face wet with sleet and rain. Death shadows had gathered in his eyes and cheeks; his breathing was labored, his chest rising and falling with every shuddering gasp.

Kane kneeled beside him. He took off his slicker, rolled it up and placed it under Sam's head. "Take it easy, old-timer," he said, attempting to smile. "You'll be fine."

"Not fine, no, Logan. They've kilt me." His eyes dropped to the front of his shirt where blood gleamed. "I'm shot through and through, Logan." He lifted a thin, blue-veined hand and touched Kane's chest with his fingertips. "I held on—figgered you'd be back." His eyes met those of the younger man. "Get yore sorrel back?"

"Sure did. Brung the dray back too."

"Take care of that mustang, Logan. He ain't a bad hoss." Sam's hand fell to his side and for a moment Kane thought he was gone, but then the old man whispered, "Cullen?"

"Dead."

"Did he have iron in his hand?"

"He did, and he had his face to me."

"Then you done what you had to do, Logan."

"Maybe so." He brushed a wisp of gray hair from Sam's forehead. "What happened, old-timer?"

"Ol' Buff called me over to the wagon, tole me Joe Foster was awful sick because o' that kick in the head you gave him. The kid was groanin' an' carryin' on, an' I set my scattergun down and stepped over there."

Sam was fighting for breath, desperately clinging to life.

"You take it easy, Sam," Kane said. "You can tell me later when you feel up to it."

It didn't matter how it had happened; the prisoners were gone and Sam was dying. The circumstances told their own story.

But the old man shook his head. "Listen . . . Buff grabbed me and held me against the bars. Then he yelled, 'Now, Jack!' Next thing I know, a bullet hits me atween the shoulder blades an' they'd done gone an' kilt me." He smiled weakly. "I didn't have no Colt or I would have drawed it an' at least plugged ol' Buff."

Kane's voice was tight in his throat. "Which way are they headed?"

"North, Logan. They got a heap o' friends in the Indian Territory." Sam let out a long, pained sigh. "My talkin' is done, Logan. Hey, know what I'd like?"

"What's that, old-timer?"

"A cup o' coffee."

Then all the life that had been in Sam Shaver left him, and he died quietly and without fuss as was the way of the Western men of his generation.

Kane struggled to his feet, a hot, killing rage in him. He fought it back. That was not the way. He was a sworn lawman, not a good or admirable one, but a lawman nevertheless. It was time to step up. He'd arrest Jack Henry for murder and throw him in the cage with the others. Let Judge Parker kill him. Kane was done with it.

The marshal led the horses into the trees and unsaddled the sorrel. There was a patch of good grass close to where Mae had bathed and he turned them loose to graze. He stood near the stream and remembered how lovely the woman had looked that morning. Now, buried at the base of the oak, she would no longer be beautiful.

Here the trees kept out the worst of the sleeted rain and Kane managed to scrounge up some dry wood. He built a small fire in the hollow base of a massive boulder a ways back from the creek and then limped back to the camp.

Kane removed his slicker from under Sam's head and spread it over him. He checked the wagon, but all the food had been taken, along with the spare rifle, a box of shells and the scattergun. For some reason, the prisoners had not taken the coffeepot that was still sitting on cold ashes. The pot was full. The old man must have been making coffee before he was shot.

Kane took the pot back to his fire, set it to boil and built himself a cigarette, then another. Only then, afraid of what he was about to see, did he slip his suspenders off his shoulders and shrug down his pants to look at the wound in his thigh.

It was bad. He could tell that, and immediately he felt a twinge of fear. He was in a hell of a fix.

The bullet had entered the front of his thigh and exited at the back, a few inches under his hip, but had missed bone. The wounds looked raw and red, like the open lips of a hog ranch whore. Kane wished Sam were at his side. The old man had patched up dozens of marshals and he would have known what to do with an injury like that.

The coffee bubbled, and Kane poured two cups. He pulled up his pants and slipped one suspender over his shoulder. Then he lifted Sam's cup. He hobbled to the old man's side and carefully laid the steaming cup beside him.

"Here's your coffee, old-timer," he said, smiling. "An' I sure hope you know I brung it."

Kane returned to the trees and drank his coffee. He built a smoke, then poured himself another cup. He was in no hurry to do what had to be done.

An hour before sunup the sleet and rain stopped and the clouds parted. The morning was cold; Kane shivered and threw a few more sticks on the fire. The effort left him gasping and he huddled closer to the flames for warmth.

He glanced through the tree canopy at the brightening sky, turquoise enamel rippled by bands of lilac and gold. A gusting wind talked among the branches and set the fire to guttering.

It was time. He'd have to get it done and then move on.

Kane slipped a shell from his cartridge belt and pried the bullet out of the brass with his pocketknife. He poured the fine-grained black powder onto the wound in the front of his thigh, figured he didn't have enough and did the same thing with another cartridge.

He'd heard the old mountain men had done this to cauterize wounds, but he didn't know if that was true or not. He'd find out soon enough.

Kane reached for a brand from the fire, gritted his

teeth and applied the flame to the powder. It flared, sizzling, sending up a cloud of greasy, white smoke. The pain was a living entity that clawed viciously at Kane's leg. His body slammed into a rigid board and he hissed through his teeth as he desperately tried to hold on. But then darkness took hold of him and he knew no more.

Kane drifted back to consciousness. The fire was burning cheerfully and the morning light was still the same. He had only been out for a few minutes.

The pain in his thigh was now a dull ache and he looked at the wound. The skin had been blackened and it was difficult to tell if the burning powder had made a difference. Maybe it seemed a little less inflamed, but that may have been wishful thinking. The burn would probably have killed any infection and that could only be good.

Now he had it to do all over again, this time on the back of his thigh, an awkward place to get at.

Kane poured more coffee and smoked another cigarette. When he was done, he opened up a couple more cartridges, lay on his left side and poured a mound of powder onto the wound.

It is said that pain leaves no memory, but Kane remembered. A lump in his throat, his heart pounding, he lit the powder. His bellow of agony sent the jays exploding from the trees and made the horses whinny in alarm. Kane's open mouth grabbed at air like a drowning man and his fingers dug deep into the soft dirt. But this time he stayed awake, arching his back until the worst of the pain passed.

He sat up again and with trembling fingers built a smoke. He puffed hurriedly, again and again, then lay back on the grass. It was done. He had no idea if the burn had really helped, but he hoped so. He was already wasting daylight and he had a burying to do. Then it would be time to ride.

Reluctantly Kane struggled to his feet. To his relief, his leg was stiff but not overly painful. He doused the fire with the last of the coffee, then, with a pang of regret, remembered that he had no Arbuckle and little chance of finding any. It was a depressing thought.

It took a tremendous effort to dig a grave for Sam. Kane had not realized how much his wounds had weakened him and he had to pause often and rest on the shovel. After an hour, he judged the hole deep enough to keep out coyotes and he laid the old man to rest.

The marshal stood at the side of the grave and in a tuneless baritone sang "Shall We Gather at the River?" His singing was not great, but his respect and affection for Sam Shaver was.

> Shall we gather at the river,
> Where bright angel feet have trod;
> With its crystal tide forever
> Flowing by the throne of God?

His voice cracking with emotion, Kane struggled to finish the rest of what he remembered of the hymn.

> Yes, we'll gather at the river,
> The beautiful, the beautiful river;
> Gather with the saints at the river
> That flows by the throne of God.

He had, he decided, given Sam a crackerjack send-off and if the old man had kin and he ever ran into them, he'd be sure to tell them so.

Kane led the horses from the trees and hitched the mustang to the prison wagon.

Only Jack Henry had a horse; Stringfellow and the others would be walking. Men wearing boots didn't cover a lot of ground fast, and even with the wagon he'd catch up with them before they reached the mountains.

He saddled the sorrel and tied it behind the wagon. Then he climbed stiffly into the driver's seat and moved out. The Little River lay just to the north, and the marshal figured the convicts would have already crossed, unless it was running white water. They would then be in the southern reaches of the Ouachitas. By the end of the day, if Kane was lucky, the higher peaks and ridges of the mountains should be in sight.

It all depended on the current mood of the capricious Little.

Chapter 17

Kane was lucky, and that meant the convicts had been too.

The heavy summer downpours had ended and the fall rains had not yet begun in earnest. No longer swollen by flood waters, the river was slow moving and sluggish. Heavy vegetation grew down to the banks, including cottonwoods, hardwoods and a few enormous bald cypress trees, some of them a hundred feet high. Mallards and wood ducks floated in the sloughs and oxbows, and Kane caught sight of a huge tom turkey that waddled out from the brush, spotted him and dashed into cover again.

His leg had stiffened up badly and he climbed down from the wagon with difficulty. He untied the sorrel and swung into the saddle. At this point the riverbank was high and deeply undercut and ran with maybe four feet of water. Kane rode downstream and after a few minutes found what he was after.

Here the water flowed only through a central channel, hemmed in on both sides by wide sandbars. The banks sloped gradually to the river and although the channel churned with a stretch of white water, it was shallow and would not impede the wagon.

Kane rode back the way he'd come but stopped and slid his Winchester out of the scabbard when he sighted a deer picking its way through the brush to drink at the river.

He shot the deer at the water's edge. It meant he'd have to drag the carcass back through thick brush, but he needed meat and had to take the shot when it was presented to him or go hungry.

It took Kane twenty minutes to drag the deer onto flat grass and by then he was used up. His wounded leg throbbed and he felt dizzy and sick. No question now of heaving the carcass behind his saddle. He'd have to dress it right where it was and pick up the meat when he returned with the wagon.

The marshal skinned and butchered the deer and wrapped the meat in the hide. He rode back to the wagon, tied the sorrel and climbed into the seat. There were coyotes lurking around when he loaded the venison into the back of the wagon.

"You'll get your share," he yelled. "Plenty left for everybody."

Then he drove the wagon down the shallow bank and crossed the Little. The river gave him no trouble and even the sandbars held firm under the wheels. Behind him the coyotes were already quarreling over what was left of the deer carcass.

*   *   *

The marshal drove north for three hours, keeping in sight a wide creek to the east. Through a screen of cottonwoods and pine he caught glimpses of white rapids, but mostly the water was smooth and shallow, eddying into narrow sloughs and small, oxbow lakes.

The sky was clear and a long-sighted man like Kane could look ahead for miles. Already the Little Cow peak was in sight, and beyond that, the thin blue spine of Walnut Mountain rose eighteen hundred feet above the flat. These mountains had once rivaled the Rockies in height and majesty, but, long since eroded into nubbins, were now only apologetic shadows of their former selves.

Kane had seen no sign of Stringfellow and the others. It was as if they had vanished from the face of the earth.

The sun had just begun its slow slide into afternoon when Kane pulled closer to the creek. He was tormented by hunger, something his growling stomach would not let him forget.

He unhitched the mustang and let it and the sorrel graze. He lit a fire among the cottonwoods and to his joy discovered that at some time Sam had spilled salt in the supplies drawer. It was a small amount to be sure, a few grains, but enough to flavor the venison steak he broiled over the fire. Wishful for coffee, but having none, he drank muddy creek water.

After he ate, Kane sat against a tree and smoked a cigarette. Much addicted to the habit Texas waddies had eagerly borrowed from Mexican vaqueros, he was immensely displeased that his tobacco was getting low. He might not be able to buy more until he reached Fort Smith. The unbidden thought came into his head, as though spoken by someone else: "*If you reach Fort Smith, you mean.*"

Kane scowled. That thought didn't please him either.

Gloomy as he felt, he decided to compound his misery by checking his leg. To his surprise the wound was no longer as angry and red, and there were no maggots, which were always a sign of infection. The gunpowder had blackened the skin and burned him, but the pain was less and for that he was thankful.

He rose, adjusted his gun belt and doused the fire with water. He hitched the mustang and tied up the sorrel, then climbed into the driver's seat.

Where were the convicts?

He must surely be gaining on them—unless they had doubled back and were now hightailing it for Texas. Or they could have headed west, into the broken, hill country south of the blue-smoke Kiamichi Mountains. If they had, he'd never find them, not trying to cross rough country with a heavy wagon and a played-out mustang dray.

An hour later, as Kane tried to remember the location of the thread of trail that led over a saddleback ridge on Walnut Mountain, his eyes scanned the rolling land ahead of him and the banks of the creek, anywhere men might camp or a bushwhacker might hide. He had hunted men before and he watched for signs—a sudden movement, a change in the shadow patterns, a glint of steel—but the marshal saw nothing, only the lonely tossing of the long grass and the movement of the cottonwoods. Ahead, he could make out the oak, hickory and pine forests on the slopes of the Walnut, a dark green mantle that allowed only a few glimpses of iron gray rock to show.

He hoorawed the mustang up a gradual slope scattered with late-blooming wildflowers, and when he topped out on the rise he saw the wagon. It had been pulled up near the creek and beside it stood a woman and a child. The girl clung to her mother and they looked helpless, aimless, like people just standing around because they had nowhere else to go.

Even at a distance Kane recognized them, Lorraine Hook and her daughter Nellie. There was no sign of Barnabas.

Kane drove toward the woman, a flurry of quail scattering from under the mustang's hooves. He waved, but Lorraine did not wave back. She and her daughter stood where they were, emotionlessly watching him come.

The marshal drew rein on the mustang and looked down at Lorraine. He tried for levity and smiled. "Lost?"

The woman just stood and stared at him, and Nellie's eyes were wide and frightened in her pale face.

Kane studied the wagon. It looked as though it had been thoroughly looted, a few items of women's clothing scattered over the grass.

"Six men," he said, "only one of them mounted. Another missing a thumb. Am I right on that?"

"The man on the horse was called Jack," Lorraine said. "He killed Barnabas."

Kane climbed down from the wagon and stood opposite the woman. "How did it happen?"

Lorraine's face was like stone, her eyes steady, betraying no feelings of any kind. She looked tired, older. "They came down on us and said they would take our horses and whatever else they needed. Barnabas was always a hothead. He cursed them and went for his shotgun. The man called Jack threw a loop on Barnabas. Then he dragged him from the wagon. He rode up and down, dragging Barnabas behind him. Over there in the long grass. The others were laughing, slapping their thighs. They thought it was funny."

Lorraine's voice was flat, almost disinterested, her face locked tight, like a company secretary reading the minutes of the last board meeting.

"When Barnabas was dead, and it took a while, they unhitched the team and cleaned out my supplies. They took the shotgun and a revolver with them."

"Did they . . ." Kane searched for a way to say it, but his face revealed what he was thinking.

"To me? No, Marshal Kane, they didn't. They

wanted to be cruel. They wanted so much to be cruel. A couple of them said they'd take me, but a big, bearded man with hollow eyes—"

"Buff Stringfellow."

"—laughed and said, 'Hell no, she's too damn ugly to . . .' Well, I'm sure you know the word. It was cruel, and the others thought it was funny, so they left me alone."

"Nellie?" Kane asked. He dreaded the answer.

"Nellie doesn't talk anymore. Nor does she know who I am."

Sickness, and a ferocious, clawing anger, crawled in the marshal's belly. He did not want to know more. Like the endless killing, it was the path to madness. He looked around him, not trusting himself to speak.

Finally he said, "Sam is dead. They killed him too."

Lorraine's face looked hurt, her eyes showing sadness at the news.

"Where's Barnabas?" Kane asked. He'd been about to say, "the body," but changed it to the man's name at the last moment.

"He's buried over there, by the bend of the creek. They left a shovel for me to bury him, but I didn't have the strength or the will, so he lies shallow, and when the coyotes come they'll find him."

Kane now asked the question he realized he should have asked earlier. "When did this happen?"

"Just after sunup. We had broken camp and were about to ride out when they came down on us."

Kane glanced at the sky and the falling sun. It was about three in the afternoon. They were only six or seven hours ahead of him. "Which direction?"

"North. They headed north for the mountains."

Kane looked toward the sharp backbone of the Walnut. The draft horses they'd taken were big, strong animals. They could ride two-up on the Percherons and with the fifth man up behind Henry they'd cover ground. There was no hope of catching them before they cleared the ridge and rode down into rolling country south of Rich Mountain, yet another rocky rampart that rose more than two thousand feet above the flat.

Lorraine interrupted his thoughts. "You are going after them." It was a statement, not a question.

Kane nodded. "I'll bury Barnabas deeper and camp here the night." He looked at Lorraine. "I can't leave you here. You and Nellie will have to come with me."

At the mention of her name the child looked up at Kane with blank eyes. Then she buried her face in her mother's shoulder. Lorraine put her hand behind the girl's head and held her closer.

"We'd only slow you down. You'll leave us here and go after them, Logan Kane, and you'll kill every man jack of them."

Again, Kane hunted for words. Finally he said, "Ma'am, I intend to arrest those men and take them to Fort Worth. Judge Parker and the law will kill them."

Malice flashed in the woman's eyes. "What's the

matter, Marshal, have you lost your belly for killing?"

Now the words came easily. "Yes, exactly that. Lorraine, a few nights ago I killed men. One of them . . . I saw my bullets explode his face into blood and bone. I never want to see that again. I don't ever again want to take a brave man's life like that."

The woman shook her head. "You're not hunting brave men. You're hunting animals. Do you want me to tell you what they did to Nellie? Do you? Do you?" Something inside Lorraine's head snapped and her small fists pounded on Kane's chest. "Find them, damn you!" Now she was screaming, "Kill them! Kill! Kill! Kill!"

Kane, feeling too big and too awkward, pulled Lorraine close to him and held her, whispering sounds he hoped were soothing. Nellie had walked away from them and she was turning in slow circles, crooning a song the marshal didn't recognize, her arms out from her sides. Probably one of her own. The girl was in a different world, a far-off place where no one could reach her or hurt her ever again.

"Lorraine," he said softly, "I'll find them. And they'll hang, I promise you."

The woman laid her head on Kane's shoulder and dissolved into tears. Time seemed to be standing still for the tall marshal, and the wide land around him held its breath and made no sound.

Chapter 18

Logan Kane had buried Barnabas deeper; and when he asked Lorraine if she wanted to say the words, she shook her head and answered, "I have nothing to say."

The marshal couldn't let it go, not like that. "Ma'am, he was your man. And he had sand. He proved that at the end."

"Then you've said all that needs to be said. Let that be his epitaph. 'He had sand.'"

"Hard, ma'am. Mighty harsh."

"And you know nothing of hardness and harshness, Marshal Kane? You who has put a dozen men in the ground?"

There was a time, a recent time, when Kane would have defended himself. But he knew what the woman had just said was true, and he'd no longer use lies to protect himself from the truth.

He threw down his shovel and walked to the

wagon. Every scrap of food was gone, and with it the coffee.

Lorraine was staring at him. "They didn't find it, if that's what you're looking for."

"You mean the money Barnabas killed to get? He took it from a man who stole it in New Orleans?"

"Then you know the whole story?"

"Three men rode into my camp, brothers by the name of Provanzano. They want their money back. I think one of them may have saved my life when he shot a gunfighting man off me." He smiled. "I think they planned to keep me alive, hoping I'd lead them to you."

"And that's what you've done, you think?"

"You asked me, so I'll say yeah, I reckon it could shape up that way."

The woman was quiet, turning something over in her mind. Then she said, "Those men are Mafia. Have you ever heard of that? It's a crime organization in New Orleans immigrants brought with them, from a place called Sicily, I think. Barnabas, when he thought on it and got scared to death about what he'd done, told me the Mafia never forgets harm done to them—never. The other side of the coin is that they never fail to repay a favor either."

"The Provanzanos look like dangerous men, Lorraine, men who would go about a killin' as just taking care of necessary business."

"You're right, Marshal. Murder is a big part of their business, along with bribery and corruption. Barnabas said that was how they took over the New

Orleans docks and then the police department and city hall."

"Barnabas never looked to me like he was running scared."

"Oh but he was. That's why he wanted to lose himself in the Indian Territory where the Mafia couldn't find him."

"He could have given the money back."

"A crippled man who made his living as a hangman and had killed for thirty thousand dollars doesn't return money willingly. He told me it was ours, for a new life together. He said in the future the hangings would only be something extra, a thing he'd do for the fun of it. Barnabas loved to see fear in other men's eyes when he put the noose around their necks. He was cruel, in the way a cat tormenting a mouse is cruel."

"Right nice feller," Kane said without a trace of humor.

"Barnabas Hook was a killer hiding behind the law," Lorraine said. She hesitated only a moment, looking at Kane, then shrugged. "There are a lot of those around."

If that was a barb directed at him, the marshal let it go. "Did you know he killed a man for the money?"

"Of course I knew, but only after the killing was done." A small anger in her eyes, Lorraine said, "Yes, I could have left him then. But go where?"

Kane's eyes moved to Nellie, who was now sitting on the grass, watching them. "It might have been better if you had," he said. He waited for an answer and when none was forthcoming, he said, "Where is the money?"

"In the wagon. It has a false bottom."

"We'll take it with us. When the Provanzano brothers catch up to us I'll give it to them and hope they just ride away."

Lorraine shrugged. "As you wish."

"You're not going to protest?"

"Why should I? It's blood money and I want no part of it."

The money, all in high-denomination bills, was where Lorraine had said it would be, stuffed into a burlap sack hidden under the wagon's false bottom.

Kane transferred the sack to the prison wagon, then unhitched the mustang. He turned both horses onto good grass near the creek, then set about building a fire.

Nellie watched him intently and after the fire was lit, he smiled and held up a piece of wood. "I need more firewood," he said. "Can you get me some, Nellie?"

The girl understood. She got to her feet and began to hunt among the trees for fallen branches. The marshal nodded to himself, looking at the girl. It was a start.

He rooted around and found some wild onions and cow parsnip, stripping off the tender, smaller leaves and flower stems. The bottom stalk of the plant was used by Indians as a salt substitute and this he cut up into tiny pieces.

Stringfellow and his looters had overlooked a skillet in the Hook wagon, and in this Kane prepared a stew of venison, onions and parsnip and set it on the fire to cook.

They ate from the skillet just as the day was shading into night, sharing Kane's knife to spear the sizzling meat. Nellie stayed close to her mother, but she ate with an appetite and the marshal considered that another good sign.

The night was cool and they slept close to the fire. Kane had gotten his blanket from his bedroll, covered Lorraine and Nellie, then lay on his back, his head on his saddle, smoking, looking at the stars. The plains to the west were a dusky purple, bladed by moonlight, and the creek ran over its pebbled bottom, chuckling at stories told by the wind. Kane closed his eyes and slept.

He dreamed of his mother. She stood in the shadows, just beyond the reach of the firelight, her arms stretched out to him. He smelled the lavender water she always wore and saw her pale lips move.

"You left us, Logan. Come back for us, Son, come back."

"I'll find you, Ma," he said. "I'll bury you decent."

A great wind rose and his mother slowly shredded into the darkness, streaming piece by piece away, like a tattered banner.

"I'll find you, Ma, I swear it," Kane whispered.

The smell of lavender water lingered sweet in the air. He slept on. . . .

*   *   *

Logan Kane woke with a start, but remained still, listening into the night, alert for any sound. What had wakened him? Kane dropped his eyes to the fire. It had burned down to dull red coals and he estimated he'd been asleep for only a couple hours. Far off, coyotes were yipping, but that was a small, remembered noise that had not entered his subconscious.

Something, like an invisible finger tapping on his shoulder, was putting Kane on edge. But the darkness pushed against him and would not reveal its secrets readily. He sat up, put on his hat and rose to his feet, bending to pick up the rifle that had been lying beside him. He tossed some small twigs and pieces of tree bark onto the fire, then added a few thicker branches.

Kane backed out of the firelight and drifted into the trees beside the creek. He stopped and listened. The wind played in the branches, the creek babbled and the moon picked out runnels of white water. The night was assuring him that it harbored no threat; yet the marshal's mouth was dry and he felt jittery.

What was out there?

Kane picked his way through the cottonwoods, walking south. He crossed a treacherous stretch of open ground, splashed with moonlight, then with relief entered trees again. He was a ways from camp now and had seen nothing. The marshal was angry at himself. He was acting like an old lady, afraid of every rustle in the bushes.

Then he heard the scream—a woman's shriek, quickly muffled.

Kane's instinct was to run back to the camp, but he forced himself to walk slowly through the trees, rifle crossed over his chest at the ready. He stumbled into a patch of Texas prickly pear, and a thorny pad scraped cruelly across the front of his wounded thigh. The marshal bit back a cry of pain, but, no matter, he had been heard.

A yell came from the darkness ahead of him. "Come on in, Kane. Quickly now, damn you, or I'll scatter the woman's brains."

He knew the voice. It was Joe Foster. Kane hesitated. Were the others with him?

Foster answered his question, or appeared to. "You got no call to be scared, Kane. I'm alone."

"Where's Stringfellow?" Right then the marshal didn't care about a reply. He was playing for time, trying to discover if Foster was alone as he claimed.

"He ain't here. It's only me an' me's enough. You quit bein' a yellow-bellied cur an' come on in now, or I'll kill the woman and the kid."

"I'm comin' in," Kane said.

"You ain't got an old man and a woman to hide behind, Kane," Foster yelled. There was a laugh in his voice. "I'm gonna kill you fer sure and enjoy doing it."

Kane stepped into camp. Foster stood a few steps beyond the fire, his arm around Lorraine's throat. He held a Smith & Wesson .38 to her head, presumably the one he and the others had taken from Hook's wagon.

Nellie sat on the ground, her scared eyes on Foster. Kane didn't know, or care to know, what the man had done to her, but the girl was terrified. She remembered.

"Drop the rifle, Kane. Throw it away from you," Foster said.

The marshal did as he was told. "Let the woman go," he said. "Your fight is with me."

Foster giggled. "You're so right, Mary Ann." He threw Lorraine away from him. She sprawled on the ground and Nellie immediately ran to her. The man's gun was steady on Kane's belly. "Now it's just between me an' you."

"Drop the iron, Joe," the marshal said. "There's no need for killing here." The thought flashed into his head that he wasn't afraid, but he knew he should be. Foster was said to be fast and the ranger had told him he'd killed six men. He was no bargain. "Go with me to Fort Smith, peaceable like, an' take your medicine."

"Damn you, Kane, I'm going nowhere with you on account of how I plan on killing you. Look what you done to my face. I ain't pretty for the whores no more."

Foster was right about that, Kane decided. His kick had smashed the man's cheekbone, and his left eye socket looked deformed, giving him a strange, wall-eyed look.

"I regret that, Joe," Kane said with as much sincerity as he could muster. "I'm not like that no more."

"You're yeller, Kane, just like I always knew you were."

The Smith spun in Foster's hand, its blue barrel catching the gleam of firelight. The gun slammed into his palm and he shoved it into the waistband of his ragged pants.

Kane recognized the fancy work for what it was, a grandstand play meant to impress and intimidate a scared man. It was the action of a wannabe, not a professional. Foster had killed seven men, or so he claimed, but what manner of men were they? One way to run up a score and gain a reputation was to gun drunks, scared married men and green farm boys. Flashy Joe Foster seemed the type.

He was talking war talk again, grinning. "I always knew I was faster than you, Kane. Now I plan on proving it, to you, to me, to the whole damned world."

The marshal was aware of the frightened faces of Lorraine and Nellie, staring at him. "Joe I don't want to kill you," he said. "You can back away from this."

"Let's see what you got, Kane," Foster said. "When this is over I plan to walk a wide path. Men will look at me and say, 'That there is the man who killed Logan Kane.' Why, folks will come from miles around and . . ."

A talking man, Joe Foster went on and on, but all Kane's talk was done. There was no way out of this and he knew it. He'd experienced similar scenes too many times in the past. Now all that was left to him was to—

Draw and fire.

If Foster saw it coming, he didn't show it by making much of a play. His hand had just closed on the handle of his revolver when Kane's bullet hit him square in the chest.

Foster staggered from the impact of the hit and took a step back. His shocked eyes wide, he was a man who had just wakened to a terrible reality. . . . He was still on his feet but was already a dead man.

The gunman tried to lift his revolver, but the gun seemed too heavy for him. He dropped to one knee and rested the Smith on his crooked left arm, desperately working to bring the weapon to bear.

Kane held his fire. The kid was game and he didn't want to put another bullet into him.

Foster fired, then fired again. A bullet whiffed past Kane's ear and the second kicked up a startled exclamation point of dirt at his feet. The man screamed, not from fear but from rage and frustration. His eyes lifted to the marshal's face. "Only the devil is that fast," he gasped, blood red on his lips. Then he pitched forward onto his face, and all that had been Joe Foster was gone.

Kane punched the empty shell from his Colt and reloaded from his belt. He shoved the gun into the holster and stood, a tall man, terrible in the darkness, his head bent as though in prayer.

There was no end to it. No matter how he tried,

there would be no end to killing. For as long as he wore Judge Parker's star on his belt he would be trapped in an endless cycle of violence. "I don't send lambs after coyotes," the old judge had told him when he signed on. "It takes violent men to stand up to violent men. That, my young friend, is unfortunate, but, alas, it is the way of things."

Then so be it. Kane's eyes searched the darkness and saw there was no new, bright day to come aborning with the morning light. And wishing it so would not make it happen.

"He's dead."

Kane looked at Lorraine. She was kneeling beside Foster's body.

"Chest shot, square on the third button of his shirt, destroys the heart and kills a man," he said. "He doesn't come back from that."

"This is mine," the woman said, prying the revolver from Foster's fingers. "He took it from the wagon."

"See if he has more shells in his pocket and let me reload it then," the marshal said, stretching out a hand. "Where we're headed, you're probably going to need it."

Chapter 19

Logan Kane found the Percheron tied to a tree a hundred yards to the north of the camp. He'd considered the idea that Stringfellow had sent Foster to kill him, but that was unlikely. Now four convicts and Jack Henry would be forced to share two horses. Under those circumstances, Stringfellow would not willingly have parted with the draft horse. Foster must have cut out on his own, confident that he'd return with Kane's scalp.

Unluckily for him, it hadn't worked out the way he'd planned.

At daybreak, Kane hitched the Percheron to the prison wagon. The trail to the summit of Walnut Mountain was steep in places and ill defined. The big, strong draft horse would handle it better than the eight-hundred-pound mustang.

The marshal turned the little horse loose. It was tough, well used to rough living, and could take its chances on the plains.

He shared what was left of the venison stew with Lorraine and Nellie, then prepared to move out. The woman threw some of hers and Nellie's clothes into the back of the cage and insisted on taking the reins of the Percheron. The girl climbed up beside her, silent and withdrawn. Kane leading the way on the sorrel, they headed north.

For the next hour they crossed open country, much of it swampy, the innumerable streams and shallow creeks lined with cottonwoods, willows and a few hickories. In the distance the short-grass plains rolled away to the edge of a sky free of cloud. They passed Little Cow Mountain, the air scented by the pines on its slopes, and Kane led the way through a shallow valley that angled to the northeast, then opened onto the lower reaches of the Walnut Mountain ridge. Kane decided to give the horses a breather before tackling the peak and unhitched the Percheron.

"Looks high enough from here," Lorraine said, her eyes lifted to the rise as she worked a kink out of her back. "Like a wall at the end of the world."

Nellie had already jumped down and was gathering wildflowers, lost in her own secret existence.

"There's a trail," Kane said. "Not much of one but a trail nonetheless. The Apaches used it and so did the Army, and it's seen its share of Texas herds." He smiled. "We'll be all right. It ain't fur, except it's straight up."

Lorraine shrugged. "I never doubted that for a minute." She looked at Kane. "I could sure use some coffee."

"Me too, but I'm tryin' not to study on it too much."

"How's the leg?"

It was the first time Lorraine had mentioned it, and Kane was surprised. "Fair to middlin'. It punishes me some though."

"Sit on the grass and let me take a look at it."

Kane was taken aback. "Ma'am . . . I—I'd have to drop my pants."

Lorraine gave him an old-fashioned look. "You think I've never seen what you have before?" She shook her head. "I swear, the way some men go on, you'd think they'd never had a mother."

Well, she had him buffaloed, Kane decided. He sat, slipped his suspenders off his shoulders and pushed down his pants, covering himself as best he could with his shirt.

Lorraine looked at the wound critically. "What in God's name did you do to this?"

"Poured gunpowder on it an' then set it alight. Figgered it would stop the poisons."

"It's a wonder you have a leg left. Is there water in the barrel?"

Kane nodded. He felt naked and exposed, and his face burned, something he couldn't remember it doing since he was a boy.

Lorraine found a white, frilled garment in the wagon that the marshal could not bring himself to look at. The woman hesitated a moment, shrugged, then tore it into strips.

She bathed Kane's leg front and back, then bound it tightly with the strips of cloth.

"It doesn't look too bad. That should hold you for a while," she said.

"I appreciate it, ma'am," Kane said, quickly yanking up his pants. "I swear the leg feels better already."

"Don't go explodin' gunpowder on it again."

"No ma'am."

Kane slipped his suspenders over his shoulders and rose to his feet. "Now we better be goin'."

The trail wound upward through a dense forest of pine, hickory and oak. In places where the going was steeper the Percheron strained into the harness, its huge hooves digging deep into the dirt underfoot. But Lorraine handled the reins with a quiet assurance and the big horse hauled the heavy prison wagon with relative ease.

Kane scouted ahead and guided the woman around flat, massive slabs of sandstone that had slid down the slope during earlier cloudbursts. Up here, nearly two thousand feet above the flat, the air was crystal clear, heavy with the scent of pine resin. Kane caught glimpses of the sky through the forest canopy, a patch of clear blue laced around with dark leaves.

The quiet of the mountain descended on the marshal like a blessing, the song of the wind in the trees a descant only an octave higher than the sound of the silence.

That made the angry roar of the black bear all the more shocking in its earsplitting ferocity.

Unlike the grizzly, the black bear seldom attacks humans. Grizzly assaults are usually defensive, but when the black bear does strike, its attacks are always predatory. You can lie down and play possum and the grizzly might leave you alone. Try that with a black bear and nine times out of ten it will kill you.

The bear charged out of the trees, closing on the Percheron. Terrified, the big horse reared, then swung to its right, galloping along the slope. The thud of its great hooves seemed to shake the mountain. Fighting the scared sorrel, Kane couldn't reach for his holstered gun. He watched helplessly as the wagon's left-front wheel hit a slab of sandstone, then toppled on its side. Lorraine and Nellie were thrown clear, but the Percheron went down, kicking wildly, tangled in its harness.

The sorrel was completely out of control. It reared and Kane was thrown, landing heavily on his back, all the breath knocked out of him. The horse pounded up the slope, then vanished from sight behind a row of pines.

Now the bear was at the wagon. The iron door had swung open and the animal reached its head inside. It emerged with what was left of the hide-wrapped venison in its jaws and bounded into the surrounding forest.

Kane was on his feet, gun in his hand, enraged beyond measure at the theft of their meat and possible hurt to the draft horse. He thumbed off two useless shots into the trees where the bear had disappeared and yelled, "Damn you, Ephraim! Damn you to hell and all the way back again!"

"Marshal! Over here!" Lorraine was standing near the Percheron. "I don't think he's hurt real bad."

From long habit, Kane reloaded his Colt before stepping to the woman's side. Nellie stood a ways off, her face pale with fright.

It took ten minutes to untangle the big horse from the harness and help it to its feet. Kane saw some cuts and scrapes on its flanks, but when he ran a hand over the animal's legs there were no breaks. Righting the wagon would be a more difficult matter. The iron cage and steel axles made it heavy, and when he put his hands on it and pushed, the wagon barely moved.

Defeated, Kane stepped back, cursing softly under his breath.

Lorraine had an arm around her daughter's shoulders. She looked at the marshal. "The bear attacked us because it smelled the meat?"

"Probably. But ol' Ephraim tends to be notional an' there's no way to tell what he's thinkin'. This time o' the year, when he's due for his winter sleep, he can get plumb ornery."

Lorraine glanced around her and shivered. "Will he come back?"

"I doubt it. He's got meat and he heard the gun. I reckon he's long gone."

"The wagon?"

Kane glanced up the slope. "I'll find my hoss, then

dab a loop on the Percheron, see if he can pull it upright."

"The wheels don't seem to be damaged." The woman smiled. "That's lucky."

"Yeah," Kane said. "We've been nothin' but lucky today." He took off his hat, wiped the sweatband with his fingers, then angrily slapped the hat against his knee. "I better go find that damned hoss."

Kane found the sorrel grazing a few yards from the summit of the mountain. He swung into the saddle and rode to the top, looking out at the vast land spread out before him. In the clear air he felt like he could see forever.

South of him lay the country he'd crossed to get there. To the north stretched rolling hills, then the bulk of Pine Mountain. After that were a couple miles of flat plains, cut about by many creeks, and beyond the plains, the smoke blue parapet of Rich Mountain.

Somewhere out there was Jack Henry, and with him the convicts, and it was his job to find them and bring them to justice. Burdened by two females and no food, he faced a tall order. Kane shook his head, his eyes bleak. No matter, he had it to do. Judge Parker expected it of him. And for some reason, loyalty maybe, or stiff-necked pride, he could not let the old man down.

The marshal swung off the ridge and rode down the slope. Lorraine and Nellie were stroking the Percheron's neck, attention the massive horse seemed to be enjoying.

He stepped out of the leather and stripped the rig from the sorrel. He threw the saddle onto the draft's broad back and cinched up, barely making it. Kane tied one end of his rope to the side of the wagon, then climbed into the saddle and looped the other end around the horn.

"Hi-ya!" Kane kicked the big horse's ribs and it moved forward, but stopped as soon as it felt the strain. The wagon rocked back into place, a wheel spinning. "Ya! Ya! Ya!" Kane kicked again. The Percheron seemed to understand what was required of him. His hooves dug into the slope and he lurched ahead. Kane felt the saddle slip backward and for a moment he thought he would go right over the horse's rump. But to his joy he heard the wagon creak, then thump onto its wheels, the iron door clanging open and shut like a discordant bell.

The marshal clambered out of the saddle and moved to the Percheron's head. "Easy, easy, boy," he said. He smiled. "I'd give you a carrot, if'n I owned a carrot."

He switched his rig back to the sorrel and Lorraine helped him hitch the big horse to the wagon again. "Once we get to the top, you an' Nellie will see a great view. I swear, the land stretches out into tomorrow." He looked at the girl. "How about that, Nellie? You want to see forever?"

The girl made no answer and when Kane looked into her eyes, all he saw was a world of pain.

Around three in the afternoon they made camp in a grove of trees near the east bank of Pigeon Creek because Kane wanted to spend some time hunting before it got dark. But his efforts came to nothing. He took a potshot at some mallards cruising the creek close to camp, but missed badly; the flock scattered and fluttered away.

Empty-handed, Kane returned with nothing to show from his hunt but a headache and a vile mood.

Lorraine had built a fire, in anticipation Kane guessed sourly, but when she saw the dark look on the marshal's face she wisely said nothing.

He unsaddled the sorrel, then sat by the fire, his knees drawn up to his chest. He looked at the woman. "Damn that ol' Ephraim," he said. "Robbed us of our supper."

Kane was hoping for soothing words of some kind. They wouldn't fill his belly, but they might ease his vague sense of guilt. Man was meant to be a great hunter and keep his womenfolk fed. Didn't it say that in the Bible, or was it written down in some other famous book? He didn't know.

It didn't matter much, because Lorraine would not have answered. She was looking intently over the marshal's shoulder into the distance.

Kane followed the woman's gaze and saw what she was seeing. Three riders were coming toward them, leading a packhorse. Even far off, he recognized the broadcloth suits and the tall, blood horses.

It was the Provanzano brothers. They were here to take what was theirs and punish those who had denied it to them for so long.

Lorraine rose to her feet, watching the men come.

Kane stood and stepped beside her. He adjusted his gun belt and eased the Colt in the leather.

They were three tough men who believed right was on their side against one who was no longer real sure about anything.

Kane swallowed hard. He wasn't confident he could beat the odds.

Chapter 20

The riders drew rein a few yards from Logan Kane, their dark, cold eyes weighing him.

The marshal did the same, looking over the three men closely, summing up their potential with the iron. It was not idle curiosity on anyone's part. They were practicing the first law of survival among men who lived by the gun: know your enemy.

Kane saw no sign of gun belts, but city men like these would carry some kind of hideout gun. He'd heard of shoulder leather but had never seen it. A campfire conversation he'd listened to back along some forgotten trail returned to him, a waddie saying that Hardin was fast from the shoulder holster. He'd never seen John Wesley either, and that was probably all to the good.

"Remember me? Name's Carmine Provanzano." The oldest of the three waved a hand. "My brothers, Teodoro and Vito." The man leaned forward in the saddle, staring at Kane. "Last time we met was in the dark and you looked different, Marshal," he said. "Bigger, maybe, and younger. Better looking too."

Kane said, "Darkness makes every star shine brighter."

Carmine absorbed that, then smiled. "Then that must be the reason."

He looked around, missing nothing, including the empty prison wagon. Then his stare fixed on Lorraine. "If I don't miss my guess, you must be Mrs. Hook." His tone was not friendly, but neither was it threatening. "Where is your husband?"

"He's dead," the woman answered, with a defiant tilt to her chin.

Kane saw the face of Vito, the youngest brother, stiffen, his skin drawing tight against his cheekbones. The young man had a wild, reckless look, and the marshal figured that if this ended up in a shooting scrape, Vito would be the first to draw. He filed that away, for later.

Kane had thought Carmine's next question would be about the money, but the man surprised him. "I don't know what the laws of hospitality are in the West, no, but in New Orleans we usually invite visitors to set and eat."

"Please to step down," Kane said, "but as you can see, we don't have any coffee or grub. When the convicts escaped they took everything with them." Then, sensing that he might appear shiftless, he added, "Shot a deer a few days back, but a bear stole the meat."

"Never seen a bear," Carmine said. He turned his head. "Vito!"

The young man immediately stepped out of the saddle. He walked to the packhorse and began to untie canvas-wrapped bundles. He filled his arms with a slab of bacon, a sack of coffee, another of flour and some smaller packages wrapped in wax paper. Vito dropped the food beside the fire, then returned with a coffeepot and a skillet.

Carmine nodded his approval, then looked at Kane. "I'm happy to accept your kind invitation." He stepped out of the saddle and behind him his brother Teodoro, a saturnine, lean-cheeked man, did likewise.

Holding the reins of his horse, Carmine looked over at Nellie, who was sitting by the fire, her knees drawn up to her chin, taking an interest in nothing. "What ails the *bambina*, Marshal?"

Kane didn't understand the Italian word, but he caught Carmine's drift. He sought for a way to answer him, then said simply, "The convicts caught up with her and Mrs. Hook."

Carmine Provanzano took a quick breath. "How many?"

"All of them."

"And now she casts a dark shadow that will stay with her a lifetime."

"I'd say that's how it shapes up unless something changes."

"Marshal, some men should never have been born. What do you do with men like that?"

"You find them and kill them."

Carmine nodded. "Yes, that is our way also." He

looked at the girl again and shook his head, then said, "I must see to my horse."

The brothers had removed their coats and Kane saw he'd been correct. All three wore a Smith & Wesson .38 in a shoulder rig and he had no doubt they knew how to use them well.

The marshal felt no threat, at least not yet, but he stayed on alert, his nerves tangling themselves in tight knots.

The brothers carefully folded their coats and laid them on the grass and then began to strip their saddles. Kane noticed that the men spread out in a semicircle around him, making sure they could catch him in a crossfire should the need arise.

The Provanzano boys were careful men, and Kane had the feeling that in a gunfight they wouldn't back up and would be hard to kill.

Vito filled the coffeepot and brought it to Lorraine. She had found sourdough starter in a package and was baking biscuits in her own deep skillet, frying bacon in the other. Soon the wonderful smell of boiling coffee added to the odors that were making Kane's empty stomach rumble.

The day had shaded into night and stars scattered across the sky. A wind off the plains danced with the flames of the fire and a pair of hunting coyotes were calling to each other in the darkness, scenting the cooking food.

Kane was on edge for two reasons: the close, uncomfortable presence of the Provanzano brothers and the worry that Stringfellow and the others might come back to see what had happened to Joe Foster. He thought it would be inhospitable and a sign of distrust to keep his Winchester close. He also unbuckled his gun belt but kept it near him, something he was sure Carmine had noticed. The man had looked, but had said nothing.

After they'd eaten and the brothers had graciously declared Lorraine's biscuits the best they'd ever had, Carmine rose and reached into his pack. He returned with a bottle of bourbon and held it out to the woman. "A shot in your coffee, ma'am, to keep out the chill of the evening?"

Lorraine gladly accepted and so did Kane.

As they drank, Vito seemed to be moved by the beauty of the night. He tilted back his head and sang a song in a fine, tenor voice. Kane didn't understand a single word, but the tune was plaintive and touching, and it pleased him immensely.

After the last note died away, Carmine smiled at Lorraine and said, "He sang an old Sicilian folk song called 'Ciuri Ciuri.' It is about a girl who chides her sweetheart for not loving her enough, but the young man says, 'I have taken all the love you have given me and returned it to you.'"

"It's beautiful," Lorraine said. "And very sad in a way."

"Sometimes love is a sadness in the soul," Carmine said. "The saddest thing of all is to still love someone who used to love you. That I have known, and I have remembered it."

"Do you want to talk about it?" Lorraine asked, a womanlike question.

Carmine eagerly went on talking pretties about the heartbreak of unrequited love and Kane grew numbingly bored. Horses, guns and bad men he understood, but all this talk of romance and moonlight and roses had stranded him on an island of his own ignorance. In the past, he'd taken women wherever and whenever he could find them and love had never entered into it. But he liked women and they seemed to like him, and that was enough for any man.

Finally he spread his blankets, laid his Colt on his belly under the blanket and tipped his hat over his eyes, questions troubling him. Why had Carmine Provanzano not mentioned the money? Was he waiting for morning, planning to start shooting and then search the wagon? Kane didn't know and the not knowing was a worrisome thing.

He drifted off to sleep, the musical murmur of Carmine's voice lulling him.

The morning light pried Kane's eyes open and, his pulse pounding, he sat erect, looking wildly around him. Nearby Carmine was saddling his horse. He looked at Kane and smiled. "Sorry, did I wake you?"

Coffee was smoking on the fire and Lorraine was bent over, cooking breakfast. Nellie sat close to her, looking very calm and pretty.

How long had he slept?

Kane's gun had slid off his belly when he jumped

up. He holstered it, put on his hat and gun belt and rose to his feet. Behind Carmine his brothers were loading the packhorse.

"Pullin' out?" he asked Carmine.

"Heading back to New Orleans."

Now it was time to say it. "Then you'll want to take your money with you."

"Yes. Most of it is there, Teodoro assures me."

"You knew it was in the wagon?"

"Yes, I knew it would be there if the convicts hadn't taken it." Carmine looked at Kane with something akin to a perplexed admiration. "You're a remarkable man, Marshal, a police officer who believes the law should be enforced only with the gun and the boot. Watching from afar, I had come to think of you as just as cruel, cold-blooded and reckless as the outlaws you hunt." The man waved away Kane's unspoken protest. "But above all, reckless. You would have died the night you attacked the Texas drovers who had hanged the lady rancher. Don't be so surprised. We shot men off your back that night—two, three men."

Kane was stunned. "You were shooting?"

Carmine smiled. "From the trees. In the darkness and confusion everyone was firing. The drovers had their hands full with you and were not even aware of us."

Kane opened his mouth to speak, but Carmine held up a hand. "Hear me out. I have said hard things about you. Now I will add that I believe you to be honest with your own, shall we say warped, code of honor. I knew you would eventually lead us to the money because you would not think about keeping it for yourself. That's why Vito shot the fast gunman who threatened you at the cow camp. We could not afford to lose you."

Kane shook his head. "I didn't lead you to the money. I was going after the escaped convicts when I happened to come across Lorraine and Nellie on the trail. Sooner or later you would have found it yourself."

Carmine smiled. "We followed you, and now you are here and the money is here. It is enough that it will be returned to my family. By this time I am sure they are growing increasingly anxious."

"You already have the thirty thousand in your pack?"

"No, not yet. We waited to see if you would indeed part with it."

"Provanzano, Lorraine is out of this. She didn't want to keep the money either. She says it's blood money and she wants nothing to do with it."

"Blood money soon launders clean, my friend. But I harbor no ill will against the woman. She is not responsible for her husband's actions."

Kane nodded. "Good. If you'd felt otherwise I would've taken it hard."

The marshal turned on his heel and walked to the wagon. Without looking at Lorraine and without a word to Carmine, he handed the man the burlap sack.

Kane accepted the cup of coffee Lorraine poured

for him, sat by the fire and built a smoke from his dwindling supply of tobacco. Carmine joined him.

"Marshal Kane," he said formally, "you have done me a favor and my family will honor you. Among us, a favor must be repaid and that is why I am leaving Vito behind. He is the best of us with a gun and he will help you recapture the convicts who escaped you."

Kane began to protest, but Carmine stopped him. "Please," he said, "do not dishonor me by refusing what I give freely."

"Vito is all right with this?"

"My brother realizes the honor of his family demands that he stay. Yes, he is all right with this."

Kane stuck out his hand. "Then I accept. And thank you."

Carmine took the marshal's hand and smiled. "If you are ever in New Orleans . . ."

"I know. Sure, I'll look you up."

The man rose to his feet and dropped to one knee beside Nellie, looking at her intently. The girl seemed not to notice him. Carmine reached behind his neck and undid a silver chain with some kind of pendant. He fastened the chain around Nellie's neck and she immediately took the pendant in her fingers and bent her head to look at it.

"She is the Holy Virgin, little one, the Mother of God," he said. "She will protect you from all things harmful."

The girl's eyes met Carmine's and she smiled. "Pretty."

Carmine nodded. "Yes, she is very pretty indeed."

He rose to his feet and his head turned to Kane. "I have no medal for you, Marshal. But I leave you with Vito and he will be your guardian angel."

"Much obliged," Kane said. "I've got a feeling I'm going to need one."

Chapter 21

When they moved out, Logan Kane took the point and Vito rode beside the wagon, smiling now and then when he saw Nellie admiring her new necklace.

Kane kept just to the east of Phillips Mountain, then led the way into rolling country that stretched ahead for several miles, some of it low-lying marshland, teeming with wading birds.

By noon they'd reached the south bank of the Kiamichi River and stopped to rest the horses among a forest of pine, hardwood and beech that grew all the way down to the water's edge.

At this time of the year the river channel was low and narrow, and the wagon would make the crossing fairly easily, barring an encounter with deep mud.

Vito began to build a fire and Kane took the coffeepot to the river's edge. He kneeled and dipped the pot into the water . . . and the mud bank erupted around him, kicking up sudden Vs of dirt. Three shots, close together, had come from the other tree-lined bank.

Kane dropped the pot, drew fast from the leather and rolled to one side. Firing from a prone position he pumped a couple of shots into a drift of smoke on the opposite bank. Then he rolled again and fetched up against the base of a pine, painfully jarring his wounded thigh into a projecting root. A bullet chipped bark an inch above his head and another drove mud into his face.

From his left he heard the spiteful crack! crack! crack! of Vito's .38.

Shots rattled into the trees around Kane and he fanned his gun dry, intent only on laying down a field of fire.

"Kane," Vito yelled, "you hit?"

"I'm all right. You?"

"I'm not hit, no."

"Can you see them?"

"I can't see a damned thing."

Kane reloaded from his cartridge belt, scanning the trees opposite for a target. But the gun smoke had drifted away and only the wind stirred the pine branches.

His gun in hand, the marshal rose to his feet. "They've gone, skedaddled," he said.

Vito walked toward him, feeding shells into the open cylinder, his head bent over his revolver. He closed the gun and slid it into the shoulder holster.

"Who do you think?"

"My guess is that a man called Jack Henry was leading them. He's kin to Buff Stringfellow, one of my prisoners. It was Henry who broke them loose and killed my driver."

"Well, they know we're close."

Kane nodded. "They'll run for a while, then stop and try to bushwhack us again. From now on ride with eyes in the back of your head."

The man smiled, showing remarkably white teeth. "Sicilian boys are born that way, Marshal."

"You're handy with the hideout gun. You were also born knowing how to shoot?"

"Not that, no. But when the family business is at the New Orleans docks, a man learns the way of the gun and the knife very quickly. If he doesn't, then he soon dies."

Kane smiled. "Your brother was right. You're a handy man to have around."

The marshal meant that sincerely. Vito could have left him to his fate when the shooting started, but he'd exposed himself to fire and stood his ground. The kid had sand.

"Logan, are you all right?"

Lorraine was at his elbow, her face concerned. He nodded. "Someone took a few pots at me from across the river."

"A few pots? It sounded like a war," the woman said. She had the warm tips of her fingers on the marshal's arm.

Kane shook his head. "Lorraine, I got a feelin' the war is just about to begin."

*   *   *

The sun was beginning its slide into afternoon when Kane led their climb over Rich Mountain, three thousand feet of pine and hardwood-covered slope with treacherous outcroppings of sandstone and shale. He took a switchback route that spared the Percheron but was hard on the wagon. Several times the wheels slipped off shallow ledges of hidden rock among the trees, abruptly tilting the wagon at a precarious angle. When that happened, Lorraine and Nellie had to cling desperately to the jolting seat.

A few narrow game traces wound through the pines, but these were impossible for a wagon and Kane, like a man lost in a maze, had to blaze his own trail, a slow, laborious process with a deal of backtracking.

The marshal had spent much time among rough, profane men and he knew three dozen spectacular curses, but even these seemed inadequate to express his feelings about the climb up Rich Mountain.

Vito was riding higher up the slope, his rifle across the saddle horn, but his horse was not bred for mountains and was finding the going difficult. All his attention was given to his unruly mount—none of it to his watch for Jack Henry and the convicts.

But worse was to come.

Kane noticed the mist drifting through the trees like a gray ghost and at first ignored it. But within a few minutes an ashy pall cloaked the mountain and around him, one by one, the surrounding trees were vanishing.

"Marshal Kane!" Provanzano's voice, hollow in the fog, sounded from higher up.

"What do you want?"

"I'm coming down. I can't see a thing. Keep yelling so I can find you."

"Lorraine, are you all right?" Kane hollered. He was damned if he was going to stand there shouting pretties at Vito.

"I'm all right." The woman's voice was behind him and closer than Kane expected.

"Stay right where you are. I'll come to you," he yelled so Vito could hear him.

Kane stepped out of the saddle and, like a blind man, felt his way forward, leading his horse.

"I can hear you, Logan," Lorraine cried. "You're real close."

Kane heard a crashing in the brush and Provanzano emerged from the mist, almost bumping into him. He was also leading his horse. "Hell, couldn't you sing or something?" he said, trying to make out Kane through a curtain of gray. "I damned near got lost up there."

"I don't sing, and anyway, you found me. I was making enough noise." He lifted his head. "Lorraine, where are you?"

The answering silence looped in the motionless trees like Spanish moss.

"Lorraine!" Alarm had crept into Kane's voice.

There was only the quiet and the mist.

The marshal drew his Colt and stepped into the

somber fog that coiled close around him. Behind him, he heard Vito's breathing, coming quickly.

"Lorraine!"

Nothing.

"Nellie!"

Kane walked closer and, like a man parting a gray curtain, he made out the square outline of the prison wagon. The Percheron was gone from the traces. He moved nearer, every nerve ending tingling. There was no sign of Lorraine and Nellie. It was as though they'd vanished off the face of the earth.

Kane scouted around the wagon. He kneeled and saw the tracks of boots and parallel gouges in the grass where someone's feet had dragged.

Stringfellow!

Vito stepped beside Kane, leading both horses.

"They've been taken," the marshal told him. "They came out of the mist and grabbed them before they could even cry out."

"The convicts?" It was plain from the tone of Vito's voice that he already knew the answer.

Kane forced himself to remain calm. "Seems like."

Vito walked to the wagon and looked around. "At least they left the food," he said.

The marshal sounded bitter. "Know what that is, Vito? That's what's called mighty small comfort." Then with contempt he repeated what the man had just said. " 'At least they left the food. . . .' "

"Sorry. I just thought you'd want to know that."

Kane knew the food was important and that he

should apologize for his rudeness, but he let it go. He and Vito were both under strain. He looked around, seeing nothing. "As soon as this lifts, I'm going after them."

"We're going after them, you mean."

Shaking his head, a gesture Vito couldn't see, Kane said, "From now on, this could get downright nasty and it ain't your fight."

"I made it my fight, remember," Vito said. "I'm not backing away from it now."

It took an effort, but Kane managed it. "Thanks. I sure appreciate it."

"When do you think—" Vito's question broke off abruptly as a man called from higher up the slope.

"Logan Kane, you hear me? This is Stringfellow."

"I hear you."

"We got the woman an' the kid."

"Stringfellow, if you harm those—"

"Listen, Kane."

There was a moment of silence. Then Nellie screamed, a shriek of pain that set the marshal's teeth on edge.

"You hear that?" Stringfellow had a laugh in his voice and another man close to him guffawed. "That's only a taste, Kane. We got an Apache up here with us and by the time he's finished with the woman and the girl, they'll be begging me to kill them and cursing you for bringing them here."

"What do you want, Stringfellow?"

A rifle shot rattled through the trees. "Damn your eyes, Kane, I'll do the talking. Now listen, you back off or I'll set the Apache to work. You give us three clear days. If I see hide or hair of you before then, the women start screaming so you can hear."

The marshal made no answer, his mouth under his ragged mustache a tight, hard line.

"Did you hear me, Kane?"

"I heard you."

"After three days we'll leave the women at a one-horse settlement on the Poteau River called Baines Flat. You know the place?"

"I know it."

"Three days, Kane. A minute less and the Apache gets a gift of the women."

"Stringfellow! If Lorraine and Nellie are harmed I'll hunt you down and kill you."

Another shot chipped its way through the trees, this one closer. Somebody up there was shooting at the sound of Kane's voice.

"Three days, Kane! Say yea or nay."

"Yea, you got three days. And damn you to hell, Stringfellow, and those with you."

There was a shot, a mocking laugh and afterward only a ringing silence.

Chapter 22

"You think that's true, I mean about the Apache?" Vito asked. "I read in the New Orleans papers that all those feathered fiends were dead or locked up."

"Apaches never favored feathers," Kane said absently, thinking. "I don't know. They could have picked up a renegade somewhere, or a breed."

"What do we do, Marshal? Stay on this mountain for three days?"

"Hell no, we're going after them."

"But—"

"They'll be slowed by Lorraine and Nellie. We head for Baines Flat and get there before Stringfellow does."

"If that's where he's really going. He could be lying."

Kane shook his head. "He'll go there all right. There will be guns and horses in Baines Flat, and Stringfellow and the rest want to kill me real bad.

They'll lay up for me in town fer sure. He won't miss that opportunity."

"How do we follow them without being seen?"

"Stringfellow will want to make the most of his three days, so he'll head due north. If he does have an Apache with him, he'll know this country. My guess is he'll guide them over Black Fork Mountain"—Kane pointed into the mist-shrouded slope—"about three miles thataway. After that, he's got the Black Fork River to cross, then miles of open country where he can make good time."

Vito, city bred, looked confused. Then he said, "Wait, I've got it. We follow them over the . . . whatever it's called . . . and keep out of sight, huh?"

Kane smiled. "No, we go around. Two men on good horses can cover ground in a hurry. We take the Eagle Gap valley between Black Fork and Shut-in mountains, then ride hell-for-leather north until we reach the Poteau."

"Sounds easy."

"It's not. There's a fur ride and some mighty rough, unforgiving country ahead of us. And when we reach Baines Flat we still have to take Stringfellow and the rest into custody. And them boys will be a handful."

"Then we'll gun them and be done."

Kane lifted his head and looked into the mist creeping above his head for a long time. Finally he said, "Vito, if you'd said that a couple of weeks ago, I'd have said, 'Yeah, that's what we'll do, gun 'em.' "

He turned to the man. "Now I'm not so sure anymore. I'm no longer sure of stuff I was dead certain of when I started out on this trip."

"Men change," Vito said.

"But maybe not always for the better," Kane said.

If anything, the mist had grown thicker and it was impossible to see more than a couple of feet in any direction. "We'll make camp here," Kane said. "The fog should be lifted by morning." Vito was just a vague shape. Kane talked to it. "Think you can find us some wood without getting lost?"

"What are you going to do?"

"Unsaddle the horses and see if there's enough water left in the barrel for coffee."

"Well, if I don't come back soon, sing."

Despite the worry eating at him, Kane smiled. He threw back his head and started in on "Brennan on the Moor."

> Brave Brennan on the moor,
> Brave Brennan on the moor,
> A brave, undaunted robber,
> Was Brennan on the moor . . .

"Enough!" Vito yelled. "Oh Blessed Mother, please, no more. If I need help I'll yell."

"But that's only the chorus." Kane grinned. "I can give you at least a dozen verses."

But Vito was already crashing through the brush, his hands over his ears.

Kane shook his head and stepped beside his horse.

"Well, at least you like my singing, don't you big feller, huh?"

The sorrel pretended it didn't understand.

Kane and Vito ate a supper of coffee and bacon and shared the last sourdough biscuit. The mountain grew colder; they spread their blankets close to the fire and slept in mist-wreathed darkness.

An hour passed, then two, then more. The night grew colder and the fire glowed dull red, without flame.

"Logan . . . Logan . . ."

The marshal's eyes fluttered open and he lay still, listening.

"Logan . . ."

His mother's voice, calling out to him from somewhere along the shadowed tunnel of the fog. Kane sat upright. He looked at Vito. The man was sound asleep, a forearm over his eyes.

"Ma! Where are you, Ma?"

"We're lost, Logan. We're lost in the mist. Come for us, Logan. Come for us."

"I'll come, Ma." Kane rose to his feet. "Wait for me."

"Come to us, Logan . . . come to us. . . ."

Kane stumbled forward into the gray wall of darkness. Ahead of him he saw crows hunched on the tree limbs, orange beaks gaping as they watched him with black, glittering eyes.

"Ma?" he yelled into the gloom. "Where are you, Ma?" The crows hopped and flapped and screeched.

"Maaa . . . maaa . . . ," they mocked him. The fog pressed against Kane's chest, making it hard to breathe.

"Marshal!"

Kane heard Vito crashing toward him. The man emerged from the mist. "Where the hell are you going? You were yelling like a crazy person."

Kane turned, blinking. "Going? I—I don't know where I was going."

"Look," Vito said. He pointed above him where the mist was clearing, slim tendrils of gray fading in the morning light.

"Coffee's on the fire," Vito said. There was an odd uncertainty in his voice, as if he were confronting something he did not understand. "Then we have to ride."

Like a man in a daze, Kane allowed himself to be led back to the fire, Vito's steadying hand on his elbow. He didn't realize it then, but he would later: it was the only time in his adult life that he'd allowed another man to touch him.

Kane sat by the fire, accepted the coffee Vito handed to him and built a smoke from his thin sack of tobacco. "Mist is almost completely gone," he said.

The other man nodded. The ridge of the mountain was already visible, a line of stunted oaks revealing their struggles with cold, wind and thin, rocky soil. "Sun's coming up," Vito said.

Warm light was blading through the pines, and flying insects danced among them like tiny scraps of white paper.

After a tremendous struggle with himself Kane said finally, "I reckon I was sleepwalking, huh?"

To his surprise, Vito shook his head. "I heard it too, I think. In my sleep, I heard a woman's voice calling out for you. I thought maybe it was Lorraine, but it didn't sound like her."

"The crows?"

"I didn't hear the crows, no."

"It was my ma's voice. She . . . died when I was fourteen."

Vito hurriedly crossed himself. "Marshal, when we are awake or asleep, we are surrounded by spirits. Some come from heaven, others from hell, but the ones that disturb us the most are the ones born of our own conscience."

"You think my mother is one of those?"

"That is for you to know, not me."

Kane looked at Vito over the rim of his cup. "My ma and pa and my two sisters died of the cholera. I left them lying, unburied, in the cabin and ran away." He drew deep on his cigarette. "We lived in a valley back in east Texas where my pa tried to farm. It was cattle range, an inch of soil lying on top of bedrock. In the end the land killed him, and Ma as well. When the cholera came, they were too wore out from hard work to fight it."

"And your sisters?"

"They were frail little things from the beginning. They couldn't fight it either."

"And now your mother calls out for you."

"Yeah. She and the others want to lie under the

ground. A proper burial with the words said over them. See, the farm was in a place nobody ever visited, except maybe a Comanche passin' through. Ain't a living soul going to go there and see to a burying. Only me."

"You'll go back one day?"

"I was thinkin' maybe right after I deliver my prisoners to Fort Smith." Then, as though the words had a will of their own, Kane said, "I was also thinking of askin' Lorraine and Nellie to come with me."

Had he actually said that? He must have, because Vito was smiling at him.

"You could do worse. Lorraine is a fine woman, and her daughter needs love and care."

Kane threw his cigarette butt into the fire. "Damn it, you city folks get into a man's head. I haven't talked this much since I was a younker."

Vito laughed. "I'm Sicilian, and that's what we do best, talk. Of course we like to eat and sing and fight and lie with women, but most of all, we love to talk."

"Must be right lively, that family of yours back in New Orleans, with all that talkin' and singin' and fightin' an' lyin' with women."

"It is." Vito grinned. "And I have a large family."

Kane rose to his feet. "Let's ride, talkin' man. We got ground to cover."

"Feeling better now, Marshal?"

"Right now, I'm feelin' about as good as I ever get."

Kane and Vito Provanzano rode down from the mountain under a broken sky where storm clouds were gathering. The rising wind that had dispersed the mist was blowing hard and cool from the north, and a few drops of sleet tumbled in the air. Despite the morning light, the land around the riders was a uniform dull gray, streaked with black shadows, like a smeared watercolor.

Kane shrugged into his slicker and Vito retrieved a wool coat of dark blue with caped shoulders. The garment was, he assured Kane, an English coach coat tailored by Simpkins & Sons of Bond Street, London. It had been given to him by his family for services rendered at the docks, and was expensive, even by New Orleans standards.

"Suits me just fine, doesn't it?" Vito asked, looking down at himself as he preened the fine cloth against his chest.

The marshal wanted to tell him that he looked like an Eastern dude who'd come to the West for his health. But he contented himself with a vexed harrumph that said nothing but implied everything.

"Well, anyway," Vito said defensively, "I think it looks just dandy."

Kane led the way around the great southern loop of Rich Mountain, crossing the Arkansas line, then swung north. An hour later they rode through Eagle Gap, the looming, forested bulk of Shut-in Mountain rising to their east, its ridge hidden by low clouds.

Drifting northeast across rolling, long-riding country, Kane fretted about the worsening weather. From horizon to horizon the sky was iron gray and there was more sleet cartwheeling in the wind than rain.

The marshal reckoned the temperature had plunged twenty degrees since they'd left Rich Mountain and fingers of icy air probed inside his slicker. The healing wound in his thigh was throbbing, from cold he guessed, and his cheeks and lips were starting to chafe, rubbed raw by the wind.

Despite his thick coat, Vito seemed chilled and uncomfortable, and when he turned questioning eyes to Kane, he looked what he was—a city boy completely out of his element.

There was a time when Logan would have kept silent and let the man suffer, but now he was moved to say, "We may have to find a place to hole up until this blows over."

"Can't be soon enough for me," Vito said, shivering. He looked at Kane. "What kind of godforsaken country is it that can be sunny one day, freezing the next?"

Kane smiled, unwilling to bend any further. "The West ain't easy—it's hard, and it sure introduces a man to himself. Fact is, the only easy place you'll find in this country is the grave."

"Well, Marshal Kane, that cheers me up to no end," Vito said. "You got any more words of wisdom?"

"Yeah, I do. I been smelling smoke in the wind for the past five minutes. And smoke means people, and not too fur away either."

Vito's voice sounded a note of alarm. "You reckon it could be the convicts?"

"I doubt it. We're way to the east. Like I said earlier, I'm sure Stringfellow and his bunch will head north, strike direct for the Indian Territory."

Kane drew rein, pointing to his left. "And lookee there. If that ain't a settlement, then I'm seeing things."

Chapter 23

The two men rode closer and Kane realized that calling the place a settlement was a gross exaggeration. Two adobe-fronted structures, which looked to be a saloon and a small general store, were dug into a steep hillside. A pole corral sagged out front and a screeching windmill pumped water into an open ditch that ran too close to an outhouse and a few storage sheds. A lean-to stable with a tar-paper roof stood beside the corral, and under its lean protection there were already four saddled horses, mustangs by the looks of them.

During the Apache wars the saloon may have prospered since army supply wagons and cavalry patrols often passed this way. But now, in a time of peace, the place looked seedy and run-down, an impression that grew stronger as Kane rode nearer.

The wind drove stinging sleet into their faces as Kane and Vito rode up to the front of the saloon. A balding man wearing a filthy white shirt, open black vest and a surly expression stood in the doorway, a matchstick bobbing in the corner of his mouth.

"Howdy," Kane said, prepared to be civil. "We need a place to put up our horses, an' hay if you got it, an' oats."

"Stable's over there." The man indicated with a slight movement of his head. "Surprised you didn't see it as you rode in. It's big enough."

Kane held his temper. "How about the feed?"

"I don't have no oats, but there's a bale of hay in there." The man's sly eyes had run over the two good horses and booted Winchesters, and it seemed he'd decided to be friendlier. "Name's Ben Levering. I'm the proprietor of this establishment. I got whiskey inside and three young Lipan gals. Take your pick, boys, or take 'em all. I guarantee there ain't one of 'em older than fifteen."

Kane ignored that. His gaze moved to the general store where its buffalo skin door was swaying in the wind. "We need supplies, coffee, sugar, bacon an' flour, enough for three, four days. Oh yeah, an' rolling tobacco."

Levering elbowed off the door frame. For the first time Kane noticed the Remington stuck in his waistband under the vest. "Can do ye tobacco, salt pork an' coffee. There ain't nothin' else. It's the same grub I serve up inside."

"Then it will have to do," Kane said. He glanced at the angry sky. "We'll rest here until this clears an' then ride on."

Levering shrugged. "Suit yourself." He vanished

inside, the rough, unplaned pine door slamming shut behind him.

"Friendly place," Vito said.

"It's out of the sleet an' cold," Kane said. "It'll do."

They put up their horses in the lean-to, threw them a generous amount of hay and walked back to the saloon.

The inside of the saloon was as unprepossessing as the front. It was small and narrow, the roof beams hung with rusty bear traps and scraps of mildewed horse harness. The bar, a pine plank thrown across a couple of barrels on the dirt floor, was opposite the door. A shelf behind the bar held several bottles, all without labels, and an embroidered sign in a frame that read HAVE YOU WRITTEN TO MOTHER?

Four bearded hard cases, dressed in long fur coats and battered hats, crowded around the only table, playing poker with greasy cards. A bottle sat in the middle of the table and glasses filled with raw whiskey stood at every elbow.

The three Lipan girls huddled together in a corner, their hair filthy and tangled, and their dead, black eyes looking at Kane and Vito without interest.

The place was rank with the smell of sweat, spilled whiskey and the green wood smoking in the potbellied stove to the right of the door.

But, Kane told himself, it was warm and dry. No— it was downright hot. He opened his slicker and flapped it back and forth.

Beside him, Vito looked stunned, as though he'd died and had caught his first glimpse of hell.

The marshal smiled to himself. Vito Provanzano was a long way from the fancy women and luxurious restaurants and bars of New Orleans.

"Now, what can I do fer you gents?" Levering had his palms on the counter, looking at them. He was smiling, showing a few blackened stumps of teeth. "If'n you want the girls and desire some privacy, take 'em into the store." His smile widened into a grin. "Cost you two dollars American per girl. Should you kill one, accidental like, it will cost you a hundred dollars or a horse."

"Just coffee," Kane said. He was beginning to nurse an intense dislike for Ben Levering.

"Ah, very good. Coffee it is."

That set the marshal back. He'd expected a surly comment at least, but the man seemed too cheerful and accommodating. Kane felt a tingle of alarm, sensing a threat. Levering didn't come across as the accommodating type. What was the man up to?

Levering reached behind him, found two tin cups and looked inside each. He shook his head and tilted out what looked like a dried-up moth from one of them. Then he set the cups in front of Kane and Vito.

A coffeepot steamed on the stove and Levering brought it to the bar and filled the cups. "Anything else, gents?"

"Smoking tobacco," Kane said. "An' papers if you got them."

"Sure do," Levering said. He was smiling, a network of wrinkles forming around his mud brown eyes.

The man seemed friendly, but the marshal knew he was taking his measure, maybe summing up in his mind Kane's likelihood of meeting violence with violence.

Levering disappeared into the store, and Kane became aware that one of the card players at the table was watching him intently. The man was huge, made bigger by the bear fur coat he wore. His eyes were steel blue, cold and calculating, and a deep, knife scar ran from his left ear to the corner of his mustache. The man's coat was open and the marshal noticed the black, scalp locks decorating the front of his buckskin shirt.

Kane had met the big man's type before, frontier riffraff who lived by plunder, murder and rape. A few years ago, the man and the three others with him had likely been scalp hunters, avoiding Apache warriors but killing women, children and old men for the bounty the governors of Sonora and Chihuahua paid for Indian hair. The going rate had been a hundred dollars for a boy's scalp, half that for a woman and twenty-five for a child. Since there was little difference between Apache hair and that of Mexican peons, gringo scalp hunters had wiped out whole peasant villages in Sonora, sparing neither old nor young.

Now the scalp trade was gone, Kane had the feeling that Scar Face was hunting for another line of work.

Levering laid a tobacco sack and papers in front

of Kane, then moved down the bar. The man seemed tense, waiting for something to happen.

It wasn't long in coming.

Kane had just lit a cigarette when the big man rose from the table. The others got to their feet with him. Dirty, shaggy and coarse-skinned with knuckles the side of silver dollars, they looked as though they'd been spawned by the same wild animal. The three men spread out behind Scar Face, their coats open, revealing Colts in crossdraw holsters. All four were staring at Kane, grinning, with no more than a dozen black teeth between them.

"Kane . . ."

The marshal nodded, acknowledging Vito's whispered warning.

Sleet drifted through the closed shutters of the saloon's only window and the two oil lamps hanging from the roof beams swayed in an intrusive wind, a string of smoke rising from guttering orange flames. The day had grown dark and parts of the room were lost in shadow. The three Apache girls still stood in the corner, motionless silhouettes in the gloom.

Logan Kane smiled, looking at the big, scarred man. "What can I do for you boys?" he asked.

He heard Levering laugh.

"Mister," Scar Face said, "my name is Zeke Clum. Mean anything to you?"

Kane shook his head. "Not a damned thing."

The man grinned. "Well, no matter. Here's how it's gonna work anyhow. You two leave them

Winchesters right where they're at on the bar, and beside them you lay your belt guns. Then, nice as you please, you walk out of here an' keep on walkin'." Clum's jaw tightened, muscles working under his beard. "Now, I spoke real slow an' laid it out plain, so there would be no misunderstanding." He hesitated a heartbeat, then said, "Now, set them irons on the bar."

Kane heard Vito's feet scuff on the dirt floor as he opened distance between them.

Slowly, Kane moved his slicker away from the star on his gun belt. "You understand this, Clum," he said. To his relief his voice was steady. "My name is Logan Kane, deputy marshal out of Fort Smith, Judge Isaac Parker's court. Now, back off or I'll arrest you for threatening a peace officer."

"I don't give a damn who you are," the man answered.

A man standing to his right laughed. "Hey, Zeke, it's been a while since we gunned a lawman, huh?"

"A fair spell I'd say," Clum said. His voice hardened. "Put your belt gun on the bar." His eyes shifted to Vito. "You too, pretty boy. I know you got iron under that fancy coat somewhere."

Clum's thumb was tucked behind his belt, his hand close to his holstered Colt.

This was the last thing Kane wanted, meaningless death in a dugout saloon that had turned out to be an annex of hell. Desperately, he tried to make it go away.

"Levering," he pleaded, "can you do something?"

The man was grinning. "None of my concern."

Kane said, "Yeah, I had you figgered for a no-good tinhorn."

"Ah, the hell with all this talk!" Clum went for his gun.

Kane drew and fired, and a black hole appeared in the middle of Clum's forehead. The man still stood, dead but on his feet, swaying, a thin trickle of blood running over his nose. Clum's eyes turned back in his head, showing yellow traced with fine lines of red.

Vito's .38 barked spitefully. The man to the right of Clum fired, his bullet kicking up dirt at Kane's feet. Then he staggered and took a step back, Vito's lead in him. Kane fired again and again. Clum crashed his length on the floor, and the wounded man next to him, this time hit hard by Kane, threw up his arms and went backward over the table, its spindly legs splintering under him.

The concussion of the guns had put out one of the oil lamps and Kane saw Levering's Remington flame in the smoke-streaked gloom. The man's bullet split the air beside the marshal's ear. Levering stood behind the bar, his gun two-handed at eye level. Kane and Vito fired at the same time, and Levering slammed against the shelf, smashing bottles, and fell, screeching.

Three men were down, and the other two wanted no part of it. If they drew, they'd die. It was a simple premise to understand. The men had backed into a corner, their hands high. One of them screamed,

"No, no, don't shoot no more! For God's sake, we're out of it."

His ears ringing from the gunshots, Kane motioned with his Colt. "Unbuckle them belts an' let them fall to the floor. Now, damn you! Or I'll drop you right where you stand."

The two men hurriedly did as they were told. "Right, out the door and start walkin'. An' I'd advise you to walk real fast."

"Mister," the man who'd done the talking said, "we need time to get our horses."

Kane's smile was not pleasant to see. "You were gonna make me walk. Now you'll find out how it feels."

"But it's a long ways to anywhere from here."

"Yeah, it's a fur piece, so you'd better get goin', hadn't you?"

The writing was on the wall and the man read it clear. "All right, we're leavin', an' be damned to ye," he said.

"You too," Kane said to the other man who'd been very quiet, his face ashen. On his way to the door he glanced at Clum's grotesque face. Then his eyes lifted to the marshal. "Zeke was fast on the draw an' shoot. Always reckoned he was anyway."

"He wasn't even close to bein' fast," Kane said. "You should find another line o' work, the hardware business maybe."

The man nodded. "Yeah, maybe that. I sure ain't makin' it in the hoss-stealin' business."

After the men left, Kane looked at Vito. "You done good. Stood your ground an' got your work in."

Vito seemed to understand that this was high praise indeed from the big marshal. "Thank you," he said, smiling. "I appreciate it."

"Yeah, well, afore you start gettin' too uppity, bring them four ponies around front. I've got a purpose fer them."

Vito's smile grew into a grin. It was just like Kane to tie a compliment on a man, then immediately undo the knot. "Sure thing, Marshal. Anything you say."

Kane waited until the door closed behind Vito and stepped over to the three men sprawled on the floor. They were all dead. The HAVE YOU WRITTEN TO MOTHER? sign had fallen from the shelf and lay across Levering's chest.

"She must be right proud of you," Kane said.

A tin box was lying beside the dead man and the marshal opened it. Inside were thirty-seven dollars in bills and some change. Kane tipped the contents of the box onto the bar, then stepped into the store. He found another ten dollars in a drawer and this he put with the rest of the money.

The door swung open, letting in a gust of sleet and cold air. "Horses are outside," Vito said.

Kane nodded, picked up the money and walked to the Lipan women. They shrank back from him, their eyes wide and apprehensive. He reached out, grabbed the arm of one of the women and thrust the forty-seven dollars into her hand.

He smiled, trying to put the women at ease, and pointed to the door. In his halting Spanish he said, "*Hay fuera de los caballos.*"

Uncertain, the Apaches did not move, their unblinking stare on Kane's face. The woman he'd given the money to opened her hand, looking at it. The marshal tried a smile again, reached out and gently closed her fingers around the bills. Again he pointed to the door. "*Caballos.*"

Now the Lipan women understood. They walked to the door and, Vito holding it open for them, stepped outside. By the time Kane walked into the sleet and cold, the women were already mounted, one of them leading the spare horse. The Lipans rode away and were soon swallowed by distance and the brawling storm.

Vito looked at Kane. "Think they'll make it in this weather?"

The marshal nodded. "Better than we will. They've got money and four horses and they're going back to their people rich."

"Where are their people?" Vito asked, his eyes on Kane's face.

"Who knows. If any of them are still alive, the women will find them."

Kane stepped to the door. "We'll load up with whatever supplies we can find. I don't want to stay around with dead men."

Vito's quick nod and the hurried cross he made on his chest were all the agreement the marshal needed.

Chapter 24

The storm was driving cold and hard from the north, and Kane and Vito Provanzano rode right into its bared teeth, heads bent against the brutal force of the wind.

Five miles south of Walker Mountain, in rolling, forested country, they picked up a large pack of red wolves that kept pace with them for an hour, slipping through the pines like phantoms.

Kane saw Vito look in the wolves' direction and he raised his voice to be heard above the roar of the blizzard. "They'll give us the road. They don't usually tackle anything bigger than a jackrabbit."

"Yeah? Well just maybe they're feeling a tad unusual today," Vito yelled. Sleet had frozen on his mustache and eyebrows, giving him the look of a worried old man.

The marshal laughed loud and long, and it felt good. Finally he said, "If they get close, the wolves may spook the horses, so ride careful."

The wolves left them when they crossed fast-running Jones Creek and rode into flatlands where the sleet storm loomed ahead, coming at them like a broken plaster wall. Kane swung to the west, toward the foothills of Walker Mountain, signaling his move by thumping Vito on the shoulder, since talk was impossible over the shrill shriek of the storm.

It took Kane an hour to find shelter. He saw a deep hollow where the spreading branches of a couple of tall, twin pines were keeping away the worst of the sleet that was now mixed with wet snow.

There was room enough for the horses, and wood aplenty among the trees. And Kane built a small fire in the overhang of the hollow where it would reflect heat. He filled the coffeepot with handfuls of the sleety snow that had piled up around them.

"Soon be as comfortable as your grandmother's parlor," he told Vito, grinning. But the man merely shivered, pulled his coat closer around him and said nothing.

Kane had found salt pork and a small sack of army biscuit in Levering's store. The flat hardtack was as solid as iron and the marshal guessed it had been stored by the Army since the War Between the States and reissued during the Indian wars.

He wetted down the biscuit and pounded it into crumbs with the butt of his rifle. He dredged slices of salt pork in the crumbs, then fried them in the sizzling hot fry pan.

"This," he promised Vito, "is going to be good eatin'."

The man glanced at the sputtering pork and shrugged. "If you say so, Marshal."

"Hell, don't turn up your nose at good food," Kane said. "What do you boys eat in New Orleans anyhow?"

Vito thought about it, smiling at what could only be pleasant memories. "Lots of pasta of course, and minestrone soup often. Veal Sorrentina, Lobster Fra Diavalo, Shrimp and Portabella Crostini, focaccia bread." Vito raised baleful eyes to the marshal. "Served by a waiter wearing white gloves and the key to the wine cellar around his neck."

Kane smiled. "Well, I don't have none o' that stuff, but I'll be your waiter." He lifted the pan off the fire and waved the smoking salt pork under Vito's nose. "Shuck your knife an' get dug into that."

The storm raged with increasing ferocity throughout the long, cold night. Kane and Vito huddled as close to the feeble fire as they could while the trees above them rocked in the wind and icy gusts of sleet splattered over them. The storm sounded like a passing freight train and the air smelled like a steel blade, razor sharp and cutting.

Once Kane woke from a shallow sleep and thought he heard the haunting howls of hunting wolves among the pines. He sat up and listened into the night: nothing—only the clamor of the storm. Uneasy now, Kane lay on his back, his eyes staring at darkness. Had he heard wolves or the wails of the unburied dead?

One, he decided, disturbed, was as likely as the other.

Like a child's tantrum that ends in tears, the storm blew itself out an hour before daybreak and only a steady, raking rain remained.

The fire had long since sizzled into a tendril of smoke. Kane and Vito drank cold coffee, then took to the trail.

Baines Flat was on the other side of the Poteau River, an hour's ride to the north. A trellis bridge, built for a railroad that had never arrived, spanned a stretch of white-water narrows and now carried only horse traffic. Beyond the town rose the rugged barrier of Poteau Mountain and fifteen miles to the west lay the badlands of the Choctaw Nation.

As far as Kane could recall, and this he told Vito, the population of Baines Flat was mostly hard-rock gold and silver miners, hoping to strike it rich along the sprawling ridge of the Poteau. Like the railroad, the gold had never materialized, yet a few hardy souls were still searching for the mother lode, but finding silver only in their hair.

Talking above the angry-cat hiss of the rain, Kane said, "To the west, in the Choctaw country, there's a standing stone on the Poteau with some kind of writing on it. One time Judge Parker talked to me about it. He said the letters were called runes and were carved by Viking men who crossed the big eastern ocean in ships hundreds of years ago." He smiled. "I don't know about that, but the writing is on the rock fer sure, an' it wasn't ciphered there by no Indian."

"You've seen it?" Vito asked.

"Yeah, I've seen it. Strange to find that rock in the middle of a wilderness where there's nothing and nobody. Kinda like Baines Flat. It shouldn't be where it is either."

The river came in sight through the shifting steel curtain of the rain, and in the distance Poteau Mountain shouldered hugely against the gray sky. As their horses' hooves thudded across the pine bridge, Kane looked ahead, taking stock of the town as his eyes roamed restlessly for any hint of Stringfellow and the rest.

Even by the modest standards of the West, Baines Flat was not much of a town. And it was made even shabbier by the glowering black sky and streaming rain that was gradually turning its only street into a river of mustard-colored mud.

The centerpiece of the settlement was a false-fronted, two-story building that proudly proclaimed, TONTINE HOTEL and under that, BEDS & EATS.

Flanking the hotel were a couple of saloons, the Alamo and the Bucket of Blood. A hardware store, livery stable and corral, a blacksmith's shop and what looked to be an adobe jail were the only other buildings. On either side of the town, scattered tar-paper shacks and smoking, crooked iron chimneys poking through sod roofs appeared to have wandered into the plains and then lost their way.

Adding to the dreariness of the place was a rickety

gallows standing outside the jail, decorated with red, white and blue bunting that slapped against the rough timbers of the platform, wet and forlorn in the wind.

"Friendly place," Vito said, eyeing the gallows as he and Kane left the bridge and splashed through the mud of the street.

"I've been here only oncet," the marshal said, "an' that was in summer. Didn't look near so bad then."

"Making up for it now though, huh?"

"I can't disagree with that. But if they have decent grub and hot coffee, my opinion of Baines Flat might improve considerable."

They rode into the livery stable and dismounted. Apart from a few leaks in the roof, the stable was relatively dry and smelled of horses, dung and old leather. A wide-shouldered man dressed in buck-skins walked out of the shadows, and it took a minute for Kane to realize he was in fact a woman. Lank, blond hair fell over her shoulders, spilling from under a battered felt hat. She wore a holstered Colt on one hip and a huge bowie knife on the other. Her brown face was traced by wrinkles from the sun, but her blue eyes were bright and friendly.

"Stalls for a couple of days, hay an' oats if you got them," Kane said.

As rain ticked from the top of the door, the woman looked the marshal over, from the toes of his scuffed boots to the top of his hat. Then her eyes flicked to Vito.

"You boys need a bath and a shave," she said.

"Winded you as soon as you rode inside. I said to myself, I said, 'Katie, look what the cat just drug in.' "

"The bath can wait," Kane said. "Right now we need a place to put up our horses, then get grub an' coffee."

"Suit yourself. It will cost you two bits a night, including the oats. That's each. You fellers got two bits?"

Nettled, Vito snapped, "Madam, where I come from, we don't stop to pick up two bits lying on the sidewalk."

"Took ye fer some kind of Eastern dude," the woman said.

Vito drew himself up to his full height. "Madam, I'm from New Orleans, the fair magnolia of the Southern cities."

The woman called Katie screwed up her face, as though deep in thought. "Nope," she said finally, "I've studied on it, but I don't recollect that I've ever shot anybody from New Orleans."

Kane grinned. "Pay the lady, Vito."

Vito dropped four silver dollars into Katie's open palm. "Tell me when we've gone through that."

The woman looked at Kane. "It ain't none of my business, but I'd say you boys are here for the hanging tomorrow."

"First I've heard." The marshal was surprised. "You got law here?"

Katie shook her head. "Ain't no law in Baines Flat. Well, unless you count Hulin Green. He kinda keeps the peace around here."

Kane was surprised a second time. "You talkin' about Hulin Green out of Wichita?"

"He rode into town about six months ago on a played-out hoss. That's all I can tell you."

"Big feller, wears his hair long an' has a red beard down to his belt buckle."

Katie shook her head. "That don't sound like Hulin."

Vito looked at Kane. "Do you know this man?"

"I've heard of him. Robbed banks and stage-coaches for a while, then became a lawman. Last I heard he was a peace officer in Wichita. He's good with a gun an' he's killed his share."

"This man who's gettin' hung," Kane said to Katie, "he get a fair trial?"

The woman laughed. "Bless your heart, stranger, Frank Dawson didn't need a fair trial or any other kind. He was caught red-handed."

"How did it come up?"

"We had a gal here in town, name of Lily LaBelle, at least that's what she called herself. She hung out at the Bucket of Blood and entertained the miners in a shack out back, and anybody else who had two dollars. Well, four days ago she was found strangled. Hulin Green caught Frank Dawson here at the livery stable, trying to steal a hoss. When Hulin searched him, he found Lily's silver locket, garter and gold ring in his pocket."

"Katie, were you here when Green caught Dawson?"

The woman looked hard at Kane, apparently wondering why he was so interested in the murder of a two-dollar whore. "No, that night I was over to the hotel, eating supper."

"So we have only Hulin Green's word for it."

"His word is good enough for this town," Katie said. "That's why we're hanging Dawson tomorrow. Lily was way past her best and after Baines Flat her next stop would've been a hog ranch, but, even so, she didn't deserve to die the way she did." The woman rubbed the velvety nose of Vito's horse. "Don't feel bad about Dawson, Mister. He's always been strange, a bit tetched in the head, you might say."

"He deserved a fair trial nonetheless," Kane said.

"He won't get it, not around here. We don't have a judge," Katie said.

"Marshal, I'm sure in need of coffee," Vito said.

And Kane threw him a look.

Katie was taken aback. "Hell, have I been standing here talking to a man pinned to a tin star?"

"I'm afraid so," Kane said. He pulled back his slicker. "Name's Deputy Marshal Logan Kane out of Judge Isaac Parker's court with jurisdiction over the Indian Territory." He smiled. "Since we're in the Territory, that would make me the law in Baines Flat."

Katie's jaw dropped in her long face. "Here, what are you planning, Marshal?"

"I'm takin' Dawson back to Fort Smith to stand trial for murder."

The woman was dismayed. "What's it to you? He's as guilty as hell and he done it here, so let him swing here."

Kane nodded. "Maybe a couple of weeks ago, I'd have done just that," he said. "Now I've come to realize . . . well, I don't know . . . maybe I've come to realize that I'm a sworn peace officer and I should start behavin' like one."

Katie's tone was skeptical. "You gonna start behavin' like a peace officer around Hulin Green?"

"I guess so."

"He'll take it hard, an' when Hulin takes things hard it always leads to a killing."

Kane shrugged. "I'm the law. I'll tell him that an' it will make a difference."

"Not to Hulin's way of thinking, it won't."

Katie led the horses to stalls at the rear of the barn and Kane followed her. For a few moments he watched her expertly unsaddle the sorrel, then said, "If five men and a woman with a young daughter ride in, let me know right away, huh?"

"Are they outlaws? If they are, they might be friends of mine," Katie said.

"I doubt it. Ever hear of Buff Stringfellow an' Jack Henry?"

"Can't say I have," Katie said.

"Then they ain't friends o' your'n," Kane said.

"And the gals?"

"They're friends of mine."

Katie thought it through. Kane could hear wind-driven rain raking across the roof.

"I'll let you know," the woman said finally.

"You won't mistake Stringfellow and his men. One of them will be riding a Percheron and one of them"—he held up his right thumb—"is missing this."

"From the war?"

"No, from me."

Katie began to fork hay to the horses and Kane said, "The girl is around twelve or thirteen an' she don't talk anymore. She was roughly handled by those men an' it done something to her mind."

The woman straightened, her eyes level on Kane's. "I'll let you know."

Chapter 25

The front door of the Tontine Hotel opened onto the dining room, partitioned from the rest of the building by gray army blankets hanging from a sagging string. There were three roughly sawed pine tables and benches, the walls covered in old newspapers and, cut from mail-order catalogs, buxom women wearing corsets.

At the end of the room, jammed against the wall, was the kitchen—a stove and a single shelf stacked with chipped white plates and cups. A huge, blackened coffeepot smoked on the stove, improving Kane's first impression of the place considerably.

Not so Vito, who looked around with disdain, breathing through his nose as he took in the pervading odor of coffee, mildew, ancient man-sweat and unwashed feet.

Kane smiled. "Well, they got coffee."

"Wonderful," Vito said smoothly, as though his voice had just been planed.

A blanket pulled back and a stocky man in striped pants, a dirty red undershirt and a stained apron knotted around his waist stepped into the room. The man was in his mid-fifties and walked with a limp; Kane pegged him for an old ranch cook. He waved a careless hand. "Sit anywhere, gents. As you can see, we ain't exactly busy."

Kane and Vito took a seat, and Kane said, "Coffee first. Then breakfast."

"Coffee I got. As to breakfast, I can rustle you up elk steak an' beans if you care to make a trial of it. You fellers like beans?"

"Elk an' beans will do," Kane said, ignoring Vito's disapproving glance.

The cook left to get the coffee, and the young man said, "I swear, if I survive the Western food, I'll never leave New Orleans again."

Kane grinned. "Your brothers knew what they were doing when you were the one they left behind."

"That is the duty of the youngest. Besides"—he leaned back while the cook placed a steaming cup in front of him—"I'm the best of us with the revolver."

Kane was puzzled. "Vito, what exactly is it you do at the docks?"

The man thought for a moment, then said, "I'm an enforcer, you might say. I keep the peace and see that our business affairs run smoothly."

"So, you're like a police officer in a way."

"You could say that, yes. But the law I enforce is Provanzano law. Above all, I preserve the interests and honor of the family."

"Lorraine told me your family is called . . . what was it? Yeah, I remember, the Mafia."

Vito's face hardened. "It is a word recently come into use by certain New York newspapers. It's nonsense. It means nothing."

Kane shrugged. "Meant nothing to me to begin with."

The food was surprisingly good and the two men ate with an appetite. After he pushed himself away from the table and smoked a cigarette, Kane called the cook over. "We'll need rooms."

The man nodded. "Dollar a night for a double. The single luxury suites cost two bits extra."

"We'll take the single suites," Vito said quickly.

"Dollar for the breakfasts, an' if you gents will follow me I'll show you to your rooms."

With a long-suffering expression, Vito paid, since Kane made no effort to reach into his pocket.

The cook pulled back a blanket and the two men followed him into a narrow hallway that ran the full length of the building. Rooms lay on either side, closed off by more blankets on strings.

"Your suites are at the end of the hall," the cook said.

Kane stepped through the blanket that served as a door and wall for his room. The suite consisted of an iron cot, a battered dresser with a basin and pitcher, and a shelf for clothes. The pillow and blankets on the cot seemed reasonably clean and the pine floor was swept.

He walked back outside. Vito turned and saw him, the expression on his face that of an animal at bay.

"Hey, I've seen worse," the marshal said.

Vito was incredulous, his face long in surprise. "Worse? Where?"

"Places. Over to Kansas way. I seen worse places over to Kansas way."

"God help us," Vito said.

"Walk with me." Kane grinned. "I want to talk to that Frank Dawson feller."

"Sure. Anything to get away from here."

As they stepped back to the dining room, Kane stuck his head into every room he passed.

"What are you doing, Marshal?" Vito asked, his irritation evident.

"I wanted to see what the regular rooms looked like."

"Any different?"

"Yeah, they got two cots instead of one."

Outside, the rain was still coming down hard. The iron gray sky hung so low, it looked like a tall man could walk along the street with his feet in the mud, his head in the clouds. The wind was cold, still out of the north, shredded into shrieking gusts by the ragged ridge of the Poteau. Kane bent his head against the downpour, water dripping from his mustache.

"Wait!" Vito had glanced in the hardware store window. Now he turned and dashed inside. "I'll be right back," he said over his shoulder.

The man emerged a couple of minutes later and pushed open a large, black umbrella. He swung the umbrella over his head and it was immediately made noisy by the kettledrum rumble of the rain.

"Ah, that's better," Vito said. He looked at Kane. "Want to share, Marshal?"

Kane shrugged. "Sure, why not." He moved closer to the other man and walked with him a few steps. But when two men share an umbrella, both get wet. He gave it up and resumed his place beside Vito.

"Don't poke me in the eye with that thing," Kane growled. "You're waving it around my head."

Vito had a white-knuckle grip on the handle, like a kid holding on to a silver dollar. "I can't help it. It's the wind, Marshal, bumping it around."

Kane put space between him and the other man until they reached the jail.

The adobe had a single barred window to the front and Kane stood next to it. "Dawson," he said.

He heard a cot creak, then the sound of feet squelching through mud. A man's face appeared at the window and a timorous voice said, "I'm Dawson."

Kane looked at the man and what he saw did not impress him. Frank Dawson was a small, skinny rat of a man with sly, black eyes and thinning brown hair. He wore a white, collarless shirt and black pants, both stained with mud.

"Name's Deputy Marshal Logan Kane out of Judge Isaac Parker's court. I plan on taking you to Fort Smith to stand trial for murder."

Dawson had a reedy, whining voice as unattractive as the man himself. "Parker? The Hanging Judge?"

"That's what some folks call him."

Urgently now, Dawson said, "I didn't murder Lily LaBelle, Marshal. You have to believe me. I liked her, I liked her a lot." He took a half step back from the window. "Look at me. How could a man who looks like me ever get a woman like Lily? All it took was two dollars, when I could scrape it together."

Rain hammered on Kane's hat and he wiped water from his mustache with the back of his hand. "Dawson, you were caught trying to leave town on the night of the murder. And you had Lily's locket and ring in your pocket."

"I wasn't trying to leave town. I went to the livery to bed down for the night. Katie Gordon lets me do that when I have nowhere else to sleep. Hulin Green came in and he'd been drinking. He's mean when he drinks, Marshal, mean as a curly wolf. He dragged me out of a stall, beat me with his fists and boots and then told me he found the locket and ring in my pocket."

Dawson swallowed hard, his prominent Adam's apple bobbing. "They're going to hang me, Marshal."

"No they're not. That will be up to a jury and Judge Parker."

Vito tried to shelter Kane under part of his umbrella but succeeded only in tipping the marshal's hat over his eyes. "Git away from me with that," he growled. "Go fur away, Vito, or I swear, I'll bend the infernal thing over your head."

Vito shrugged. "Then I'll let you get wet."

"Yeah, you do that."

After Vito left, Kane stepped closer to the jail window and a vile stench assailed his nostrils. "What you got in there, Dawson?" he asked.

"A bucket. There's mud on the floor and rats, a lot of rats. They bite me." His own rodent eyes lifted to the tall lawman. "Green won't feed me, Marshal. When I asked him for grub, he said there was no point in feeding a dead man."

"I'll get you out of there," Kane said. He waved a hand. "I'll be back."

Alarm edged Dawson's voice. "Where are you going?"

"To get the key for this here juzgado from Hulin Green."

"Then you'll not ever come back." More than just words, it was a primitive wail of despair.

Chapter 26

Logan Kane joined Vito on the boardwalk. "Now what?" the man asked.

"We go look for the man called Hulin Green."

"What are you planning, Marshal? You going to gun him?"

Kane shook his head. "Nope, I plan on asking him for a key."

Vito's brown eyes clouded as he thought that through. Then he smiled. "Right, let's go get the key to the outhouse."

"The jail."

"Close enough," Vito said.

They found Green in the Bucket of Blood. He was drinking coffee at a table, a silver pot and china cup and saucer in front of him.

Kane's first impression was that the man was big, very wide and thick across the shoulders, his hands resting on the table like huge hams. Kane had expected to see a buckskin-clad ruffian, but Green affected the dress of the frontier gambler/gunfighter. He wore black broadcloth, a clean, frilled shirt and string tie. His hat was also black, low crowned with a flat brim. Red hair hung in ringlets over his shoulders and he'd curried his facial hair back to a mustache and the pointed imperial that adorned his chin.

Despite his finery, especially when he lifted cold gray eyes to Kane as he stepped through the door, Hulin Green looked what he was—a dangerous gunman who had killed his man.

The bartender, a plump, rosy-faced man in a brocade vest, was decanting whiskey from a barrel into bottles. Four men, hard-rock miners by the look of them, were nursing beers at a table, and a couple of others stood at the bar.

Oil lamps were lit against the gloom of the morning and a potbellied stove glowed cherry red in a corner. The bar was mahogany, out of place in a tar-roofed shack, and it had a wide mirror of veined French glass, imported from the East at considerable expense.

Like everything else in Baines Flat, the Bucket of Blood had anticipated the coming of the railroad. Now it seemed shabby and worn, like a tired old hag who had never recovered from being jilted at the altar.

"What can I do for you boys?" the bartender asked, smiling with practiced affability.

"Coffee," Kane said.

"Coming right up."

The man found a silver pot under the bar, filled it

from the huge pot on the stove and set it on the bar. He produced china cups and saucers and set these beside the pot.

Kane poured coffee for himself and Vito, then said to the bartender, "I'm looking for a feller, Hulin Green by name."

Before the man could answer, Green spoke up, his tone early-morning surly. "That would be me. What do you want?"

Kane tried the coffee, holding the cup by the rim. He quickly replaced the cup on the saucer. "Hot, hot, hot," he said, shaking his fingers.

"I said, what do you want?" Green repeated. The man was not in a sociable frame of mind, that much was obvious.

"All I want," Kane said, "is the key to the juzgado."

Green's smile was a white grimace under his mustache that never quite reached his eyes. "And who might you be? You kin to Frank Dawson maybe?"

"I'm on your right," Vito said softly.

Kane nodded without taking his gaze from Green. Slowly, he moved back his slicker with his left hand, revealing the star on his gun belt. "Name's Logan Kane, Deputy Marshal out of Judge Parker's court. I plan to take the prisoner to Fort Smith to stand trial for murder."

Named gunfighters were few in the West and their reputations spread far. From the end of the War Between the States to the closing of the frontier, perhaps fifty men who had the readiness to kill and the necessary hand and eye coordination to do it well, earned such a distinction—only twoscore and ten out of the millions who at one time or another carried a gun. It was little wonder such men inspired fear and were avoided at all costs.

Hulin Green was not scared, but his eyes flickered in recognition when he heard Kane's name. Wherever Western men gathered, they talked about gunfighters and would argue their merits endlessly as they attempted to place them in a lethal hierarchy. Green would have heard of Wes Hardin, Luther Bishop, Jim Masters, Clay Allison, Wesley Barnett, among others . . . and a gunfighting deputy named Logan Kane.

If Green was intimidated, he didn't let it show. His voice steady, he said, "I'm hanging Frank Dawson in the morning." He waved a hand, like a man shooing away a bothersome fly. "Now, be about your business, Marshal, and leave me to mine."

Kane felt a familiar quick start of anger, but he held himself level. "Green, Dawson may not be alive in the morning unless I get him out of that stinking, rat-infested hole you call a jail."

The gunman shrugged. "His funeral."

Kane drank coffee and built and lit a cigarette, he and Green eyeing each other like wolves. The marshal was giving himself time, planning what he was going to say next. Now he said it. "Green, you have a choice. Either you give me the key to the jail or I'll get an axe and cut the door down."

Hulin Green was a short-tempered man. He rose
to his feet and brushed his frock coat away from
the Colt on his hip. "Kane, I wouldn't try that if I
was you."

But the marshal was not a man to back down and
everybody in the saloon knew it. He could not walk
away from it and let it be known that Green had put
the crawl on him.

"Hulin," he said, using the man's given name as
a peace gesture, "you've made your war talk. Now
say something else that makes sense." He shook his
head, his eyes cold. "Don't make me draw my
pistol."

Rain throbbed on the saloon roof, and a log of
wood fell in the stove. The saloon clock ticked into
the silence, loud as rocks falling into a tin bucket.
The men behind Green got up hurriedly. Chairs
scraped across the pine floor and one tipped over.
They stepped to the bar, out of the line of fire. One
of the miners was suffering from a lung disease and
his breath wheezed like an out-of-tune harmonica in
his chest.

In a close-range gunfight luck is the bastard child
of skill, and on that day Hulin Green didn't seem to
be feeling particularly lucky. "If I draw, you'll kill
me," he said. A pulse in his throat was throbbing.

"Probably," Kane said. "Seems to me you've got
a choice to make."

Green exhaled through his teeth. "Key's in my left
coat pocket."

"Slowly," Kane said.

Green reached into the pocket and laid the key on the table.

"I'm beholden to you," Kane said, smiling.

The gunman swallowed hard, and his struggle between pride and common sense was obvious to everyone in the saloon. Finally sense prevailed. His face like stone, without a word he brushed past Kane and walked outside.

Wary, Vito changed his position, moving away from the bar to the opposite wall where he could keep an eye on the door and guard Kane's back.

The bartender looked at Kane. "Mister, I hope you're as fast with the iron as you think you are. Hulin Green won't let that go."

The marshal smiled and thumbed over his shoulder at Vito. "I've got help."

"Hulin Green don't need help," the bartender said.

Kane walked outside to the jail, Vito following him. He called out to Dawson, then turned the key in the lock. A wave of stink hit them like a fist.

Vito gagged. "Oh, geez . . . oh, my God . . ."

Out in the open, the man looked even smaller. He was about five foot tall and couldn't have weighed ninety pounds. His hair was matted, his pants and shirt filthy and his bare feet were caked with dirt and black mud.

"Where are we taking him, Marshal?" Vito asked.

"Back to the hotel."

"He stinks like a hog."

"I'll take care of that," Kane said. He looked at Dawson. "How long have you been in there?"

"About a week, since Lily was murdered." The little man looked nervously around him. "Where's Hulin?"

"He's sulking," Kane said. "You've had no food or water?"

"I had water. There was a jug in the jail, but I finished it yesterday."

Kane nodded. "Right, come with me."

"Where are we going, Marshal?" Dawson asked.

"The hotel."

The marshal grabbed the little man by the back of the neck and marched him through the mud of the street toward the Tontine. There had been no letup in the rain and a thin wind gusted cold.

At the last moment Kane veered away from the hotel to a zinc horse trough standing outside. He lifted Dawson bodily and threw him into the ice-cold water. The man shrieked and tried to struggle out of the trough, but Kane held his head under. He looked at Vito. "Get a blanket from the hotel."

Vito was grinning. "Hell, Marshal, you're drowning him."

"He'll be all right. Get the blanket."

After the other man left, Kane let Dawson up for air. He spluttered and coughed, his eyes wild, and tried to climb out again. The marshal pushed his head under the water, ignoring his pleas for mercy.

When Vito returned with a blanket, Kane reached into the trough, grabbed Dawson by the front of his shirt and dragged him to his feet. "Feel cleaner now?" he asked.

The little man's teeth were chattering so much he couldn't answer.

"Now strip those wet rags off'n you."

Dawson hesitated, but Kane said, "You do it, or I cut them off with a bowie."

Quickly Dawson stripped. His skinny, white body, covered in sparse, black hair, had erupted all over in goose bumps.

Kane took the blanket from the grinning Vito and threw it over the little man's head and shoulders. "Let's get you something to eat," he said.

Vito shook his head. "Marshal Kane, you surely have a gentle way with prisoners."

Kane nodded. "Sometimes a man has to be cruel to be kind."

"I wonder what you'd be like if you were concentrating only on the cruel part."

Kane grinned, pushing Dawson through the hotel door. "Vito, you don't want to ever find out."

He pushed Dawson into a chair and when the cook appeared he said, "Feed him." Kane turned to Vito. "See that he gets his grub and coffee. I'm going to talk to that Katie gal at the livery."

"You have something on your mind?"

"Yeah. It's on my mind that this little man didn't murder Lily LaBelle."

Chapter 27

Katie Gordon was standing at the stable door, looking out at the rain when Kane stepped beside her.

"Well, if it ain't the man who put the crawl on Hulin Green and lived to talk about it," she said.

"I didn't talk about it," Kane said.

"Maybe not, but the whole town is." The woman's eyes searched Kane's face. "Is it right what I'm hearing, that you challenged Hulin to draw and he backed off?"

"No, it's not right. I asked Mr. Green for a key and he gave it to me. That's all there was to it."

"Uh-huh . . . Well, that's not how the story was told to me."

"Well, half-truths have a habit of growing up to be whole lies."

Katie knew she wasn't going to get anywhere with the taciturn lawman. She said, "What can I do for you, Marshal? It ain't much of a day for riding."

"I don't need my horse. I just want you to answer a question for me."

"Shoot."

"What kind of gal was Lily LaBelle? Physically I mean."

"She was a slut and she had a big pair of bobbers if that's what you're driving at."

"Was she large all over?"

"Sure, she was a big girl, well shaped and as tall as me"— the woman smiled—"but not near as pretty."

Kane played the gentleman. "That goes without sayin', Miss Katie."

Pleased, the woman said, "Why are you asking me this?"

"First, one more thing. Would you say Lily was strong?"

Katie laughed. "I seen her beat up on a drunk miner a time or two over to the Bucket of Blood. And about a month before she died, she shot a saddle tramp who was passing through and tried to get for nothing what she had for sale. Lily shot about five balls from a .31 pepperbox into his hide and damned near killed him."

"She had a pepperbox?"

"Sure, a six-shot Allen and Thurber. She carried it in her purse and sometimes in a garter."

"Was the gun found after she was murdered?"

"I don't know. Maybe Hulin Green took it." Katie looked hard at Kane. "I'm trying to catch your drift here, Marshal. What trail are you following?"

"I took Frank Dawson out of the jail earlier. He's

this tall"—Kane made a gesture with the flat of his hand level with his waist—"and he can't go a hunnerd pounds. How could he have strangled a woman who was strong enough to beat up on miners and carried a belly gun in her purse?"

Katie's eyes lifted to Kane briefly, then moved to the rain slanting across the stable door. Finally she said, "I don't know."

"Frank Dawson didn't murder Lily LaBelle. Somebody else did, somebody a lot bigger and stronger than him." Kane listened into the hissing silence for a few moments, then said, "Why was Hulin Green in such an all-fired hurry to pin the murder on Dawson an' so set on hangin' him tomorrow?"

Katie thought about that. Kane studied her, thinking that she wasn't a beautiful woman, not even a pretty one, but she had sky blue eyes that could grow on a man and the blond hair escaping from under her hat had a sheen that was all its own. Her small breasts pushed against her buckskin shirt, budding in the cold air.

"Hulin was sparking Lily, everybody knew that, and they had screaming fights all the time," the woman said. "But I never knew him to get physical with her."

"Until the day he snapped and strangled her, huh?" Kane said.

"Why would Hulin kill her?" Katie said. "She was his meal ticket. He took a cut of every dollar she earned."

"Maybe he found out that she was holding out on him."

"Lily became real close with Hank Stafford, the man who owns the Tontine and the Alamo saloon." Katie shrugged. "Hulin is a dangerous man when he's drinking. He could have got jealous."

The woman took off her hat and her hair cascaded over her shoulders. She rubbed her temples, then shoved her hair under the hat again. "Marshal, you're giving me a headache." She sighed her resignation. "What are you planning to do? Arrest Hulin Green and take him to Fort Smith? If that's what you have in mind, forget it. It isn't going to happen."

"I think Green murdered Lily LaBelle. But thinkin' a thing isn't proving it. So far I've got nothing on him."

Exasperation flickered in Katie's eyes. "Marshal, all you're going to do is dig a grave for yourself. Does a little weasel like Frank Dawson matter that much? Step away from it and let events take their course."

Kane shook his head. "I won't see an innocent man hang just because it's convenient. And if Dawson doesn't matter much, then Lily didn't matter much either." His raw-boned face tightened and his voice grew a little louder. "Where does it end, Katie? One day will someone decide that you don't matter? What will happen to you then?"

The woman looked out at the rain. Without turning she said, "Marshal Kane, I've listened to you talk and I've seen the struggle in your eyes as you yourself try to believe in what you're saying. I have the feeling that you're a man attempting to change his ways, desperately trying to be what he is not. I think, for whatever reason, you've come to this recently." Now Katie turned and her level gaze met his. "Instead of the hired gunfighter, you're all at once the upright, noble lawman. This is all very honorable, but it's not a plan for survival."

Kane opened his mouth to speak, but the woman held up a hand. "Hear me out. When I scouted for the Army, I met Judge Parker at an officers' ball in Fort Smith. He told me he had to keep the peace in seventy-five thousand square miles of the Indian Territory with fewer than two hundred deputies. For that, the old man said he didn't need knights errant in shining armor—he needed gunfighters, men who had killed and would not hesitate to kill again if the need arose. Why do you think so many of Parker's deputies have ridden owlhoot trails?" She waved a hand. "Kane, you ride out into the Territory still wearing that halo around your head, the outlaws will use it for target practice." She touched her hat. "Well, I've got work to do, but here's some advice: go back to what you were when Judge Parker hired you, or get the hell out of the peace officer business."

Katie turned on her heel and walked into the barn.

"I still won't let an innocent man hang!" Kane yelled after her, his anger flaring.

The woman waved a dismissive hand and was then swallowed by the gloom.

The marshal felt like a little boy who had just been scolded by his ma and had pitched a temper tantrum. It was not a good feeling. And to make matters worse, she could have been in the right.

*   *   *

Kane returned to the hotel and stepped into the restaurant. Frank Dawson still sat at the table, wrapped in his blanket, and the cook and Vito stood looking at him as if he were some kind of strange species that had wandered in from the high plains.

Vito glanced at Kane and grinned. "He's eaten three elk steaks, a dozen eggs and drunk a gallon of coffee."

The cook shook his head in wonderment. "I fed hungry Texas punchers for nigh on twenty years, but I ain't never seen the like. He's skinny as a bed slat, but the little feller'll eat anything that don't eat him first."

Still angry from his encounter with Katie, Kane did not crack a smile. "Vito, take him to the store and see if you can buy him a shirt, pants and shoes. And see if they got some kind of coat he can wear. I ain't takin' him to Fort Smith nekkid."

"I'd be happy to oblige, Marshal," Vito said, "but I think we're in trouble." He was standing at the window and he nodded to the outside. "Take a look."

Kane was at the window in two quick strides. He looked outside and something inside him went cold. Six riders stood their horses in the street, dark, menacing outlines behind the gusting, gray curtain of the rain. Behind them, on foot, their bare heads bowed, were Lorraine and Nellie. Both had their hands tied in front of them, and loops around their necks roped to the saddle horn of a long-haired man wearing a flat-brimmed black hat, its domed crown circled by a wide band of blue, Apache beadwork. Somebody said something to the man and he grinned, and jerked on the rope, pulling both women off their feet and sending them sprawling in the mud. He turned in the saddle and yelled, so loud Kane could hear, "Women! No talk!"

This time the others laughed.

As the wind shifted and parted the curtain for a moment, the marshal recognized the horses four of the men rode. The slender threads of civilized behavior that lay buried within Logan Kane and kept him together snapped one by one, hastening his descent into barbarism.

Nothing that was human remained of Kane as he bellowed his teeth-bared rage and sprinted for the door. Behind him he heard Vito yell, "No!" But, now beyond hearing, he ignored him.

The Apache, more wary than the others, saw Kane as the hotel door burst open. The man lunged for the booted Spencer under his knee, but Kane shot him out of the saddle. Hick Dietz, missing his right thumb, made a play with his left hand. Kane fired, missed, fired again and Dietz fell into the mud, screaming.

Now Kane was aware of the wicked *crack! crack! crack!* of Vito's gun. He saw Amos Albright, the man who enjoyed killing women, reel in the saddle.

Jack Henry was shooting and Kane felt a tremendous blow to his left side. To his surprise, the boardwalk rushed up to meet him and slammed into him with sickening force. He was on his belly, his face in the dirt. He tried to raise his gun, but it was too heavy for him. Vito was out in the mud, firing, his gun at eye level. But then Kane saw only cascading rain and an empty street. And then he saw nothing at all.

Chapter 28

"He's coming around."

Lorraine's voice.

Kane's eyes fluttered open. The woman's face, blurred in the lamplight, swam over his. "How are you feeling?"

"How do you think I'm feelin'?" he said with the querulous tone of an invalid. Kane recognized it and tried to make amends. "What happened?"

"You got shot," Vito said. He sounded cheerful enough.

"Where?"

"Out on the boardwalk."

Kane allowed himself to sound peevish again. "I mean, what part of me got shot?"

"You took a bullet through your side," Lorraine said. "You've lost a lot of blood, but I'd say there's nothing vital damaged inside you." She laid a hand on his forehead. "But I don't know for sure."

Kane struggled to sit higher and the woman

plumped pillows behind him. He was naked under the blanket, his waist bandaged by what looked like a torn-up sheet. He looked around him. He was in his room in the Tontine Hotel, a glowing oil lamp hanging from a beam above the bed, an orb of orange light that did little to banish the darkness. Vito stood across the room, Kane's Winchester in his arms.

The marshal looked at him. He felt as weak as a kitten. "I don't remember much after the shooting started."

"You killed two of them, an Indian and a man missing a thumb. I wounded another—I don't know how badly." Vito smiled. "It took the thumbless bandit a while to die and he cursed some. He sure didn't like you very much, Marshal."

Kane ignored that. "Stringfellow and Henry, where are they?"

"Skedaddled." This from Lorraine.

Kane struggled to rise. "I have to go after them."

The woman pushed him back onto the pillows. He was so weak he couldn't resist. "You stay right where you are, Logan. Catching those two can wait."

"There are four of them, though I think the one I hit will be out of it for a while," Vito said.

"That was Amos Albright. He's made a career of murdering women."

Vito smiled. "Well, a most singular man. I'm very glad I shot him." He hesitated a moment, then said, "Marshal, they all saw you go down. You're all shot to pieces, a hole in your thigh and now another in your side. I don't think those bandits rode too far, knowing you're bound to be feeling poorly."

"You think they might come back tonight?"

Vito lifted his arms, showing the rifle. "What do you think?"

"Shot through and through or no, I have to get out of this bed," Kane said.

"No you don't," Lorraine said, pushing him back again. Her face was clouded by worry.

Kane's head was spinning and he gratefully sank back on the pillows. "My revolver?"

"Right here on the floor, beside you," Lorraine said. "I reloaded it."

The marshal nodded wearily. "Thank you."

Guilt didn't creep up on him slowly; it hit him like a fist. He had been so preoccupied with his own concerns that he hadn't asked Lorraine about what had happened to her and Nellie.

Now, fearing the reply, he said haltingly, as though speaking in a language foreign to him, "Lorraine . . . you and Nellie . . . what . . . ?"

The woman's face betrayed nothing. "Stringfellow promised us to the Apache, but only after you were dead. He starved us, beat us and dragged us behind his horse, but that was all." She looked hard at Kane. "Does that answer your question?"

"Where is Nellie?"

"She's helping Mr. Pitt."

"Who's Mr. Pitt?"

"The hotel cook. He and Nellie are making you soup. It will build up your strength."

"Lorraine, when Stringfellow rode in, did he know we were here?"

"Yes, he did. He didn't really think you'd give him a three-day start, so the Apache was always riding out to keep track of you. He found the dead men you left behind at the dugout saloon. At least, I suppose it was you."

"What happened to the Lipan girls?" Kane asked, letting go of the woman's comment. "Stringfellow and the others were riding their horses."

"The Apache found them." Lorraine's skin tightened against her cheekbones and she shook her head. The gesture said it all.

"Logan, the Apache told Stringfellow he could kill you and Vito at any time," Lorraine said. "Stringfellow said he didn't want that. He wanted to kill you himself and make sure you knew you were dying."

"Sounds like him," Kane said. He extended an arm and lightly touched Lorraine's cheek. "You look tired, woman. You've come a fur piece on foot across some mighty hard country. Have you eaten anything?"

"Nellie and Mr. Pitt are bringing me food."

The cook, Nellie in tow, appeared a few minutes later, bearing a loaded tray. It seemed he'd made an extra effort for the ladies. "Beef sandwiches, ma'am," he said to Lorraine, "on sourdough bread I baked my ownself. An' tea. You like tea?"

The woman smiled her thanks and Vito said sourly, remembering his own meal, "What happened, Mr. Pitt, you run out of elk?"

The cook was not fazed. "I always push game

meats. If'n you wanted beefsteak an' taters, you should have asked fer beefsteak an' taters."

Kane smiled. "Vito, never start an argument with a woman or a ranch cook. You can't win against either one."

For his part, the marshal was happy with his soup, a broth of beef, onions and some kind of wild greens. Lorraine was right; it would give him strength. But the question was, when?

Heavy, booted feet sounded in the hallway outside, then stopped. "Marshal Logan Kane!" A man's voice, made rough with years of whiskey and tobacco.

"Who is it?" Vito yelled, bringing up the Winchester.

"Got a message fer Kane. Who I am, don't matter."

Vito pushed the blanket aside and stepped into the corridor. Kane heard him say, "What's the message?"

"Buff Stringfellow says for him to look at the gallows."

"That's it?"

"That's it."

Vito stepped into the room just as Kane was lowering the hammer of his Colt. "I heard what he said. You ever see that man before?"

Vito shook his head. "No. A miner maybe? That's what he looked like."

The wound in his side had slowed Kane, not only physically, but mentally. Cursing himself for not asking the question earlier, he said, "Where's Dawson?"

"At the livery. He said he always slept there and Katie Gordon wouldn't let anything bad happen to him."

"Give me my hat and my clothes," Kane said. He swung his legs out of the bed and immediately the room around him spun wildly.

"Logan, you're not fit to go anywhere," Lorraine protested.

"Damn it, woman, do as I say."

Vito shook his head. "Ma'am, you can't argue with a woman, a cook or a mule. Better do as he says."

Kane put on his hat, then his clothes, and stomped into his boots. He buckled on his gun belt, swaying like a sailor on the deck of his ship in a storm. The left side of his waist bulged with the thick pad Lorraine had placed under the bandage. He saw blood seeping through his shirt. His head was throbbing and the pain from his wound chewed at him.

"For pity's sake, Marshal, you're shot to doll rags," Vito said. "You got to find a hole to crawl into until this is over."

Kane gritted his teeth. He was aware of Nellie looking at him, her eyes huge. "It will not be over until I get Buff Stringfellow, Jack Henry, Amos Albright and Reuben Largo to Fort Smith." He looked at Vito. "Then I'll find that hole."

"Logan . . . please . . . don't get killed like Sam did." Nellie was looking at him, her eyes damp.

Lorraine and Kane exchanged a surprised glance. Then the woman took her daughter in her arms and held her tightly, their tears mingling.

"Nellie," the marshal said, "I'm a mighty hard man to kill." He smiled and laid his hand on top of the girl's head. "Once this is over, we'll go to Texas. Would you like that?"

Nellie nodded and Lorraine's eyes lifted to Kane's. "All of us?"

"Of course, all of us. I wouldn't have it any other way."

Vito finally coughed into the stretching silence that followed. He said, handing Kane his slicker, "If you're all set on heading out there, Marshal, let's go. I don't want you out of my sight."

Kane tore his eyes away from Lorraine's face. "Step careful, Vito," he said, the pain making him sick and tired beyond anything he'd ever known before. "I don't know how much good I'll be in a shooting scrape. It'll be like drawing against a full house."

Vito nodded, grinning. "Know what this reminds me of, Marshal? We're like the heroes in the dime novels they sell in the railroad station in New Orleans. You know, about stalwart frontiersmen who triumph over impossible odds."

"I'm a shot-up, poor excuse for a lawman and you're a city slicker who shoots fair to middlin' with a belly gun. Where do we fit in?"

"Why, right there on the cover. You and me, looking stalwart."

Despite the tormenting ache in his side, Kane managed a smile. "Let's go, Dan'l Boone."

Lorraine's cries of protest still ringing in his ears, Kane walked into the rain-lashed darkness. Lamps were lit in the Alamo and Bucket of Blood saloons, spilling rectangles of yellow light on the soaked boardwalks that glistened like wet paint. Driven by hunger, the coyotes were yipping close to town, a dreary counterpoint to the snake hiss of the rain.

The body hanging from the gallows swayed in the wind, the hemp rope creaking. Frank Dawson had strangled to death, his swollen, black tongue sticking out between pale lips. His eyes were open, staring accusingly at Kane.

"Look," Vito said. "A message for you." He was pointing to a board nailed to the gallows platform beside the steps. The writing was done, badly, in white paint.

KANE
YURE
NEXT

"The spelling leaves something to be desired," Vito said. He was consciously keeping his tone light, but his face was grim. "However, the intent is clear enough."

Kane, almost dead on his feet, felt the hair on the back of his neck rise.

And the unnatural, derisive laughter that rose from somewhere in town did nothing to make him feel more at ease.

Chapter 29

Logan Kane swayed on his feet, looking around him into rain and darkness. "Vito!" he whispered urgently.

The man knew what was expected of him. He took the marshal's arm and draped it over his shoulders, taking as much of his weight as he could. "You're going back to bed," he said.

"No," Kane said. "Help me to the livery. Katie Gordon is there."

A proud, stiff-necked man, Kane would have asked no other person alive for the help he demanded of Vito Provanzano that night. But Vito, a proud man himself, was aware where the parameters of another man's pride lay and he would not step over the line. To Kane, that made the difference.

Half dragging the marshal through the mud, Vito managed to get him to the livery stable. The place was in darkness.

The marshal disengaged himself from Vito and

stepped to the door, supporting himself by a hand on the frame. He drew his Colt and yelled, "Katie!"

No answer.

Rats rustled restlessly in the corners, rain rattled on the roof and a horse blew through its nose, then fell silent. The tin-rooster weather vane on the gable turned this way and that, uselessly trying to point out the shifting direction of the squalling wind and screeching in flustered protest.

"Katie!" Kane called again. And again the answering stillness mocked him.

Beside the marshal a match sizzled into flame and Vito lit the oil lamp he was holding. He held the lamp high, casting orange light into the barn, deepening the angled shadows.

Katie Gordon lay on her back, half in, half out of a horse stall. She was naked. Kane lurched toward her, stooping to his left against the biting pain in his waist. Lost in the uncertain lamplight, the woman's face was in shadow. He stepped into the stall.

"Vito," he said, "bring the lamp closer."

A moment's hesitation, then, "That might be difficult, Marshal. I've got a gun pointed at my head."

"Turn real slow, Kane. And keep your hand away from the iron."

Kane straightened up, his back stiff. He turned and saw Hulin Green standing next to Vito, the muzzle of the man's Colt screwed into his temple. "I see anything fancy, anything I don't like, and I scatter his brains," Green said.

"Why are you here?" Kane asked. "Come back to admire your handiwork?"

"Her? I didn't kill her. A man called Amos Albright did that. He likes to strangle the ladies while he's about his business."

"You're a liar, Green," Vito snapped. "I put a bullet in that man."

"You grazed him, is all." Green pushed on the Colt, forcing Vito's head to the right. "And listen, you damned dago, you call me a liar again and I'll blow your head clean off."

Roughly, Green opened Vito's coat, slid out the Smith & Wesson from the shoulder holster and tossed it into the dirt. "Buff told me you carried a hideout there. Now, lay the lamp at your feet and get over beside Kane. After me and him have it out, maybe I'll let you live." He shrugged. "But, again, maybe I won't."

Vito did as he was told and the marshal said, "I'm callin' you a liar as well. You murdered Katie Gordon an' before that, Lily LaBelle."

Green smiled. "Kane, you stupid hick, I've never killed a woman in my life. I told you, Albright killed Katie. And Lily was murdered by . . . well, why don't you guess."

Kane was desperately trying to hold on, battling pain, dizziness and waves of nausea. "I don't have to guess. It was you."

Green shook his head. "Wrong again. Katie murdered Lily, and I helped cover it up for her, repaying old favors you might say. Besides, Katie owned the livery and she'd be missed. Frank Dawson, now who would miss him?"

"Katie had no call to kill Lily LaBelle," Kane said.

"Had a sheltered upbringing, huh, Kane?" Green took a single step back, a gunfighter seeking his comfortable distance. But he was still talking. "Katie didn't like men, at least not in her bed. But she didn't have the same feelings about women, especially Lily. When Lily told her she was leaving her and heading east to Boston town, Katie couldn't take it. If she couldn't have Lily, then no one would. So she strangled her."

Green moved his frock coat away from his holstered gun. "I took some things from Lily's cabin and said I'd found them on Dawson. All but a sweet little pepperbox revolver. That I kept for myself."

Now Green's smile slipped. "Kane, I'm all through talking and I don't much care if you believe me or not, on account of how you'll be dead real soon anyhow."

"Like I told you afore, Green, don't make me draw down on you."

"Big talk from a man who's half dead already. You've been stepping a mighty wide path since I wouldn't fight you in the saloon," Green said, his eyes luminous in the lamplight. "Men talk, and there are some saying you put the crawl on me. Well, I've never enjoyed killing a man before breakfast and that's all there was to it, why I let it go." His gaze hardened from gray to ice blue. "It's way past break-fast now, Kane."

"Damn you, the man is dead on his feet," Vito yelled.

"You shut your trap! He's getting an even break."

Kane was falling apart. He was so weak his knees trembled and he saw Green through a haze of glimmering yellow light and purple shadow. He had to hold on, just a minute longer. . . .

"Any time you feel like it, skin the iron," Green prompted. His face had a grinning, predatory cast, like a lobo wolf that has just hamstrung an elk. "I want this thing done right."

"Hulin," Kane pleaded, "please be reasonable. I'm not in any condition to—"

He drew and fired.

The bullet slammed into Green's belly, low down, an inch under the navel. But the man was fast, very fast. He fired a split second later and the big hunk of .45 lead struck the cylinder of Kane's revolver. The slug caromed off the gun, flattened and tumbling, then slammed into the upper part of the marshal's chest. The deformed bullet smashed its way across ribs and exited through the top of Kane's left shoulder, exploding out of the collarbone in a ragged spray of scarlet blood.

Green's face was ashen, his lips drawn back from his teeth in a grotesque grin. Gut-shot, knowing he was a dead man, he dropped to one knee. He shot again—a miss.

The cylinder of Kane's gun was loose and out of line. He held it in place with his left hand, thumbed the hammer and fired, hitting Green in the belly again. The gunman got off a shot, into the floor. He tried to get up, his eyes, terrible with hate, meeting Kane's, then just rolled over.

Kane limped to Green's side and stood above him, his arm with the shattered gun hanging at his side. "Damn you," the man whispered, "you are fast."

"Faster than you'll ever live to be," the marshal said, no pity in him, his anger a red and black fog in his mind.

Green struggled to talk through the blood that filled his mouth. "I hanged Dawson, me and Buff. You couldn't save him, Kane. I beat you . . . you . . ."

Then Hulin Green died.

Vito Provanzano's gray face betrayed his shock. "Marshal, you're hit again."

"Seems like."

"I have to get you to bed and then find a doctor, or what passes for one around here."

Kane shook his head. "No. Hell, I'll probably be dead afore sunup. It's got to be finished tonight." He tossed his mangled revolver aside and nodded to Green's body. "Give me his gun."

Vito picked up his own revolver, wiped it off, then did the same with Green's Colt.

Kane reloaded the gun, filling all six chambers, and shoved it into his holster. "Rip that shirt off'n him an' see if you can use it to stop my bleeding." Vito hesitated, looking at the dead man. "Hurry up," the marshal said. "We're running out of time. I don't know how long I can stay on my feet."

Vito bent to the body, but stopped, his alarmed eyes on Kane.

From outside came the sound of booted men running through rain and mud.

The marshal drew his gun and staggered to the door of the barn. Four men were charging toward him, the bulky shape of Buff Stringfellow in the lead. Kane shot rapidly, fanning the Colt. He knew his chances of hitting anything were remote, but the flying bullets had the desired effect. Stringfellow and the others broke and ran.

Vito was beside him, his revolver in his hand. "Watch them!" Kane yelled. He could see nothing but a cartwheeling blur of darkness and rain. After a couple of minutes, he said, "Well? Where?"

"The Bucket of Blood."

"Good. Then that's where I'll find them." He looked at Vito and even managed a smile. "I took 'em by surprise. I reckon they thought I was dead."

"And I reckon that was a real good guess on their part," Vito said, looking Kane up and down . . . a tall, grim lawman, shot through and through and drenched in blood that was all his own.

The thought came unbidden to Vito's deeply troubled mind that Deputy Marshal Logan Kane was a dead man who hadn't fallen over yet.

Chapter 30

Vito Provanzano ripped the shirt off Green's body and helped Kane out of his slicker. He bandaged up the wounds on the marshal's chest and shoulder as best he could and was shocked by what he saw.

"I've seen wounded men before," he said, looking hard into Kane's eyes. "But I've never seen an injury like this. Nothing like this. Marshal, it's"—he fished through his mind for a word—"savage. Savage . . . like raw meat."

"You know how to cheer a man, don't you?" Kane said. "Button me into the slicker again to hold the bandage in place."

"It's not a bandage," Vito said. "It's just a dead man's shirt soaking up blood."

A hay rake hung from a hook on the barn wall and Vito took it down and smashed off the pegged wooden tines. He looked it over, nodded and offered it to Kane. "I'd say this is a pretty fair imitation of a crutch," he said. "I can't have you hanging on me when the shooting starts."

The marshal took the rake and propped it under his left arm. His eyes sought Vito's in the gloom. "Vito, before it's too late, saddle your hoss an' run fast an' fur, all the way to the New Orleans docks."

Vito shook his head. "I'll see this job through."

Logan Kane was a man born without the ability to back up or back down, combined with a harsh drive toward sudden, wild-eyed violence. He recognized those traits in others, and although Vito's lay hidden under a glossy veneer of city slicker sophistication, it was there nonetheless. The man would stick, no matter the consequences, and there could be no talking him out of it.

"I'm beholden to you," Kane said.

Vito smiled. "I know."

"Then let's get it done," Kane said.

He shuffled toward the door, trailing a spoor of blood behind him. His face was ashen under his tan, his blue eyes burned out, revealing his battle with pain and the waves of weakness that kept washing over him.

Kane had been weathered by a thousand difficult trails and he had known much of hardship and doing without, whether of food, water, sleep or the scented companionship of a woman. All that was not bone or muscle in him had long since melted away and the soul within his body was scarred by many wounds, most too deep to ever heal. But that night, shot to ribbons and barely able to stay on his feet, all that had gone before helped him endure and, despite his feebleness, made him dangerous, fast and deadly with a gun as few men are.

Had a man used to soft living and civilized ways taken the hits, he would already have been dead, his life ebbing away on the dirty floor of the barn. But Kane was a tough man to kill, rugged as the Western lands that had tested him time and time again and had never found him wanting. He had been bred hard, lived hard and now he was determined to die hard.

He was at the door of the barn. And he had it to do.

Lorraine, running through mud and rain, desperately tried to stop him.

"I heard the shooting and I thought you were dead," she cried.

She threw herself against him, heedless of the blood that stained her dress. She begged, pleaded, cajoled and wept bitter tears, and later Kane couldn't remember what he said to her in reply.

"Logan, you're in no shape to go up against Stringfellow and three other gunmen," Lorraine said. "We'll leave, now, tonight. I'll go anywhere with you."

She read her answer in Kane's eyes and she swung on Vito. "For God's sake tell him!"

The man shook his head. "Ma'am, I can't tell the marshal what to do."

"There's blood everywhere," Lorraine cried, looking at the scarlet shreds hanging in strips under Kane's slicker. And again she asked Vito, "How bad is it?"

"It's bad, ma'am. Real bad. Ribs broken, shoulder broken." He looked at the ground between his feet. "I don't know what else is broken inside."

"Lorraine, go to the hotel and wait for me," Kane said. "I'll be back for you and Nellie."

Lorraine was intelligent enough to realize that she'd used every womanly weapon in her arsenal, including tears, and that Kane would not budge. Ten yoke of oxen would not move him and it was pointless to attempt the impossible. "I'll be at the hotel," the woman said, her voice flat as she accepted what was now inevitable.

Lorraine turned on her heel and walked into the lashing rain. Kane called out after her, but she did not turn and soon became one with the night.

The Bucket of Blood glowed in the gloom, needles of rain spiking into its spilling rectangles of yellow light. A slight haze hung in the air, gray as winter smoke, and around Kane and Vito the muddy street hissed. The saloon crouched on the boardwalk, silent and waiting, hung with an aura of dread so real a man could reach out and grab it and come away with a handful of blackness.

Vito turned uneasily to Kane. "How are you holding up, Marshal?"

"I'm still on my feet."

"Yes, but barely."

"I've got a few minutes left in me. Then I'm done." He looked at Vito, his face drawn, haggard and suddenly old. "I don't have time for anything fancy. We walk inside and I ask for their surrender." He reached down, undid the tin star from his gun belt and pinned it to the front of his slicker. "About time I showed I'm proud of this." Kane reached out and laid a hand on Vito's shoulder. He said, "I'm sorry about getting you into it. It could all go to hell real fast."

"Your few minutes are running out, Marshal," Vito said. "Let's get it done."

Kane adjusted the hang of his gun, settled his crutch under his arm, then nodded. "I'm ready."

The younger man smiled. "No you're not, but I'm all through trying to tell you that."

The two men walked slowly through the mud to the saloon. In the darkness the rain fell around them like liquid silver.

Kane opened the door and stepped inside.

Buff Stringfellow and Jack Henry sat at a table opposite the door, a bottle between them. Amos Albright, the woman killer, stood at the corner of the bar, his sly eyes glittering with the thrill of the hunt. He held Sam Shaver's Greener against his side, half hidden by his ragged coat. Reuben Largo had taken up a position behind Stringfellow. Largo was wearing a holstered Colt, but the man was a knife artist and he'd have a bowie about him somewhere. Largo called himself a preacher, but his cold, black eyes gave no hint of any religious fervor.

"Been expecting you, Marshal Kane," Stringfellow said. "You don't look so good."

"Last I saw of you, Buff, you wasn't lookin' so good either. As I recollect, you was a-runnin' through the mud like a buckshot coyote."

Stringfellow smiled. "Yeah, well, we ain't a-runnin' now, are we?"

Kane nodded. He looked around the bar. The bartender had disappeared and there were no other patrons. Probably they'd been run off by the convicts.

"I don't have much time, so I'm going to talk plain to you men," Kane said. "I want you to surrender your guns and then come with me peacefully. I guarantee you a fair hearing in Fort Smith on multiple counts of murder and a crackerjack hanging with new hemp ropes."

Stringfellow turned, looked at Henry and both men broke into guffaws of laughter. Albright and Largo joined in the mirth, neither of them aware that they'd soon be dead men.

Logan Kane looked dreadful, like a walking corpse. But, covered in blood, his eyes burning with cold, green fire, that night he was probably the most dangerous living being, human or animal, on earth.

Jack Henry knew it. A killer himself, he recognized it in others and he showed it by the way his skin tightened like parchment against his cheekbones. Standing tall and terrible in the trembling, orange lamplight, Logan Kane was a man to step around, a man to let be. But Henry had been there many times before. There was no going back from this and there could be only one end . . . and that would be when dead men were stretched on the floor.

Henry rose to his feet, the scrape of his chair scratching across the silence.

"Kane!" he yelled. "The hell with you!"

Jack Henry, man killer, named gunfighter, drew— and died.

His gun had cleared the leather, his thumb on the hammer, when Kane's bullet crashed into the bridge of his nose. Henry's head snapped back and he did an odd pirouette on his right foot, staggered to the side and sprawled across Stringfellow. The rickety chair collapsed under the weight of both men and Stringfellow fell on his back, Henry's limp body on top of him.

Amos Albright had stepped away from the bar and he was bringing up the Greener. Beside him, Kane heard Vito fire twice. Albright staggered back, blasting the shotgun into the timber ceiling. Vito fired again and this time the man went down. In his dying moments Albright learned he'd made a fatal mistake— an abuser of women should never seek a fight with men.

Terrified, Reuben Largo took himself out of it. His gun still in the leather, he screamed and made a dash for the back door. He almost made it, but Kane cut him down with two fast shots. The man died with his boots in the saloon and his face in the mud.

Through the gray, sullen drift of gun smoke, Kane saw Stringfellow try to rise. His crutch thumping rapidly on the floor, the marshal stepped beside the outlaw. Stringfellow looked up at Kane and shrank back, like a man seeing a frightful ghost.

Stringfellow's Colt had slipped out of the holster and lay beside him. The man eyed it and Kane, out of his mind with pain and rage, roared, "Pick it up, damn you! Get to your work!"

Stringfellow jerked back his hand as if the gun were suddenly red-hot. His scared eyes lifted to Kane's face and he shook his head, struck dumb by fear.

"Pick it up!" Kane yelled. His boot crashed into Stringfellow's ribs. "Pick it up!"

At that moment, Logan Kane was no longer human. He had reverted to something that had existed a long time before in mankind's past, a creature primitive, brutish and savage. His boot thudded again and again into Stringfellow's body and face. The man writhed and shrieked, blood on his lips, his wild eyes already swollen shut.

Vito stepped in front of Kane. "Stop, Marshal!" he said. "See him hang, but don't kick the man to death."

Kane's lips were pulled back from his teeth, his face murderous. "Get away from me!" he roared.

"Damn you, Kane, he's had enough!" Suddenly the muzzle of Vito's gun was pressed into the marshal's throat. "Back off or I swear I'll blow your head off."

Like a man waking from a nightmare, Kane stared into Vito's eyes for a long moment, blinked, then looked down at Stringfellow as though seeing the man for the first time. "I'm all right," he said after a long while. He breathed hard, steadying himself. "Let somebody else kill him."

Vito waited, his gaze searching Kane's face for any sign of an untruth; then he took his gun away. He managed a weak smile. "You do get a tad over-wrought by times, don't you, Marshal?"

The door opened and a grizzled head of a miner poked inside.

"You," Kane said to the man. "Bring me the black-smith."

"Huh?"

Louder this time. "Bring me the damned black-smith!"

The old miner backed out and his running foot-steps sounded on the boardwalk.

Kane looked through the curling gun smoke at the three dead men, then the groaning man at his feet. He wanted to lie down and sleep, close his eyes and lose himself in oblivion for hours. Forever. No, not that, not forever. He had thought himself dying, but death was a luxury he could not afford. It was his duty to take Buff Stringfellow to Fort Smith to be hanged. This was what Judge Parker expected. That he was returning without his driver and five of the escaped convicts would not sit well with the old man. It would probably cost him his star.

Kane nodded to himself. No matter, he was done

with all of it anyway, the shooting and the killing. The smell of blood and powder smoke acrid in his nose, he vowed that he would never again turn a gun on any human being.

The door opened. The blacksmith, a burly man, stepped inside and looked around anxiously.

Kane pointed to Stringfellow. "Make an iron collar for him. Make it thick and strong, a padlock on one side, a ring on the other. I want it by first light."

"That fast"—the blacksmith swallowed hard—"it will cost you ten dollars."

Kane turned to Vito. "Pay the man, then help me back to the hotel." He glanced at Stringfellow. "We'll take that with us."

"What's left of it," Vito said, without even an attempt at humor.

Chapter 31

Logan Kane pulled out of Baines Flat at sunup. Lorraine rode next to him and Nellie, and Vito took up the rear. Kane dragged Stringfellow behind him by a rope looped through the ring welded to his iron collar. The man staggered through the mud, his breath hissing through his teeth. Every time he stumbled and fell, Kane jerked him to his feet again.

Apart from a groan now and then, Stringfellow was silent. The man had fallen apart completely, the iron collar a harsh symbol of his harsher fate. His arrogance had disappeared with the deaths of Jack Henry and the others, and now he seemed a broken man, content to allow himself to be dragged, like a sheep, to his death.

Logan faced a two-day ride to Fort Smith, a prospect that scared him. He had steeled himself to hold on as long as he was able. All he had to do was get close enough and Vito could take Stringfellow and the women the rest of the way.

After an hour's ride, Kane reached the foothills of Poteau Mountain. As he led the way into the pines and hardwoods covering the southern slope of the ridge, fever raged through him and he rode slumped in the saddle, Stringfellow stumbling along behind him. It seemed to Kane that the trees, swollen with a north wind, spun around him and the mountain stood on end, its prow-shaped outcroppings of rock threatening to break loose and crush him.

A couple of miles to the west soared the twenty-four-hundred-foot peak of Oklahoma High Top, lost in cloud and rain. Some said that the mountain was part of a vast territory once claimed by Vikings who traveled far across the misty ocean, only to perish in a land even more hard and unforgiving than their own.

Norsemen were far from Kane's mind, but as he climbed the Poteau ridge he would have believed, had someone mentioned it to him, that he was sharing their hardships.

The marshal heard whispered talk between Lorraine and Vito. Then they rose closer to him, supporting him in the saddle. They were near, but Kane felt alone, more alone than he'd ever been in his life. Around him, rain ticked through the pines, and the wind sang an elegy for the sun that had died somewhere beyond the leaden clouds.

Kane searched for the top of the ridge. He could

not see it through the trees, but he felt its baleful presence. Then he knew what was happening. The entire mountain was moving, rolling over him, a colossus of rock that would smash him to pieces.

He screamed, just before the mountain covered him and plunged him into darkness.

"He's coming to. His eyes are opening."

Lorraine's voice. Kane drifted back to consciousness, the woman's face an oval blur in the darkness, hovering over him.

"What—what happened?" he asked.

It was Vito who answered. "You called out, then fell off your horse. You took a nasty tumble, you know."

Panic spiked in Kane. "Stringfellow!"

"Tied to a tree," Vito said. "He's very concerned about you."

"Yeah, I bet he is."

The marshal's eyes tried to penetrate the gloom. He heard the crackle of a fire close by and the smell of coffee. Somewhere a stream made a soft, splashing sound. "Where are we?" he asked.

"My answer to that would be nowhere," Vito said. "But Lorraine assures me we're on the north slope of the Poteau ridge." He hesitated a moment, then added, "In the rain."

"How did you get me here?" Kane was surprised at how weak his voice sounded.

"I took you up on my horse," Vito said. "It wasn't

easy. You're a big man and every square inch of you has a bullet hole in it."

Kane felt Lorraine's cool hand on his forehead. She sounded worried. "Logan, your fever is not as bad as it was, but you're still burning up. Don't try to talk. You must rest."

It was a hell of a time and place to be an invalid and Kane forced himself to stay awake. "Lorraine, help me sit up and get me some of that coffee," he said.

"I'll get it," Nellie said.

The girl had been sitting near Kane's feet and he smiled when he saw her. "How are you feelin', Nellie?" he asked.

"I'm fine, Logan," she said. "Just fine."

But there was a wounded sadness about the girl that Kane recognized and he decided that only time and kindness would heal her.

Nellie stepped into the firelight as Lorraine and Vito propped his back against the wide trunk of a beech. He was naked from the belt buckle up, and he turned to Lorraine. "Woman, you surely love to take my clothes off."

"I washed your bandages and I'm drying them by the fire," she said, smiling slightly. "They were stiff with blood."

Kane wanted to look at his wrecked shoulder and the wound in his side, but he fought off the urge. Maybe it was better if he didn't know how bad it was, though the pain was spitefully keeping him up to date.

"Did you find tobacco in my shirt?" he asked.

Lorraine reached into the pocket of her dress and passed the sack and papers. "Why they weren't ruined by blood, I don't know," she said.

"Just lucky, I guess," Kane said.

He rolled a cigarette and drank the coffee Nellie brought him, then another cup. He felt a small surge of strength, but was still very weak. His head pounded and he found it hard to focus his eyes. It was an effort to talk.

"Vito," he said, "come morning you take Stringfellow into Fort Smith. Lorraine and Nellie will go with you."

"And leave you here alone?" Vito was incredulous.

"I'll make out. Tell Judge Parker where I am and he'll send someone to bring me in. It ain't such a fur piece."

Vito shook his head, the half of his face nearer the fire glowing red, the other side in darkness. "I can't do that, Marshal. Suppose you got eaten by a bear or something? Why, I'd be upset for at least a day or two."

"Then what do you propose?" Kane asked, irritated at the other man's short period of potential mourning.

It was Lorraine who answered. "Logan, you stay right where you are for a few days until you have strength enough to ride. Then we'll all head for Fort Smith and find you a doctor as soon as we arrive."

Kane shook his head. "I'll saddle up come daylight. I want Stringfellow in Judge Parker's jail where he belongs and the sooner the better."

"We'll talk about that . . . in . . . the . . . morning. . . ." Lorraine's voice grew distant, fading into the silence of his mind, and Kane closed his eyes. Suddenly he was very tired.

On the morning of their fourth day on the mountain, under a blue sky, Kane and the others rode down the slope and onto the flat.

The marshal was still weak and had been helped into the saddle by Vito. His pain was gone, and that worried him. It could hardly be a good sign. But his fever remained high—and that had worried Lorraine.

Just before dawn, as they'd drunk coffee by the scarlet light of the fire, she'd asked, "What happened to your family, Logan?"

Kane had been building a smoke, and his head had snapped up. "Why do you ask that, woman?"

"Because you've been out of your mind with fever for days and you've been talking to your mother constantly, like she was right here."

Kane smiled. "I think I've told this story before. My ma died of the cholera. So did my pa and my two sisters. I'd been out hunting, trying to lay in meat fer the winter. When I got back to the cabin, they were all dead." Kane had lit his cigarette and inhaled deeply. "I got scared an' rode away from there—left them lying in their beds, unburied."

"How old were you?"

"I was fourteen that fall. Man grown, I reckon."

"What does she want from you, your ma?"

"She wants me to go back to Texas and lay them all in the earth."

"And you will, won't you?"

Kane had nodded. "Soon as I see Stringfellow hung, I'll go back an' find the cabin." He'd stirred uncomfortably. "I still want you and Nellie to come with me."

Lorraine had smiled, looked into Kane's eyes and had laid her hand on the back of his. It was her answer to his question, and it spoke louder to Kane than a volume of Mrs. Elizabeth Barrett Browning's love sonnets.

Now Lorraine was beside the marshal as they rode north and swung around Cowskin Ridge into rolling, long-riding country cut across by dry washes and shallow creeks.

Stringfellow had recovered from his gloom and cursed Kane loudly every time he stumbled and the marshal jerked him to his feet. The iron collar was rubbing the outlaw's neck raw, and at Lorraine's insistence Kane stopped to let her bind the wound, using a strip torn from her petticoat.

If Stringfellow had it in mind to thank her, Lorraine headed him off. She looked into his eyes and said, "I'd do the same thing for a dog."

An hour later they skirted the foothills of the Sugar Loaf Mountains, then stopped among the cottonwoods of Gap Creek to boil coffee and let Kane rest.

The marshal was barely holding on to what little sense of reality still remained with him. He was scorched by fever, tormented by phantoms that haunted every shadowed hill and stand of pine. Dead men from his past stood and watched him ride past, their faces chalk white, hollow eyes without expression.

Once he saw Sam Shaver squatting on the top of a low hill, peeling a green apple, shoving white slices into his mouth with his thumb and the blade of his knife. The old man watched Kane for a long time, then rose and disappeared over the rise, limping like a man whose wounds gave him no peace.

The coffee helped Kane, or he convinced himself it did. He mounted again and the rest followed. Lorraine's face was haggard with fatigue and Vito and Nellie rode together, saying nothing. Stringfellow stumbled more often and cried out when Kane yanked on the rope and dragged him to his feet.

The day was shading into evening when they crossed the timber bridge over the Arkansas and rode into Fort Smith.

Chapter 32

"Logan, there's a gentleman to see you."

Lorraine stood at his bedroom door, lit by the sunlight that streamed through the windows. She was wearing a new dress and her hair, just washed, hung over her shoulder in damp golden ringlets.

Kane moved higher on his pillows and rubbed a hand over his stubbled chin. "I don't think I'm ready to see anybody. I'm a sight."

Lorraine smiled. "It's Judge Parker."

It had come, the meeting Kane had been dreading. He swallowed and said, "Show him in."

He looked quickly around him, making sure the furniture was in order. Before he'd left for New Orleans, Vito had rented the house for three months, calling it an early wedding present. It was a sunny, pleasant place and for the past week Kane had enjoyed the birds singing in the piñons in the yard.

The old man's head appeared in the doorway.

"Deputy Marshal Kane, would you think it amiss and me too bold if I entered?"

"No, Judge, not at all." Kane smiled.

"Please stay, dear lady," Parker said to Lorraine. "I won't impose on you for long." He stepped into the room, white haired and dignified, old before his time. "And how is the patient today?" he asked. "Much better than the last time I saw you, I'll be bound."

"I don't remember anything about that, Judge," Kane said. He wished he'd had time to shave and trim his mustache.

"Well, you brought in the escaped murderer Buff Stringfellow. Then you collapsed." Parker shook his head. "It was all very distressing, but now I can see you're on the mend and that pleases me."

"Stringfellow, is he—"

"He hangs tomorrow morning at ten o'clock. That's partly why I'm here, to see if you wish to attend the execution. The other part is, naturally, that I wanted to check on your welfare." He smiled at Lorraine and made a courtly little bow. "I can see you are in excellent hands."

Kane said, "I don't want to see Stringfellow hang. I'm done with him."

The old judge registered surprise with a raised eyebrow, but said nothing.

"All the others are dead," Kane said.

"By your hand?"

"Most of them."

Parker nodded, his tired eyes thoughtful. "You can give me a full report when you get on your feet again." He stepped to Kane and placed a hand lightly on his shoulder. "We have a difficult job to do here in the Territory, Marshal Kane, and when men die, good and bad, we must live with the consequences." The old man smiled. "I will not allow myself to judge you too harshly."

"Lorraine," Kane said.

The woman walked to the door where Kane's holstered Colt hung. His badge was pinned to the cartridge belt. "Give it to the judge," he said.

Parker took the gun belt from Lorraine, his face puzzled.

"I'm turning in my star," Kane said. "The Colt belongs to a dead man, but maybe another marshal will need it sometime."

Judge Isaac Parker was an intelligent man and he knew it was pointless to argue. "Mr. Kane," he said, using his civilian title for the first time ever, "this will stay in my desk drawer. If you ever want it back, you know where it is."

Kane smiled. "Thank you, Judge."

"Where will you go?"

"Back to Texas."

"Then all I can say is good luck." He bowed to Lorraine. "I'm a thoughtless old man and I've imposed on both of you long enough. Dear lady, I wish you good day."

After the old man left, Lorraine plumped Kane's pillows. He reached out, took her in his arms and kissed her long and passionately. When she broke free of him, the woman said, "Later, Logan. The doctor will be here any minute, though all he'll say is that you're as tough as an old boot and healing well."

"Lorraine," Kane said, grinning, "let's get married before we leave for Texas."

The woman smiled. "Of course, Mr. Kane. I wouldn't have it any other way."

Historical Note

New Orleans was the first home of the Sicilian Mafia and its roots went all the way back to the War Between the States. By 1881 the Provenzano family, made wealthy and powerful by its control of the docks, pretty much ran the entire New Orleans underworld. (In *The Convict Trail* I slightly changed the spelling of the clan name to protect the guilty.)

Around 1886 the Provenzanos lost control of the docks to the powerful Matranga family and by 1891 had ceased to be a major influence on organized crime in the Crescent City.

"A writer in the tradition of Louis L'Amour
and Zane Grey!"
—*Huntsville Times*

National Bestselling Author
RALPH COMPTON

**Available wherever books are sold or at
penguin.com**

No other series packs this much heat!

THE TRAILSMAN

**Follow the trail of the gun-slinging heroes of
Penguin's Action Westerns at
penguin.com/actionwesterns**